MOBILE LIBRARY

a novel

DAVID WHITEHOUSE

Scribner

New York   London   Toronto   Sydney   New Delhi

Scribner
A Division of Simon & Schuster, Inc.
1230 Avenue of the Americas
New York, NY 10020

First Scribner hardcover edition January 2015

SCRIBNER and design are registered trademarks of The Gale Group, Inc., used under license by Simon & Schuster, Inc., the publisher of this work.

For information about special discounts for bulk purchases, please contact Simon & Schuster Special Sales at 1-866-506-1949 or business@simonandschuster.com.

The Simon & Schuster Speakers Bureau can bring authors to your live event. For more information or to book an event, contact the Simon & Schuster Speakers Bureau at 1-866-248-3049 or visit our website at www.simonspeakers.com.

Interior design by Jill Putorti
Jacket illustration by Gray318

Manufactured in the United States of America

10 9 8 7 6 5 4 3 2 1

Library of Congress Cataloging-in-Publication Data is available.

ISBN 978-1-4767-4943-3
ISBN 978-1-4767-4946-4 (ebook)

MOBILE LIBRARY

CHAPTER ONE

THE END

Lips, sticky, not how his mother kissed. He only considered the difference in their ages whenever he tasted her makeup.

"Are we in trouble?" Bobby asked.

"No," Val said, "not anymore."

The white cliffs of southern England spread out beyond them, disappearing where the blues, sea and sky, coalesce. High up in the cab of the mobile library, they could not see the land below them, just the ocean's ceaseless loop, as if they were driving an island through the sea to a faraway place. Hemmed by a crescent of police cars to the cliff edge, bulbs flashed, helicopters chopped up the air. When the sirens fell mute, he saw her, exquisite in the dim dashboard light.

Rosa rested her head in the shallow pool of sun on Val's lap. Bobby's stomach gurgled.

"Are you hungry?" Val asked. The noise, a purr, came from another compartment inside him, one contented, not troubled by bubbling chambers of acid or some such bodily thing.

"No," he said, and kissed her again.

Detective Jimmy Samas, chase-weary but enlivened by its imminent conclusion, stood by his car. He knew the other officers were waiting for him to issue an order, but he could not conjure one. It was a high-profile investigation. His job was to lead it, and so his colleagues presumed he would know what to do. They were wrong.

At times he felt too young to do his job, though this was precisely why he was good at it. His boyish nature and blemishless skin provoked sympathy in others. Sympathy is an invaluable asset in the business of negotiation. People immediately felt sorry for the fresh-faced boy sent to do the work of a man, and it was in this second of distraction that Detective Samas was usually able to free a hostage, or talk a man down from a ledge.

The gummy gnaw of tiredness made it difficult to concentrate. He considered his priorities. Continual reassessment of the objective at hand had formed a major part of his training, and he did well to remember that now, his eyelids pinching in spasm. Chief among his concerns was the safety of the two children, Bobby Nusku and Rosa Reed, aged twelve and thirteen respectively. Regardless, a hundred and one other problems crackled in the heat of his mind. For starters, there was the woman, Rosa's mother, Valerie Reed, who at any moment might drive the truck into the sea. Who knew where her mind was? Evading the law, whether willfully or not (that remained to be seen), was a mightily stressful business. First-time kidnappers, particularly single mothers with an otherwise clean record, would feel that anxiety more keenly than most. A wrong move on Detective Samas's part could prompt disaster. He watched a live news crew setting up behind the police barrier and unstuck his collar from the sweat beading on his neck. Televised disaster, at that.

Besides Ms. Reed, of course, there was the not insignificant matter of the man Detective Samas had reason to believe was hidden in the back of the vehicle, and whose pursuit had shorn sleep from him for months. He put the bullhorn to his mouth but didn't squeeze the trigger. Instead he appreciated a calm that exists only by the sea. The jeer of diving gulls and the tide washing the rocks. He took a deep breath, trying to co-opt its serenity.

The mobile library formed the trailer of a semitruck, the type that rattled teeth as it streaked by on the highway—a real gum-tingler. Originally painted pea green, the library was so long that Val could barely see its rear end in the wing mirror, just the rusting skirt of its livery. Rolling through the countryside it appeared, to a squinting eye, as a mirage moving on the breeze. Now the white emulsion with which they'd covered it was flaking, and this original bed of color could be seen again, along with the words *Mobile Library*, returning like a memory once forgotten.

On the side was written its weight, twenty tons. Many months previously, as they had sat on the mobile library's steps watching zigzag jet trails carve a blushing summer sky, Val had said twenty tons is what a whale might weigh "if you could catch it and slap it on the scales." Rosa had hooted with delight. They had read Herman Melville's *Moby-Dick* together. To her, with the sea view now before them, it appeared that the story was, in some tiny, beautiful way, coming true. Searching the foam breaks of waves for glimpses of the whale's silver hump breaching, or a blowhole spouting, Ahab's heart (*that madly seekest him*) was now Rosa's, beating as if her imagination might fill it with joy enough to burst. How quickly, she wondered, would the mobile library sink, when the whale smashed its chassis and dragged it down into the sea? She would not need to wait long to know.

"I love you," Bobby said, and Val flinched like she had never before heard those three words strung together in that certain painful order.

As the sun rose, heat beat out the cab's cool air. Bobby's T-shirt clung to his belly, a transparent skin over the pale smirk of his scars. Bert panted, sweat collecting on the glistening black cherry of his nose.

Detective Samas had not accounted for the presence of a dog. No mention of it had cropped up in the case notes. Only now that it had been sighted by the police helicopter humming overhead, and the news relayed to him over the radio clipped to his belt, was he even aware of its existence. A dog! How had this been overlooked? Even a detective as sharp as he could not be in complete mastery of the details in such a sprawling case. This was precisely the kind of oversight he'd been desperate to avoid. Animals were far more unpredictable than kidnappers or fugitives. Generally speaking, he found that the less hairy the variable, the better. He imagined it savaging his testicles as he tried to calmly negotiate the children's release. Contemplating the job ahead had already prompted the first dreadful needling of a catastrophic migraine. Switching off his mobile phone in case his girlfriend went into labor and called, he felt momentarily guilty. Bad timing, he supposed. There was a job to do.

Nothing happened for a while. The mobile library stood strangely dormant, surrounded by police cars on the clifftop, existing in the uneasy lull before the future comes. Val had never looked forward much before. To her, the future was a Magic Eye picture, always disappearing whenever she verged on fully grasping its shape. But she could see it clearly now. It was beautiful and full of love and she wanted it, but it had never seemed further away. Perhaps it was she who was vanishing.

"We had an adventure," Val said, like it was over. "That's all we ever promised to do."

A warm film covered Bobby's eyes. "Like in a book," he said.

Bobby looked in the mirror and saw the detective's reflection as he approached. He had seen him before, on the television news, and noticed the red flecks in his moustache, a neat copper awning for his lips. The detective's shirt was crumpled, as if his clothes had gone to sleep without him.

Running through a mental checklist of everything he knew about Valerie Reed, Detective Samas realized that it amounted to more than he knew about his own girlfriend. Rather than saddening him, this epiphany buoyed the detective with renewed confidence. Perhaps, just perhaps, he *was* better equipped to handle this investigation than anybody else. Some talk had circulated, in light of how long the case had gone on, that it should be handed over to a more senior officer. *Nonsense*, he thought now.

When he got to within four meters of the mobile library, Val leaned out of the window and nixed his assurance with the devastating speed of a bullet shot through the bottom of a barrel.

"Stop," she said, "wait right there," and he did, shielding his eyes with a yellow-fingered hand and smoking a cigarette; the ash whipped in dances from the end of it.

"What does that man want?" Bobby asked.

"He wants to speak to me," Val said.

"Tell him to go away."

"He just wants to check we're okay."

"Of course we're okay." He clambered over Val's legs, put his mouth to the small gap at the top of the driver's side window and shouted, "Of course we're okay!"

"We're okay! We're okay!" Rosa said, and they both laughed.

Detective Samas took a few steps backward. Had the wind not picked up enough to extinguish his smoke, he'd have heard the collective sigh of the tired police officers standing by their vehicles, guns trained on the mobile library's rear door from where it seemed any danger was most likely to emerge. It had been a long, frustrating night chasing shadows that refused to be boxed.

Val put an arm around Bobby's waist and another around Rosa's shoulders and bunched them together, burying her head between their bodies so they could both feel wet from her face. Bobby butterfly-kissed Rosa on the forehead and she swallowed loud enough that they all heard it.

"Do you want me to go out there and tell him to go away?" he asked. Val shook her head. "Because I will. I'll protect you."

"I know you will," she said, "you're my man." She held him even more tightly, so that their bodies creaked with a realization—this might be the last time.

"Tell me a story," he said.

"All of the books are locked up in the library," she said.

"Then make one up. One with a happy ending."

"I told you before, there's no such thing as an ending."

"Then start to tell a happy story and stop before you get to the end. If we decide where it ends, than it's bound to be happy, isn't it?"

She peered into the mirror again.

Skimming the grass with the sole of his shoe, Detective Samas tried to decide his next move. Should he rap on the window, or wait for Val to open the door? There would be no benefit in trying to establish authority here. Though he wore the badge, she had the upper hand. He decided to bide his time, and hoped that whatever they were discussing in there wouldn't take much longer. His colleagues were already starting to suspect, quite correctly, that he didn't know what to do. Feeling woefully out of his depth was something he was getting used to. Impending fatherhood had seen to that.

Far from being offended, as the subjects of negotiations often were, that the force had sent a relative youngster to deal with her, Val watched Detective Samas for a few seconds, long enough to see something that she could relate to absolutely. Fear. In that moment they shared it, mournfully, like the last of the rations.

Beyond him, past the police line, on the hill that led back up into Britain, was an ice cream van emblazoned with vibrant colors. At first glance she thought it a tastelessly decorated ambulance, parked as it was behind a row of others.

"Who would like an ice cream?" she asked. Bobby and Rosa thrust their hands into the air, waking Bert from the delight of a newly entered slumber.

Val removed a note from her purse, the fake gold clasp shining a greenish hue, and held it out toward Bobby, clutching it tight, a flower in her hand that unfurled when she opened it.

"Here," she said, "take Rosa and Bert and buy us all an ice cream." Bobby shrank back into his seat, not keen on the notion that they might be parted for the first time in months. "What are you waiting for?"

"You're not coming?"

"I'll stay and guard the mobile library."

"The police will catch us," Rosa said.

"The police won't catch you because the police only catch bad people. Isn't that right, Bobby?" Bobby understood the pretense, and nodded, so that Rosa copied him with that charming delay she'd perfected. Val had made a new plan, and he trusted her, despite not knowing what it was.

He pulled on his plimsolls, then attached the dog's lead to his collar and put the handle into Bert's mouth. Lazy, even by the standards of old dogs, Bert insisted on walking himself. "Just keep going," Val said, "all the way to the ice cream van. Don't let them stop you. And make sure you get me a big one, with lots of chocolate sprinkles on top."

Detective Samas tugged the plump knot of his tie tight. Something about the situation rested awkwardly on his conscience. No amount of training could have prepared him for it. To what life was he returning the boy? He had met Bobby Nusku's father, and seen not the hollow a lost child leaves, but hints of indifference in the space where it should have been. What misery would he, in helping, inflict? There were no happy endings to this story, he was sure of it.

Val hugged Rosa, whose body loosened to fit around her mother's, and they became the same for a second, merging to make pairs of everything. Then she put her hands on Bobby's face to pull him close, and they kissed a final time. She closed her eyes and hoped that nothing would go wrong.

"I love you," she said, and he had not heard the words before either, not like that, not sewn together with such magical thread.

He climbed out of the cab and felt the air cool his ankles. Rosa came next, and then Bert, leaping to the dewy grass on the cliff-top, only a misstep from the violent drop of the edge.

The detective watched, incredulous, as the children for whom he'd been searching since before autumn came ambling past him arm in arm, followed by a dog, apparently walking itself.

"Hello," Rosa said, "I am Rosa Reed. What is your name?"

"My name is Jimmy Samas," Detective Samas said, tipping his head to the side. Rosa stopped and wrote his name down in her notebook.

Many surreal moments had punctuated his service, but none more so than this. It had more in common with a dream's wobbly oddity than it did real life.

Bobby, Rosa and Bert continued on their way. They walked past the police cars and the men and women in their smart blue uniforms, with silver badges and heavy belts so black as to blaze off reflections of the sun, past the eager news crews, past the waiting ambulances. They walked all the way to the ice cream van.

Detective Jimmy Samas approached the mobile library.

Bobby didn't turn around until the fire melted the ice cream over his trembling fingers. Smoke inked the sky.

CHAPTER TWO

THE ROBOT, PART ONE

With eyebrows drawn at an inflexible thirty-eight-degree angle, the toasted ocher of Bobby's father's girlfriend's foundation was a matte bed onto which she painted a single unchanged emotion. Suspicion. The egg-white wink of missed inner ear offered a fleeting hint of her true color, but her singing voice, a dull functional honk, was befitting of the new shade she had chosen. Few who tried could accurately guess at Cindy's age, in the same way it's difficult to know the age of a reptile thanks to its unchanging mask of scales. It was actually somewhere in the mid-twenties but could easily have been a few decades north of that, depending on the harshness of the light. She looked youngest on Saturday nights.

Despite calling herself a mobile hairdresser, people always came to her—that is, to Bobby's father's house, into which she had moved barely three months after Bobby's mother left it for the final time. Though Cindy had received no formal training, her knack for re-creating the styles worn by stars from pictures in glossy magazines was passable. Once a week she bleached her own hair over the kitchen sink. The damage she had done it was irreversible. Though permanently attached to her head, it did little to repel potential customers, lending weight to the adage that all publicity is good.

Apart from hair, her other primary interest was gossip. Bobby sat on the stairs listening to the conversations Cindy had with her clients. Soundtracked by the scissors' percussive clack, they discussed rumors and invented new ones. To Bobby, the chatter was of no concern. He concentrated on one thing and one thing only: hair, theirs, cut loose and slowly floating down onto his mother's rug. Individual strands, brown and black and brittle bottle blond, wove themselves into the wool, entwining lives that were never meant to touch. Afterward, when alone, he would pick the hairs out by hand, split them into two piles and put the piles into jars. One jar for his mother's hair, one jar for everybody else's. He could tell which hairs were his mother's because they were softer and smoother. When he held them to the light they were the same color as the glow behind an angel. Collecting them took hours and made his fingertips ache, but Bobby updated his secret files every night after Cindy's last client left and she headed to the shop for wine (she boasted of having become immune to the resultant headaches).

He kept the jars beneath his bed. He was an archivist of his mother.

Measurements formed a similarly integral part of his files, and he would meticulously catalogue them in a notebook, making the numbers as small as possible so that his father, should he ever find it in a hiding place beneath the bedroom carpet, would have great difficulty understanding what they said. With arms outstretched, walking sideways like a crab, he could make it from one wall of the house to the other in five big steps. There were eleven stairs to the staircase, thirty-eight tiles on the kitchen floor, forty-three swirls in the bedroom ceiling plasterwork and nine mini paces from the toilet to the bath. There were fifty-seven different vehicles—planes, police cars and helicopters—on the wallpaper in his bedroom, but they were only the ones he could see to count. Bobby estimated that another twenty were hidden on the far wall, behind the boxes bulging with Cindy's belongings.

Sometimes he practiced walking around the house with the lights off. If he couldn't be seen, he couldn't be punished, and so in the darkness he was closest to himself. As his night vision improved, he was able to find his way around without touching any furniture, even on the blackest of nights. If he ever encountered a burglar, Bobby planned to wait until he fell over the hairdressing chair in the middle of the lounge, then stab him through the throat with the scissors. Coagulated in the carpet fibers, the blood would make the hairs more difficult to pick out. But he would do it anyway. There could be no greater indicator of commitment to his files than that.

The rug was five feet by three feet—it said so on the label—and turned from red at one end to yellow at the other, the colors of a plate after a decent breakfast. Other rugs looked plain by comparison. No wonder she had loved it.

Houses are bodies, their memories mapped by the scars left behind. Bobby drew sketches of each room with a charcoal pencil that his mother had used to draw him, and added the pictures to a special section at the back of his files devoted to art. He knew that this was the section she would enjoy most.

The black smudge on the wall above the stove marked the time she set fire to a pan of oil when his father crept up behind her, drunk and in a state of arousal. The spot was two and a half hands wide. There was a crumbly seven-inch hole on the stairs from afterward when she ran, fell and put her foot through the plasterwork, breaking her ankle. There were the divots her fingernails dug in the headboard, and remnants of the easel Bruce had smashed.

Bobby imagined how proud his mother would be of his archives when she returned. They could use the notes to re-create the house to these exact specifications, except up on top of a mountain. Inside, it would be identical. Lime-green curtains in the lounge, chocolate-brown borders ringing the walls. Cream tiles on the kitchen floor betraying splats of dropped food. The same gap between the cupboard and the fridge, three inches across, where lost items could always be found. But when they opened the back door there would be clouds on the lawn. Eagles would nest in the drainpipes, and he'd scoop snow from the peak for pure washing water. The world would be their garden, just as she had promised.

Days felt longer with her gone. Bobby chased the slowing hours round his watch. Until his mother came home, only one other person in the world knew about his files. His name was

Sunny Clay and he was Bobby's best and only friend. He was also his bodyguard. That's why he always wore a shifting mask of bruises, the colored lumps changing, a violent ode to coral reef.

Bobby arrived at Sunny's house on the first Saturday morning of the summer holidays. Everywhere glimmered reminders of the amassed blank days ahead, on which he and Sunny could impress any fantasy they wished. Excitement's hot tickle rushed down Bobby's spine, until Sunny finally answered the door with a familiar look on his face.

"Hello, Bobby," he said.

"Hello, Sunny," Bobby said.

"Do you know what today is?"

"I know it's Saturday. Is that going to be enough of an answer for you?"

"Not really," Sunny said.

Bobby sighed. He hooked his thumbs through his belt loops and hitched up his jeans. "Then you'd better tell me."

"Today is an important day. Today is the day that we commence Phase Three."

Bobby had been dreading Phase Three. Phases One and Two were difficult enough. Bones had been broken. Blood had been spilled. It wasn't very relaxing. However, they had made a plan, a mission, and there was no backing down. When it was over, Bobby Nusku would never be picked on by anyone, at school or by his father, ever again. Sunny would become a cyborg by the end of the summer holidays, and then he'd be able to protect

Bobby with all the extra strength and speed being half human, half robot would bring.

It had been Sunny's idea, and though he claimed it a long-term ambition, it had come to him shortly after he and Bobby met. Sunny had approached Bobby in the playground at school and asked if he knew anything about making tunnels.

"Tunnels?"

"Yes, tunnels."

"Not really."

"Then you can pick it up as we go along." Bobby presumed that Sunny had an ulterior motive. He was considering running away when Sunny stretched an open palm out toward him. When Bobby finally opened his eyes he was surprised to realize that he hadn't been struck. They shook hands, and Bobby was impressed by the strength of Sunny's grip.

Sunny had been watching Bobby all week. He had watched him skulk alone around the perimeter of the fields at break time. He had watched him try to avoid three older boys, who had chased him across the football pitch. He had watched one of them trip Bobby into the mud, not once but twice, and followed him unseen into the bathrooms, where he had attempted to clean his shirt in the sink, only to make it worse.

He recognized loneliness when he saw it. Noisy crowds that swirl around the silence in the center where you sit. An irrepressible ache made by the melody of other people's laughter. The breadth of the canyon between you and someone you can reach out to touch. He too had felt as if he had radioactivity trapped in his bones.

Sunny was large for a twelve-year-old. Bobby on the other hand was slight, waspish and the color of milk. He looked like he needed a friend no matter what shape they took, and so this new arrangement was mutually beneficial.

"Come with me," Sunny said, and Bobby walked proudly behind him toward the art department, trying to match the exact timing of his steps.

"Why are you making a tunnel?" Bobby asked, as they reached a brick wall, sheltered from view of the playground by a thorn-bush.

"So that we can get out of here. You want to get out of here, right?" Bobby's first thought was of the trouble they would be in, just as his mother had raised him to think. Embarrassed, he put his hands on his hips and tried to stand up tall and straight.

"Of course."

"And you've seen prison films?" When Sunny's father walked out on Sunny and his mother he left behind a considerable library of old movies on VHS cassette. Sunny had made an education of staying up late and voraciously consuming them.

"Uh-huh," Bobby said, not sure what Sunny even meant.

"Then you'll know as well as I do that tunnels are the only way out." Sunny leaned against the wall, stroking the brickwork so that the cement turned to dust on his fingertips.

"But this is the wall to the art department. If you tunnel through this, you'll be breaking back in."

"Wrong kind of tunnel," Sunny said. He lay on his stomach

on the ground and reached into the base of the thornbush, from where he produced a box containing two stolen tins of black paint. Bobby glanced down at the ground, which he sensed move further away from him. This, he reasoned, would be his view from the gallows. Regardless, he didn't want to desert Sunny. He wanted to climb on his back and throw both fists into the air.

Sunny daubed the semicircular outline of a tunnel onto a wall, as he'd watched Wile E. Coyote do in countless *Road Runner* cartoons. This Bobby *had* seen, though he wasn't brave enough to point out where he recognized it from, hoping he might be wrong, and that Sunny wasn't crazy. Sunny thrust a brush into Bobby's hand and told him to start helping fill its empty center black.

"This isn't going to work. You do know that don't you?" Bobby said, liberally splashing the paint onto the wall.

"Incorrect," Sunny said, "this tunnel will get me out of school today." Bobby admired the fervor of his new friend's belief. Even if it was misguided, it was enough to convince him. And that was all Sunny wanted to do. He knew full well the plan was stupid, but in that hour, the timid boy he'd watched retrieve the contents of his bag from the marshes at the back of the field had scarcely looked over his shoulder. He hadn't needed to.

"Do you want to come over to my house later?" Sunny said.

"To your house?"

"Yes."

"For what?"

"For dinner."

"Your parents wouldn't mind?"

"It's just me and my mum."

"Oh. Well, okay then."

"Okay," Sunny said, "good." He rolled up Bobby's right sleeve and, with the thinnest paintbrush he could find, daubed an address onto his forearm. Then they both turned toward a rustle in the thornbush, and Mr. Oats appeared, spittle collecting in the corners of his mouth.

"What the hell have you done?" he said. Spooked, Sunny turned and sprinted into the tunnel, knocking himself unconscious. He lay spread-eagled on the floor, coated in black paint. The tunnel had gotten him out.

They spent that entire weekend watching Sunny's father's movies in the attic, thrilled by the fact that their ages were far lower than the numbers framed in red on the front of the cases, gorging on chocolate and long sherbet straws. On Bobby's insistence, Sunny fetched what toys he had from the cupboard in his bedroom. All of them fitted inside a battered shoe box, which Sunny opened with a sickly mixture of dread and embarrassment, stalling as he peeled back the lid. But Bobby, unlike any friend Sunny had invited home before, never commented on how dated the few toys were, or that some were held together with sticky tape. In his hands the green plastic soldiers came to life, and eventually even Sunny stopped seeing their missing limbs.

Neither mentioned how reluctant they were to part when Bobby slowly gathered his things and prepared for the short walk home.

"I can protect you from those boys at school," Sunny said.

"What?"

"I can stop them."

"No, you can't."

"I can. I can walk with you to and from school every day. I could come to your house and collect you in the morning, and afterward I can walk you all the way home."

"No," Bobby said, knowing that he didn't want Sunny to meet his father, "that's something we definitely can't do." They shook hands again. "But thank you."

Sunny ignored his mother's pleas to go to bed. That night he watched *Terminator 2: Judgment Day*. The indestructible metal skeleton, coated in a faux-human flesh, protected the boy, John Connor, at all costs. He had an idea and immediately began taking notes. In order to execute it properly, it would need to be done in three separate phases, otherwise he would probably die. Having his entire skeleton replaced with steel in one single operation was, by any standards, too ambitious.

The next morning, Sunny waited by the tunnel. He found that, like all his ideas, his enthusiasm for it had diminished as quickly as the paint had dried in the weekend sun. All of his ideas, that is, but this new one, which he knew he'd see through to the end no matter what as long as he had a little help.

When Bobby arrived, Sunny beckoned him from the bush. As he came closer Sunny saw that his shirt was again covered in mud, and that a mixture of snot and tears had blurred the dirt on his cheeks. A solitary droplet of blood glistened in his left nostril.

"What are you doing here?" Bobby said, forcing his foot flat on the ground to stop his leg from shaking.

"I have a plan, and I need you to help me with it," Sunny said.

"What kind of plan?"

"To protect you." He opened his mouth to say that he didn't need protecting, but no sound emerged. Sunny stepped out from behind the bush in time to catch Bobby, who sobbed with force enough to send ripples through them both. "I'm going to become a cyborg."

Even through his anguish, Bobby struggled to stifle a laugh.

Reckless as it may have been, Phase One had nonetheless gone as hoped. Sunny positioned two chairs in his garden, resting his right leg across them. They placed sandbags on either side of his ankle to hold the foot in place, then laid a sleeping bag beneath him as a rudimentary crash mat. Bobby rolled up a towel so tightly that it creaked and pushed it into Sunny's mouth, who clamped his jaws shut. Just as they had practiced, Sunny nodded three times to let Bobby know that he was ready. The third nod was Bobby's cue to leap off the shed onto Sunny's leg, snapping both the tibia and fibula clean in two. The jump was swift and accurate. Birds fled the echo.

Sunny pretended that he had fallen from the shed and landed awkwardly. The surgeon told him it was one of the cleanest breaks he had ever seen. Sunny thanked him, confusing everyone in the operating room.

With steely resolve, Sunny soldiered through the months of pain that followed, emerging with precisely what he and Bobby hoped for: beneath the shiny twist of scar tissue on Sunny's leg—six inches long and almost the shape of Italy—was a stiff metal rod. Solid. Indestructible. The first part of Sunny's skeleton had been replaced.

Phase Two wasn't nearly as successful. X-shaped scarring mapped the spot on Sunny's forearm where the smashed crumbs of bone swam around inside his skin. Though he'd had a metal rod fitted, the arm remained twisted and weak. The sledgehammer had been too unwieldy for Bobby, half its size, to control, and both Sunny's mother, Jules, and the hospital staff were more reluctant to believe his lies about what had happened. Regardless, they had achieved their aims for Phases One and Two. Having come this far, nothing could deter them from seeing the plan through to completion.

Before Phase Three commenced, Sunny declared it important that they didn't work on an empty stomach. Bobby, always pestered by hunger, was happy to hear it. Inside the fridge sulked a large lemon cheesecake. They each gobbled up a generous slice. Bobby licked his teeth until the sugar buzz subsided, methodically hunting down all residual zing. His father never allowed food like this at home. He wouldn't even let Bobby chew bubblegum. He said that if Bobby swallowed it, it would stick inside his guts for seven years. Bobby imagined his rib cage as an explosion of color. He was fine with that. When he was with Sunny it was how he felt on the inside.

They took two bottles of Coca-Cola and sat on the wall in the front garden beneath the lip of the gutter. The sky was as dirty as a pigeon wing. It started to rain. Petrol-poisoned puddles shivered on the road. Traffic crawled by, car windows steamed with muddled hieroglyphics. Sunny licked the palm of his hand and swiped it upward over his brow.

"What if you don't like me when you're a cyborg?" Bobby asked. As much as Bobby appreciated Sunny's efforts to protect him, he feared losing him as a friend far more than any schoolyard beating.

Sunny pushed his tongue against his front teeth, maggoty pink lumps pulsing in the gaps.

"That's the part of my brain I'm going to keep," he said.

His mother, Jules, appeared, draped in the shadow of her umbrella. A kind, quiet woman, she worried about only two things, the ailing health of her parents, who lived hundreds of miles away, and the remarkable talent of her only child to injure himself in such dramatic fashion. She spoke slowly, hoping that her words might worm their way inside his ears somehow.

"Are you hearing me?"

"Uh-huh," Sunny said.

"Then what did I just say?" He wriggled. She clipped him around the side of the head, but only lightly. She knew how easily he broke. "I said stay off the scaffold." The scaffold had been erected around the house while the windows were replaced. Bobby and Sunny were already conspiring—silently, as only children can—exactly how they were going to scale it. Even when she made them promise, hands on heart, they were wondering how high they might get.

"Sunny, honey, I only tell you to do things because I love you, you know that, right?"

"I know."

"Except for when I tell you to tidy your room. I do that because you make a damn mess and I'm sick of it."

"I know." Jules stroked Sunny's hair.

"I love you," he said.

"I love you too, honey." She said goodbye to Bobby and walked slowly toward town. As she left, Bobby felt guilty enough to whisper an apology she didn't hear. Guilt was an emotion he knew well. Adults mistook it for impeccable manners.

The boys climbed a plaster-spattered ladder to the third story of the scaffold and threw broken brick chippings off the side, penny-whistling bomb sounds and growling in their throats to make explosions. From there the town was a dull procession of chimneys, muted by a drizzle that made it somehow futureless, but also without history. It existed, as did its people, in a moment it wanted to escape. Sunny's tunnel didn't seem such a bad idea from up on high.

Sunny tried to take off his T-shirt, but Bobby had to help feed his head through the neck hole while he bent like a disobedient marionette. Sunny's left arm was still limp; the plaster cast had been removed only a few days before. They could feel the metal through the skin, a cold stiff lump of hard-won achievement. Wet, his body glistened. There was already something robotic about it, lithe and functional, the efficient engine of youth.

"Let Phase Three commence," Sunny yelled, proceeding to the far end of the platform three stories up. A sick feeling in his stomach, Bobby's knees buckled. Phase Three, the final phase, was to have metal plates installed in Sunny's skull. Had they waited any longer, the scant regard for danger enjoyed by young boys might have waned. Without danger, boyhood is undone.

Sunny rocked back and forth on his feet, and as assuredly as he might step into a warm bath, he began running toward Bobby. His arms rose like wings on either side of his body, but Bobby could tell by the writhing eels of the muscles in his jaw that he was already having second thoughts.

"Abort! Abort!" Sunny said, grinding his heels into the wood. But the surface was slick. There was no time for him to stop. Bobby grabbed him by the ankle and rammed a shoulder into his knee, which locked and spun Sunny's leg to the left. This only seemed to give him more momentum. Sunny seemed briefly, gloriously weightless as he left the scaffold's edge. He took to the air in near silence, scuppered only by the songbirds mocking a boy's imitation of flight. Upside down and tumbling toward the earth, he said, "I'll protect you Bobby Nusku."

Sunny cracked his head on the jut of a long, sharp metal pipe protruding from the scaffold—breaking his fall—and then dropped the remaining nine feet to the ground, where he hit the patio with the sickening thump of a boxer punching a side of beef. Blood formed a deep red maze in the cracks between the paving stones, an eerie puzzle with Sunny the prize in the middle. The balloon of nerves swelled in Bobby's craw, filling his insides and threatening to prod his guts out through his bottom.

Right then, Bobby learned of the dizzying nausea that arrives in the wake of a freshly made mistake. Mistakes are those moments when we grip the future so hard that it breaks, and we know we must build another future from the pieces, but one that shall never be as good. Bobby wondered how many pieces there would be, and if any would be too small to pick up.

Jules returned to find Bobby cradling her son's broken head. In her panic she pushed Bobby to the ground, and became blind to everything but the boy, whose skull moved beneath her fingers.

"He fell," Bobby said, "it was an accident," but it was as if she couldn't tune to the frequency he was using, that she'd changed to some emergency channel, the unique language shared by a whale and her lost calf.

"Call an ambulance!" she screamed. "Call an ambulance!" Bobby rooted through her handbag for the house keys and ran inside to use the telephone.

An ambulance spirited Sunny and his mother away. Bobby was left sitting in a puddle on the ground. Rain turned it from blood red to the gray of the others around it.

He waited there all night until Jules returned, alone, at dawn. Dark bags hung beneath her eyes. Tears clotted her lashes. Bobby threw his arms around her waist and sobbed against the warm pillow of her pelvis. He held her hands and prepared to be told that his best friend was dead.

"He was awake, for a while," she said, staring at the wall.

"For a while?"

"Long enough to say it was an accident. That it wasn't your fault." Bobby crumpled at her feet. "Come," she said, "I'll drive you home."

He cried for the entire journey, leaving a sodden clump of tissue in the footwell. As the car pulled into a space outside his house, he spoke the words he had only heard in the movies Sunny had played for him.

"I am deeply sorry for your loss." Jules pinched Bobby's earlobe and tugged, gently, as if she might produce a coin from behind it.

"Bobby, honey," she said, "I think you've misunderstood me. Sunny isn't dead. I mean, he's not well, but he's not dead." Though she was crying the chime of her laughter filled the car. "My boy is indestructible, it seems."

Sunny had never been in hospital this long before. Eventually Bobby was permitted to visit. Given his presence at her son's continuing brushes with death, it wouldn't have been unreasonable for Jules to consider Bobby a bad omen. But, knowing how happy seeing his friend would make Sunny, she slipped a note through Bobby's door the moment he was well enough to receive him.

This wasn't the first time Bobby had visited Sunny in hospital. Navigating his way to the children's ward was easy using the back corridors, past the morgue and the kitchens, one of which always smelled of boiling vegetable water and old men's skin. Bobby zipped his hood tight around his face so that only his eyes were visible and slunk into the ward behind a porter's cleaning trolley.

Three rooms down on the left he found Sunny, chemically dazed, and was quickly met by the inescapable realization that he didn't look quite the same anymore. Something had changed. He still had two eyes (peering out from the centers of bruised purpling circles), a nose (broken) and a mouth (missing five teeth). He was still bigger than all of the other boys on the ward. His head had a slight dent in it, hinted at beneath the bandages, but nothing to explain the overwhelming sense of changed physiology. Bobby couldn't be sure what, but something wasn't right.

"Hello," Sunny said. His voice was deeper and wetter and stuck in his mouth, face slack and creeping down his skull. Only then, when he could no longer use it, did Bobby realize how big Sunny's smile used to be.

Sunny offered Bobby a grape—his arm and hands still worked, evidently—but Bobby felt it rude to take it all, so he had half and gave the other back, nestling it on Sunny's tongue. It fell off and rolled under the bed. The sound of laughter came from Sunny's mouth, in time to the rhythmic jerking of his chest, but there was no reflection of it in his expression. It was as if Bobby was hearing Sunny's thoughts. The muscles in Sunny's face no longer worked, an avalanche of synapses blocking this specific neural pathway. Bobby wanted to reach inside himself, tear out whatever it was Sunny now lacked and hand it over, still bloody and twitching in his grip.

"I'm sorry," he said.

"Don't be stupid," Sunny said, "this is the best thing that could possibly have happened. How many cyborgs do you know who walk around smiling all of the time?"

"I don't know any cyborgs, apart from you."

"Well, trust me. Cyborgs don't have feelings. Like the Terminator. That's why they strike fear into the hearts of their enemies." Bobby stroked the bedsheet. It was rougher than he'd thought it would be and he hoped it wasn't irritating Sunny's skin.

"Bobby," Sunny continued, "I got my metal plate. I am complete now. Nobody can ever hurt you again."

CHAPTER THREE

THE PRINCESS

Sunny's absence proved as vivid a pain as a toothache. By day, Bobby stayed in his bedroom alone, killing time by peeling off the wallpaper. He set about unpicking the curtains thread by thread. Eventually boredom permeated everything. He could taste it in the rations from the biscuits and apples he had squirreled away. He could feel it rattle in his lungs with every breath he drew. When he slept he dreamt of nothing.

Bruce and Cindy ignored him as much as possible. Occasionally when he heard them laughing he would slip into the room hoping they would share with him what they had found so funny, but they never did. What bothered him most was not that they didn't speak to him. It was that his father always said good night before he went to bed. Of all the day's possible interactions, why had he chosen the one that brings with it such finality, one that could not really be answered at all? It was, in fact, for that exact reason.

At night when they were fast asleep, Bobby recorded, by looking at the leftovers in the bin, what his father had eaten for dinner. Changes in his culinary behavior since his mother left could then be plotted on a graph. He devoted many hours to his files, minded only by the moon through the window, the monocle of a watchful one-eyed God.

When he had finished archiving, Bobby sat on his mother's rug and watched television with the lights off and the sound muted, so the colorful amorphous blobs illuminated the walls around him. He watched the news. Fourteen police cars surrounded an old farmhouse in the countryside, the city a distant twinkling conga. The farmer's chin puckered and his lip trembled as though he only felt things with the bottom half of his face, the way men do. He was worried by what might be hiding in the hay. Across the bottom of the screen scrolled a caption, *The search continues . . .*

Bobby switched on the bathroom light. Patches of piss on the toilet seat blinked like frog spawn. His father was asleep on the floor. A zip line of drool linked his mouth to the tiles.

Bruce opened his eyes and stared at his son until he came into focus. Instinctively his first feeling was one of great shame. Bobby was this shame manifest, cowering by the laundry basket.

"You think it's funny to sneak up on your old man?"

"No."

"To spy on me?" he said, standing.

"No, I promise," Bobby said, shrinking. Bruce rubbed a thumb over his belt buckle. Bobby ran from the room, through the kitchen and up the stairs, where it didn't smell of stale beer.

For the rest of the week, neither addressed the cold space between them, as real as a prison wall. When his father did talk to him Bobby jumped like he'd just popped a blister. Soon he found it hard to get to sleep, day or night. Slumber always came anyway, but late, an unapologetic party guest.

On a drab Monday morning, Bobby ate scraps from the bottom of the cereal box, a paltry handful of beige dust, and walked to the top of the hill. Looking down, the neighborhood formed a basin with his street at the center. Soft grassy inclines rimmed the outskirts of the town, as if the whole place resided inside a dead volcano and its people fed on the warmth of lava underfoot.

Bobby headed to The Ponds, where he'd often come with his mother, to check whether it was frog season yet. No such luck. Stagnant water held aloft a sponge cake of algae, which burped pungent bubbles at the air.

The graying lady at the corner store had spruced up her chocolate selection with some new additions, a pyramid of ruby-red wrappers. Bobby complimented her on her eye for an attractive display, hoping that they might talk, that she might let him stay around a while, or perhaps put him to work restocking the shelves.

"I might be old," she said, carefully topping the pyramid with a Belgian chocolate bauble, "but I'm not a fool."

"Sorry?" Bobby said, and she turned to face him. Her perfume smelled of rosewater, the kind usually worn by a much younger woman, and Bobby was surprised how pleasant he found it.

"You distract me with your chitchat, and then the bigger boys burst in and steal all of my stock."

"No, that's not . . ."

"I've seen those boys around here." She opened the door and flipped the sign to Closed. "Get out. At your age, you should be at home with your parents." Bobby thought about throwing a brick through her window, knowing he never would.

He walked to the park fence and peered through a knothole at knee height to see if anyone was there. The three older boys from his school—Big Kevin, Little Kevin and their de facto leader, Amir Kindell—were carving their initials into the wooden posts by the swings. Though they were some distance away, Bobby recognized them instantly. Not from their features, from their gait, the way they swung—something inside them, loose, unbolted, that would emerge through their mouths or their fists in lightning. He knew that if he cut across the park they would catch him, deaden his arms with rabbit punches, and empty his bag into the mud. He closed his eyes and wished that Sunny were there now, using his superstrength cyborg arms to tear the fence to pieces and his shoulder cannons to blow them all to smithereens. Still shaking, Bobby walked back down the main road.

By mid-afternoon he'd run out of things to do and could think of only one new place to go. Five doors down from his home, on the corner, was a patch of scrubland six steps across and four long. It wasn't a front garden, it wasn't a back garden, merely a forgotten botch in town planning under no one's jurisdiction.

Weeds and flowers merged in bracken, greens and browns bullied by sharp blasts of cerise. Petals twitched and became butterflies. A bee made deliveries between daffodils, a tabby cat snatched at ballerina seeds pirouetting in the air. Bobby sat atop a moist bank of mud that supped spillage from the well-kept hanging basket above it and stabbed his fingers in deep.

From behind him, he heard the grind of rubber rolling over grit, and turned to see a girl riding a red tricycle. Not the kind of tricycle meant for a toddler, but one custom-made, the frame specially welded to wheels as wide as beer barrels. The device had a curious majesty to it, like a sturdy metal horse. Blissfully chuntering to herself, the girl had round cheeks that framed lips pocked with chapping. Her hair, the gold of crisp wheat, had been cut into a functional bowl shape, just short enough at the fringe to stay out of her eyes. She was a little over five feet tall, but, Bobby guessed, maybe a year older than he was, despite the brightly colored clothes she wore, patched with cartoon characters he had long outgrown. She pressed an open hand against her belly where it bloomed over the lip of her tracksuit bottoms and held it down hard on her distended stomach to form a pale expanding starfish on the skin.

Bobby hid in the long grass, not wanting to be seen. What he needed was camouflage, like Sunny and he had used when playing war. Muddy colors, leaves and thicket. Slivers of wintry paint streaked across his face, making him a part of the bark, a nature creature, held in the palm of earth's hand.

The tricycle came to a stop and the girl looked right at him as if they knew each other. Embarrassed, Bobby leapt to his feet, as though he had never been hidden at all.

"What is your first name?" the girl asked.

Thomas Allen, a boy in Bobby's class, did an impression of the kids with special needs from the other school, across town by The Deeps. He rolled his tongue, forced it into his bottom lip and spoke slowly in a stupid voice. He couldn't pretend that she didn't sound a bit like that.

"Bobby," he said.

"What is your last name?"

"Nusku." Bobby lurched onto his tiptoes, balanced on a rock, and peered over her shoulder down the hill. No one was coming. It had suddenly occurred to him what might happen if he was seen talking to her by someone from school. They would tease him, push him around, and until Sunny recovered to full cyborg capability, he'd be left to face them alone. He had to get away from her as quickly as possible.

Bobby had never experienced this heightened self-awareness before, and it shamed him. What would his mother say when she returned—to find Bobby the antithesis of everything she'd taught him about kindness and acceptance?

The girl pulled the elastic on her tracksuit bottoms then let it go, briefly revealing their white imprint on the flesh above her knickers.

"My name is Rosa Reed," she said. "Do you want to play?" She clambered down from the tricycle. In her hand was a black felt-tip pen. She held it out toward Bobby like a runner's baton. "Do you want to play?" she said again. He twirled a blade of long grass between his fingers.

"Play what?" he said. Teeth marks ribbed the plastic pen. "What do you want me to do with that?"

"Write your name." She reached into the basket bolted to the front of the tricycle and pulled out a gnarled notepad with *Rosa Reed Rosa Reed Rosa Reed* written over and over in a fractured jerky scrawl.

"Why?"

"I collect names."

"But you only have one."

"Bobby Nusku," she said, shaking her head, "sometimes you are funny." He took the notepad, wrote down his name and handed it back to Rosa as quickly as he could. It felt important not to be linked physically, by them touching or holding on to the same thing at the same time. Bobby shifted his weight from his left foot to his right. He began to salivate, as if his own unexpected prejudice might actually make him vomit.

"Now," he said, "you have two."

"Wait here," Rosa said. She walked over to the house on the corner and fetched a scuffed leather basketball from the garden. Bobby had had no idea it was where she lived. He'd not afforded her that level of normalcy, to live in a home on a street—his street— just like him. This made him doubly sickened by how embarrassed he remained at the prospect of their being seen together. He tried to swallow the feeling, a morsel of unpalatable meat.

They sat on the curb and bounced the ball to each other. Though she was clumsy, her fingers short and unready, they quickly established a pattern where Bobby imitated Rosa every time she dropped the ball and she laughed until her sides ached. He kept watch for people coming but no one did.

Rosa mimicked Bobby, but her movement was unwieldy. Bobby imagined she was being controlled from the inside by

someone much smaller struggling to reach the pedals. Every game
they played disintegrated into a disharmonic routine of call and
response. He raised an arm, she raised an arm. He threw the ball,
she threw the ball. There was no competition, just a strange mir-
rored dance done in silence, like they were two petals on a flower,
tickled split seconds apart by the same gentle breeze.

Bobby was having fun. For the first time since visiting the
hospital, Sunny drifted from his mind, as did the notion that he
and Rosa might be discovered. For a few lovely moments, self-
awareness relinquished its grip on him, and he was happy. This,
time spent with Sunny had taught him, is what friendship is. To
be given the key to a locked part of your soul.

The first breath of dusk cooled Bobby's skin and gave him goose
bumps. Somewhere in the distance he heard laughter. It bounced
around the air and turned soft, disappearing like an idea of no
merit. He began to panic.

"Rosa," Bobby said suddenly, "I need to go."

"Why?" she asked, spinning the ball in her hands.

"I just do. And so do you. You need to go home."

"Why?"

"Go home!" He pushed her, just gently to turn her around, but
she was stronger than she looked and wouldn't budge. "Please."

"Why?"

He heard the laughter again, rooted, nearby. They were coming. And they would see him with her. This would be *it*. Bobby
gripped her by the shoulders.

"Rosa, you have to go, now." She took the pen and paper from her pocket and scribbled *Rosa Reed Bobby Nusku.*

"No," she said, angrily, "I want to play."

In silhouette against the fall of the sun he saw them, the three boys from the park, walking up the hill.

"I'm sorry," he said.

Too late to run away, Bobby dove behind the bush, leaving Rosa on the pavement. He dug his head between his legs and wrapped his arms around his knees as tightly as he could. He held his breath.

They came, but had not seen him.

"Hello. My name is Rosa Reed. What is your name?" Amir repeated what she'd said as if it were being played back at half speed. The two Kevins laughed. Bobby wanted to run and get help but he was too scared to move. They teased her for a while but she did not understand. Their laughter dipped to a murmur, and then the sounds began to overlap.

The crash of Rosa's pen and pad hitting the road.

The sole of her shoe scraping back and forth against the curb.

Her wailing, like a freak storm.

All Bobby could do was listen, petrified, and imagine the worst. She screamed, then it cut off, as if one of them had a hand across her mouth. And the flapping of her trousers where her legs were kicking, that stopped too, as they lifted her feet and slammed her down into the soil.

The churn of mud moving.

The rustle the bush made as she reached out for Bobby and struck it.

As he discovered shame, the dark being inside us that emerges, hunchbacked and groveling, into the light, Rosa Reed, the girl he'd been too embarrassed to be seen with, was a meter away in the dirt, discovering fear at the very same time.

Only when he'd heard them run away, not laughing but crowing, was Bobby able to stand.

Rosa lay on her back, where they had pressed down on her arms and shoulders hard enough to leave an imprint of her shape in the mud. Her mouth, nose and ears were packed with dirt. The streaming of her eyes ran erratic red routes through the soil stuck to her face. Bobby took her hand and pulled her to a sitting position, then began clearing the mud from her airways with his fingers. He used his sweater to scrape clean her ears and nostrils. Rosa cried. Thin pink threads of blood teemed beneath the skin around her eyes. They were glassy where she had retreated from them, to somewhere else, somewhere better, whatever garden we go to in the mind.

"I'm sorry, Rosa," he said.

It took all of his strength to help her stand, and what loose soil remained in her hair and on her clothes quickly tumbled to the ground. He hoisted her arm around his shoulder and she sobbed so loudly that by the time they reached her front door it was already opening.

A woman stood behind it. Her skin was pale, with dark hair and eyes, the stormy design of a Gypsy Madonna. Rosa clung to the woman and for a while they cried into each other's necks, mud now stuck to them both.

Rosa had begged her mother to be let out of the house to

play, enough that she had finally, reluctantly, relented. It was that simple decision, one of millions over the years, which the woman knew she'd regret for the rest of her days. This was her experience of motherhood, something you can be good at for a lifetime, but only need be bad at for a second.

A gray cloud swallowed the sun. The woman looked up at Bobby and spoke with a will so strong he swore he could see it as a color in the iris of her eyes, the greenish purple of wet snakeskin.

"What happened to my daughter?"

"Some boys came," he said. "They held her down and filled her mouth and eyes and nose with mud." The woman went inside the house and emerged with a bottle of water. Rosa, still unable to catch her breath, held her head back and allowed her to pour its contents into her mouth and over her face. Eventually Rosa took the bottle, and the woman came toward Bobby. She put a hand around the back of his head and forced him to look up at her. Above her head the dark cloud that trapped the sun inside it formed a sullen halo.

"These boys," she said, "were these boys your friends?"

"No," he said, but, still racked with shame, even he thought it sounded like a lie. She pinched harder. "I don't know who they were. I didn't see them."

"You tell me the truth. Did you do this to her?" She pointed toward Rosa. Bobby shook his head. Two tears fell from the woman's face, hot ants landing on his hair.

"No."

"Because I will kill you if you did."

The words tumbled out of Bobby. "I was scared. I hid. And I'm sorry."

"God help me I will break every bone in your body . . ."

"No!" Rosa shouted. The woman let go of his neck. Rosa opened her dirty clenched fist and inside it was the piece of paper bearing their names. The woman took it and read aloud.

"Bobby Nusku."

"This is Bobby Nusku," Rosa said. "Bobby Nusku is my friend."

The piss stain on his trousers was lightening, but was still visible, his cowardice drying on the cloth. The woman had seen it. This circle of his shame complete, he ran as quickly as he could. When he got home, there was nobody there.

CHAPTER FOUR

THE QUEEN

Bobby opened the cabinet beneath the kitchen sink, pulled out a bottle of bleach and found that he wasn't quite strong enough to twist the child lock. The corrugated lid scored his palms. Frustrated, he grabbed the next closest bottle he could find and, with the coarsest brush, scrubbed the piss from his trousers. When his father and Cindy got home from their anniversary dinner at a local Chinese restaurant, they could tell by the smell of lemons that Bobby had used her most expensive shampoo—reserved for her best clients—and ruined her nail brush. When she got angry the skin on her neck pulled taut, bringing all of her features into sharp focus. She demanded Bobby be punished, but he ducked under his father's outstretched arm and fled as quickly as he could.

He spent the evening in his bedroom, frantically gathering things for his mother's return. It had been a while since she'd left. He wasn't sure exactly how long, but he was sure that she'd come back soon. Of course she would. She had never let him down before.

Underneath his mattress, hidden inside the lining, was a scalpel he'd taken from his father's tool belt. He used it to cut a small square of material from every one of Cindy's dresses. In the event that she ran away and changed her identity before Sunny the cyborg was up and running, robbing Bobby of his shot at vengeance, this would make life simpler. By slipping the square into the hole in the cloth, Sunny would be able to confirm her true identity. Then he could destroy her. Have fire dance in circles at her feet, scorch her skeleton, and leave nothing but a black mound of ash inside her clothes where her body used to be. Perhaps then she would feel foolish for her flammable hair.

Bobby had never been this angry before. His mother always taught him that anger was a wasted energy, that it was better turned to love. But it felt good, coursing through him, cooking his blood. He wanted to cut himself, let it out, spurt a great red arc across the room. Watch it cool on the cold windowpane where he now saw his reflection, a swarm of veins in his temples. The same as his father. But he didn't want to be like his father. Not now, not ever. How strong must a man's legs be, Bobby wondered, to always carry this deadweight of hate in his gut?

Hidden in a rusty biscuit tin at the back of the wardrobe was a wedge of old family photographs. While the scalpel was still sharp enough, Bobby cut his father's head out of each and every one.

He carefully placed all the new samples in the empty cereal box and numbered them individually for his files. Then he turned off the light and waited in the darkness for everybody else to go to sleep. It didn't take long. Their bed was creaky and old, grinding to the choppy rhythm of their brief, passionless sex. Afterward, snoring. *Happy anniversary*, he thought.

Creeping, as quietly as he could, he went downstairs to watch television. On the news they showed a helicopter chasing a spotlight through some fields. The farmhouse where the police had been looked lonely against the pinpricks of the night's celestial entertainment. Bobby switched on the subtitles so that he could understand what the man—Detective Jimmy Samas, according to the captions—was saying. He was a young man. Too young, Bobby thought, to have such an important job. Usually the news was comprised of bulldog faces talking, jowly politicians and baggy-chinned union officials. The detective didn't seem long out of school and he looked embarrassed, or perhaps just sick of the rain. Still, he reassured everyone watching at home, "While the trail has gone cold for now, be in no doubt that the hunt will go on."

Birds sang in the dawn. How glorious it must be, Bobby thought, to forget the day that went before and wake up full of song.

Drizzle, a fine cobweb veil, the streets a cobalt mirror of the sky. Bobby wandered. Flower beds half dug, empty graves on the roadside, with a sculpture, scratched and rusting, the headstone for a dead town. He walked the long way around, to nowhere specifically if you asked his legs, but his heart knew where it was going—to the place he had thought of all night.

"Bobby Nusku," said the woman. He enjoyed the way she pronounced his name. It was nothing like the way his father said it, as if hacking at the words with his tongue.

"Hello," he said, staring at his shoes. He was pleased to see his piss stains had been washed from the ground by the rain.

"What are you doing out here? You're soaking wet," she said. She hooked the wet ringlets of his fringe from his forehead with a dainty finger. "You'll get sick."

"I'm okay."

"I called the police about what happened. They came to speak to Rosa. I didn't know where to find you."

Bobby scratched the back of his leg with his toe.

"I have something to tell you."

"Well in that case, you'd better come in." Bobby hesitated. "I know that Rosa would like to see you. My name is Valerie. Valerie Reed. But you can call me Val. Everybody else does."

Val Reed draped a soft red towel around Bobby's shoulders and sat him at the kitchen table. Boiling the kettle, she let the steam stroke her face, then spooned chocolate powder into a mug and poured the hot water on top.

Rosa came downstairs from the bathroom, where Val had been bathing her.

"Hello, Bobby Nusku," she said, and he was surprised by how delighted she seemed to find him sitting there. She held his hand, and he noticed that her fingernails glowed the white of hospital linen. Bobby had never seen anyone so clean. It made him grossly aware of the dirt that had dried inside his ears. Val opened a bag of marshmallows. He took one and enjoyed how it fizzled on his tongue.

"What do you have to tell me?" she said.

"I have a friend," Bobby said. "He's a cyborg."

"A cyborg?" Val smiled. "What a useful friend to have."

"He's still being built at the moment, but as soon as he's finished, I can get him to kill those boys for you."

"Oh, well . . . I'm not sure anyone should be killed."

"Then how will we stop them from doing it again?"

"Bobby," she said, "it's very kind of you to want to look out for Rosa like that, but believe me when I say that there are many, many other ways."

A dog waddled into the room, stubby and flanked by thick tubes of flesh. His eyes were pink and drooped so that the exposed flesh beneath the fur caught spikes of light as he moved. In his mouth was Val's old wristwatch, which he had taken a liking to chewing. The mangled leather strap hung from the sides.

"Hello, Bert," Rosa said. Groaning, he dropped to the floor, having realized long ago that his survival didn't depend on his cooperation. Val wrestled her watch from his jaws and placed a biscuit close to his mouth. He scooped it up sideways with his tongue, leaving a semicircle of glistening drool and crumbs on the linoleum.

"The police won't do anything," Bobby said. "They come to your house and then they go away again."

"And how do you know that?"

"I've seen it." The screech of chair legs pushing back across the floor made Bert run away. Val stood.

"Are you hungry?" she said.

"Yes," Bobby said.

"Then let me make you something to eat."

Rosa and Bobby watched cartoons. After a while they tried to play hide-and-seek but abandoned the idea because Rosa only wanted to have whatever role Bobby assigned himself, the hider or the seeker, circumstances in which the engine of the game failed. He counted that she had written his name beside hers seventeen times in a notebook. The letters fluctuated wildly in size, never making it to the end of the page before being herded together by an invisible lasso.

Val called for them to come downstairs and they were met with a delicious-looking spread of salmon, slightly flushed, potatoes the size of eggs framing a collapsing knob of melting butter and weird green spears Bobby had never seen before. She explained they were called asparagus and would make his wee smell strange. Rosa laughed.

"Val Reed," she said, "sometimes you are funny."

"You're sure your parents won't be wondering where you are?" Val said to Bobby, a rock salt snowflake settling on her lips.

"Yes," Bobby said, pushing a wedge of lemony salmon into the well beneath his tongue.

"I'm sure that's not true. You should call them."

"My father isn't in."

"What about your mother?"

"We don't know where she is."

Val formed an O shape with her mouth, the lips undulating to make the circle bigger, then smaller. Unbeknownst to her this happened perfectly in time with Bobby's heartbeat.

"We have ice cream."

"My father says that I'm not allowed to eat ice cream."

"No," Val said, "he's mistaken. You're allowed to eat as much ice cream as you like, whenever it takes your fancy."

Rosa, Val and Bobby ate ice cream on the sofa. They watched Disney films until Rosa fell asleep. For Bobby, the hours passed quickly and happily.

When Val left the room to let Bert into the garden, Bobby watched through the window. It was dark outside and his breath made misty blooms on the glass. Tripled, his reflection chased itself around the pane. By the time she'd returned Bobby had switched off the television. There was no sound but the buzzing of appliances half-alive. The toaster. The bulb. One red eye in a shallow state of sleep, waiting, hoping to be woken.

Val looked handmade, Bobby thought. The pinched bridge of her nose glowed. It was elbow shaped at the end, and her chin was neat and square.

"That's enough TV for one day," Val said. "Our eyes will come out of our heads."

"Does that really happen?" he said.

"No, not really. At least I don't think so."

"I don't know because I don't watch much TV."

"You don't? That's unusual. I thought all kids watched lots of TV these days."

"Not me."

"So what do you do? Do you read?"

"My dad doesn't have many books."

"Oh." Val looked at her daughter, chasing a dream around behind her eyelids. "You should go," she said, "it is late."

"It's okay," Bobby said.

"You don't have a home time?"

"No."

"Then what would you like to do?"

Bobby thought about it. "We can talk."

"Talk?"

"Uh-huh."

"About what?"

"You're the lady," he said, "you can choose."

Val couldn't decide whether there was a better or worse person to confide in than a child. On the one hand, the advice he could give was limited. On the other, the solace offered was profound. It had been a long time since she'd had a meaningful conversation, and three weeks since she'd exchanged purposeful words with anybody apart from Rosa. On occasion, when Val spoke, the sound of her voice constructing sentences took her by surprise. She struggled to remember her own phone number, so unused was she to sharing it. The friends she'd had at school were gone, Rosa's birth the catalyst for their slowly backing away. They were uncomfortable with Rosa's disability and how the extra demands of it affected the group whenever they got together. She supposed they could not have been her friends at all. There was, at least, some satisfaction in that.

These days she looked forward to visiting the doctor. As cold as his hands were, small talk was a welcome respite from the otherwise lengthy nothingness. Sometimes she considered faking symptoms, just to feel that rough chill against her body and talk about the changing of the weather.

But this, sitting here with the boy, seemed like a glimpse into the world of real life, one that she never really got to be a part of. She and Rosa had an existence with its own reality. This peek at another made her curious. And talkative. Before long, Val had told Bobby a lot of what little she had about herself to tell. The warmth of his companionship lingered like the imprint of a pillow on the skin after a good night's sleep.

Though he enjoyed spending time with Val, Bobby felt strange for reasons he couldn't explain. It was as if she was staring, studying his face, and he found it difficult to maintain eye contact with her for long periods of time. As he buttoned his coat he realized why it seemed so unusual. She wasn't looking over his shoulder.

"Can I ask you a question?" Bobby said.

"Sure," Val said, "anything."

Bobby paused for a second, arranged the words in his head, checked their order and the way they sounded, what they meant in his mouth and her ears, making sure the specifics were perfectly tuned. "You promise you won't be offended?"

"How can I know that until you've said it?"

"It's just that I'm interested . . ."

"Then ask."

Bobby swallowed. "What is wrong with Rosa?"

Val thought, and for more than a minute they sat in complete silence, him wishing the words were attached to his voice box with string so that he could reel them straight back into his throat.

"Nothing at all," she said, and then held his hand.

Val fetched Bobby's shoes from the cupboard beneath the stairs. Scuffed and worn, their size reminded her how young he was, how old he seemed.

"I have an idea," she said. "Tomorrow you should come to work with me."

Val tore a blank page from Rosa's notebook and quickly scribbled a few words on it, which Bobby craned to see. As she reached across her daughter to hand it to him, the paper fluttered against Rosa's sleeping breath.

Bobby glanced at the paper, and saw the words *mobile library*, with an address. Somewhere that he had never been.

CHAPTER FIVE

THE NON-FIRE-BREATHING DRAGON

Bobby assumed the whole neighborhood could hear his father and Cindy fight. He could make it out from halfway down the street. This one was especially loud, enough that he could sneak in and retreat to his bedroom without being noticed.

Peppered by the gunfire of slamming doors, the argument had a number of false endings, only to ferociously reignite out of silence. Finally reaching a crescendo, Cindy screamed and Bruce hurriedly left the house. From the upstairs window Bobby watched him go, climb into his van and speed off down the road. This was how their fights always ended, though Bobby noticed that they were getting shorter, her eyes blacker.

Half an hour later, three of Cindy's friends arrived. The women stayed up late drinking wine and chuffing cigarettes, celebrating Saturday night in a way that suggested it was something other than an inevitability. Smoke slunk its way up the stairs, filling the corners and hanging from the ceiling. It crept beneath Bobby's bedroom door to where he lay with his ear to the carpet like an Indian chieftain listening for the distant rumble of hooves. He coughed four times with his mouth buried in the soft flesh of his arm, so that nobody would hear.

Once Cindy's friends left and before his father got home, Bobby went downstairs to collect samples for his files. More accurately, they were for a subsection of his files built around a diary he kept which detailed everything that had taken place in the time since his mother had gone. Where possible, the names of everybody who came was logged, next to simple line sketches of their face in portrait and in profile, and a brief description of what they were wearing. Bedtimes were recorded. Receipts and bank statements were salvaged from the waste bin and preserved. That night he found a precious trove of artifacts. Pocket mirrors lined with gunky white residue. A mascara wand with eyelashes trapped in it. A packet of chocolate penises, one half eaten and left out to melt. He knew that his mother would want to know every last detail of what she had missed, and the more physical evidence he had the better.

Gee Nusku had painted these ceilings. She had carpeted these floors. For Bobby, this house was her, these walls her rib cage and within it her heart. He would keep it beating until the day his own stopped dead.

Despite working on his files all night he was not tired when his father returned, though he hid beneath his duvet until Bruce again lost consciousness on the cold bathroom floor. Bobby was still not asleep when the sunshine searched his bedroom. He was far too excited for that. For the first time in weeks he had somewhere to go, and friends who would be waiting when he got there.

Early on Sunday morning, disco-ball dewdrops lit up the grass. Bobby didn't visit The Deeps often. Wide cars lined the streets. New houses emerged from the grounds as if built and held together by the vibrant flower beds that surrounded them. White marble lions stood guard, wooden beams split faux-aged façades and somewhere, in what Bobby imagined was a magnificent garden, he could hear the impatient trickle of a small fountain. Even the clouds seemed to be on their best behavior. Pearly, plump and still, waiting to be captured by a calm hand's loving watercolor. Bobby assumed that no one around The Deeps was half eating chocolate penises, let alone leaving them out to melt.

First he spotted Bert, then Rosa, then Val following behind them. Rosa gave him a tight bear hug and he tried not to show how much it hurt. Val removed a jangling cluster of keys from her handbag to unlock the gate.

"I'm glad you came," she said. "I wasn't sure you'd make it."

"I'm glad you came too," Rosa said, and Bobby smiled. They slipped through the gap one by one.

The mobile library was the biggest vehicle Bobby had ever seen. He counted sixteen wheels, a couple of spares stowed above the axles for luck. The cab at the front bore a smile in its grille of silver teeth, and twin horns of exhaust piping curved up into the sky.

"Are you a librarian?" Bobby asked.

"Oh," Val said, "I wish."

They walked to the rear of the truck, where Val twisted the key in the hole and let Rosa press the button. With a loud clunk, the giant steel door burst open and transformed into a staircase that wound down to their feet.

Inside the library, books were stacked on shelves floor to ceiling on three sides. Bobby had never seen so many, or even imagined that they existed in this number. The column of space running through the center of the truck was ribbed with sets of smaller bookcases forming a simple maze leading to the back. The carpet was woven from hostile burgundy fibers, except for an area at the rear where it was thick and woolen. To Bobby it felt equal parts forbidden and mysterious. Already, he didn't want to leave. .

Rosa sat down and emptied out the contents of her bag. She took a pen, put the lid in her mouth and forced the curled-up end of her tongue inside it. Then she wrote *Rosa Reed, Val Reed, Bobby Nusku* over and over in her notebook.

Val found cleaning fluids in the cupboard behind the counter, fluorescent and upright like fireworks waiting to be lit. While a bucket filled with hot water, she polished the tops and edges of the two smaller blocks of shelving, Science Fiction and Biography. Once the water had cooled she added a dash of bleach, and Bobby watched as she mopped the stairs. Wrung out, the mop was a perfect length for knocking down the cobwebs that had collected in the high corners around History. Then she cleaned the lavatory.

"Sometimes," she said to nobody in particular, "I worry that life is just the journey between toilets."

With the carpet vacuumed, Val invited Rosa and Bobby to sit outside on a few old deck chairs under a retractable awning above the entrance. They shared the sandwiches she'd made that morning. Bacon, lettuce and tomato on a springy rye bread that seductively reassumed its shape when squeezed. Hunger had scooped a hollow in Bobby's belly and he ate quickly. Rosa threw her crusts to Bert, who wolfed them down without even bothering to chew.

"Is the cleaning done?" Bobby asked.

"Cleaning is never done," Val said. "All the while you're cleaning, someone else is dirtying. There's always other people, Bobby, and some have grubby hands."

"I won't dirty anything."

"I know," she said, and smiled.

"Val," Rosa said, putting her head to Val's chest as if listening in on a conversation inside her rib cage. "Where does the library go?"

Bobby enjoyed observing Val and Rosa as mother and daughter. It was already obvious to him that they had established routines, ones he would never wish to interrupt, and that was how they got through the days together. He could tell by the way Rosa reclined on Val's lap and closed her eyes that she asked this question every week, even though she knew its answer verbatim.

"Well, now that it is nice and clean, somebody will come on Monday morning and drive it to a different place so that the people who live close by can come and borrow some books with their library cards. Then they will drive it to a different place every day until next Friday, when they leave it here so that we can come and clean it again on Sunday morning. Except they might stop it soon because it costs too much money." Val ran her fingers through Rosa's hair with a gentle scissor action, coming to rest at the top of her back. "Mobile libraries aren't just trucks like ours. They have them all over the world, and in some countries, they use animals instead."

"What animals?"

"Well, in Kenya, in Africa, where it is very hot all of the time, they use camels. The Camel Library Service. They have twelve camels, and the camels are big and strong so they can carry really heavy bags on their humps. Between them they can carry around seven thousand books, and they deliver them to all of the people who live in all the little villages all over the desert." Rosa twisted the fingers of her left hand in the palm of her right. "Can you imagine, all of the camels slobbering over the books with their big horrible tongues?" Val stuck her tongue out as far as she could and flapped it around. Rosa laughed. Bert retreated underneath the rear axle, licking the last of the dew from his paws. "In Zimbabwe, which is also in Africa and is also very hot, they have a library in a cart that is pulled around by a donkey. He must be a big donkey because he has to be very strong to pull all those books. Do you know what else he has to be strong to do?"

"What?"

"Ee-or!" A plane passed, lost in the swirl of the clouds, only just loud enough to drown out Rosa's giggles. "In Norway, which is always a bit cold, they have one on a boat so that they can take the books to all of the old people who live on little islands. And in Thailand, where it is warm and rainy and they have jungles, they use huge elephants to take books to all the people who live too far away in tree houses." Val brought her arm to her nose like a trunk, pursed her lips and made a noise reminiscent of a trumpet. "Which would you prefer? I think I'd prefer the elephant. It'd be able to reach all of the books on the high shelves."

"The elephant," Rosa said, then she took off and jumped into the biggest puddle she could find. Water exploded around her feet, soaking her trousers from ankle to knee.

"I like your library," Bobby said.

For a moment, Val had forgotten he was there. "Thank you for coming. You can take some books if you like."

Bobby was unaccustomed to receiving gifts, and his first instinct was that he'd need to pay. His father would never let him have the money.

"What for?" he asked.

"For reading, of course. As long as you bring them back next week."

"I can just take them?"

"As long as you promise not to lose them, or rip them to pieces." What books there were in Bobby's house had long been stashed in the attic by his father, who said they made a mess of the place. Besides a car repair manual and a Gideon Bible taken from a hotel, they were mostly picture books his mother had gotten for him as a toddler. She taught him that they were precious. He still associated the smell of their pages with her voice, and the quiet creak of a hardback spine with the warmth of her bosom on his cheek.

"I promise more than all of the other promises added together forever." He crossed his heart and showed her that his fingers were spread so as not to jinx the deal.

"In every book is a clue about life," she said. "That's how stories are connected. You bring them to life when you read them, so the things that happen in them will happen to you."

"I don't think the things that happen in books will happen in my life," he said.

"That's where you're wrong," she said. "You just don't recognize them yet."

It started to rain. Val gestured for Rosa to come inside. Picking up Bert, his body falling limp in her arms, she started toward the library. Bobby edged his deck chair a little closer to Val's, so that their legs were touching.

"It's nice to have a new friend," he said, and she agreed, already suspecting that the word *nice* didn't do his arrival in their lives justice.

Val let Bobby borrow four books, even though he didn't have a library card. He promised to take care of them, and he did, by hiding them in a place where no one would ever find them. At the back of the wardrobe behind the boxes of his mother's stuff, with his files.

One of the books, *The Iron Man* by Ted Hughes, was about a little boy and a giant robot who become friends. Bobby wondered if this was a clue about his life. He was the boy and Sunny was the robot. He wished more than anything that he could share it with Sunny. By now, Sunny would be able to scan the book with his eyes in five seconds flat and memorize it forever.

Bobby was so busy reading the books that he fell behind on

the upkeep of his files. He forgot to count the empty bottles. He failed to log what times of day the door slammed. Women came to have their hair cut and he didn't even note their names, or which celebrity's hairstyle they wished to emulate.

He wanted to be in a book, to have an adventure. But his story seemed set. There was no point in its ever being read.

When he woke the sky was newborn pink. Waiting for his father to go to work was infuriating—Bruce was always running late, funneling black coffee into his throat, mustering appetite enough to swallow breakfast. Bobby noticed the skin around his father's eyes speckling, the yellowness of his cheeks. How hilarious it would be, he thought, if on his mother's return she didn't recognize the man to whom she was still married.

As soon as his father had gone, Bobby went straight to Val and Rosa's house, Val made breakfast, comprising many things he had never tried before. Spinach. Poached eggs. A white cheese that crumbled in the warmth of his fingertips.

"What would you like to do today?" Val asked.

"I don't know," Bobby said, "what is there to do?"

"We could go to the park?" Bobby shook his head. "You don't like the park?"

"I don't like it as much as I like it here."

Every week, Val allowed Rosa to choose a book from the mobile library, and since discovering a beautifully illustrated edition of *Alice's Adventures in Wonderland* by Lewis Carroll, she had clutched it tightly to her chest. On the cover, rendered in frail gold leaf, was the image of the Cheshire Cat's grin. Each tooth carried a letter, executed in elegant calligraphy, combining to spell out the heroine's name. It took Bobby a few seconds to realize that Rosa wasn't just showing it to him, but urging him to take it, to open it and read.

"I can't read it to you," he said.

"Why?" Rosa asked.

"I just can't."

"Why?"

"Because . . ." Any excuses he could think of seemed to scatter as soon as they came to him, like a child kicking away a ball it wants to pick up. Rosa thrust the book into his lap and opened it on the first page. Bobby looked to Val for help, but she took off her slippers and reclined in her chair with both hands behind her head. Rosa mimicked her mother and they both laughed. Sighing, Bobby finished the last of his toast. He began to read aloud. Alice, bored on the riverbank, chased the clock-toting White Rabbit down the rabbit hole and got lost in a room with many doors.

"Do the voices," Rosa said. Val snatched the book from Bobby.

"Come on Rosa," she said, "give the poor boy a break."

Bert, upset by the kerfuffle, waddled past them into the living room, the mangled remnants of Val's leather watchstrap a macabre tongue hanging from his lips.

"To the den!" Rosa said, grabbing Bobby by the hand and following Bert into the living room that overnight she and her mother had completely transformed. Suspended a few feet from the ground was a false ceiling of sheets and blankets, hoisted atop upturned sofa cushions and stacks of pillows from the beds upstairs. Beneath that, a catacomb, into which Bobby crawled behind Rosa, imagining a labyrinth that expanded forever. Val listened to them laughing and wondered what was so funny.

"Val," Rosa said, forcing her head through the gap between two cushions in the wall of the den. Val was sitting on the stairs admiring their handiwork.

"Yes?"

"Can Bobby Nusku come and live here with us?" Bobby stopped dead. Val saw the hump of his back rising and falling underneath the sheets.

"Oh, I think his father would be wondering where he is."

"He won't," Bobby said.

"How do you know?"

"One time I stayed out all night because I thought I'd killed my friend Sunny."

"All night?" Bobby could tell that Val thought he was exaggerating.

"Yeah. I sat on his doorstep until the morning when his mum came home."

"And nobody came looking for you?"

"Nobody," he said. Val looked at the den and realized that she wanted to be in there with them. She felt like Alice, full of EAT ME cake, too big to fit through the door.

Bobby appeared at the far end of the room, beside the fireplace, where he had widened an entrance to the den that she would easily be able to crawl through.

"I don't think so," she said.

"Come on," he said. Val dropped down on to all fours and

shuffled, self-consciously, across the carpet toward him. With each inch she moved forward she regressed another year. "Go in," he said. So she did, reminded of how it felt when she was a little girl, when she and her father would play in the attic, and he would bury her in blankets and pillows until she giggled so much she could barely breathe. Rosa took her hand and led her to the center of the den. There, she found what they had been laughing at. Bert, licking the leather watchstrap's lacquer from his teeth, a luminous Cheshire Cat grin of his own.

On hot days they laid a blanket out on the plush grass in the garden and had a picnic. When it rained they stayed indoors and took turns reading aloud.

Bobby taught Val how to keep a ball in the air using just her head and she taught him about psychology and sociology. How people work on the inside and out. About experiences and what they make you do.

"I haven't had any experiences," he said, "I'm not old enough."

"Sadly," Val said, "that's not how experiences work."

"How do you know so much? Were you a professor before you were a cleaner?" She smiled and the tuning fork of his heart hummed.

"I wanted to be. Or something like that. Instead I clean around the textbooks and take them home to read afterward. I suppose I'm my own professor. But really I'm just a cleaner."

"Well, it's like you said, the world always needs cleaners. There is always someone making things dirty."

Val caught a laugh in her throat before it could cleave open her lips. Rosa dangled treats in front of Bert's nose, but he remained unimpressed by their half-hypnotic twizzle.

When the weather was warm enough they went to town. Every time Bobby recognized somebody from school, he walked beside Rosa with his jaw pointed upward at the sky. For the first time in his life, he felt pride and confidence, those twin spires that rise from the soul when you have a good friend.

One day they saw Cindy drinking coffee and eating chocolate cake with another woman, her hair not even slightly reminiscent of the film star's it was intended to be. The indistinct memory of a tattoo had blurred on her forearm, a permanent dark green mess. Bobby slowed to hide behind the ballooning ruffles of Val's dress as they passed by, and though convinced he'd made it, they had moved out of step. He had been seen.

Two thoughts entered Cindy's mind. The first was how odd it seemed that Bobby was with the woman and her disabled daughter who lived at the end of the road. She considered calling Bruce, but knew better than to disturb him while he was working. The second was that she should finish her cake, which was delicious.

As the end of the summer approached, Val received the news she had been dreading in the form of a letter from a man she had never met. It said, as succinctly as it was possible to put it, that the mobile library was closing down. Funding had expired, and despite a small but vocal campaign to save it, belt-tightening had cut off blood to the head. It would be mothballed, starved of the resources needed to operate. In return, Val wrote a letter of complaint to the local council. She received no reply.

To her surprise, her immediate concern was not the loss of wages. This was important—without the money she earned for cleaning she would need to quickly find another way of supplementing the pittance she received from the state to help look after Rosa. If she couldn't secure a job with hours so suited to Rosa's care, then she would need to consider moving into a smaller house, perhaps an apartment with one bedroom, like the place where they'd lived before she worked at the mobile library. But that was not what kept her awake at night. Instead, she lay in bed counting the memories she cherished, more of which had happened in the last six weeks, in the mobile library, than at any other time in her life. The stories they had shared. The discoveries made in them. How they had cheered a victorious hero and willed on a villain's comeuppance, as if these were tales of their own existence. Parts of themselves they'd never noticed absent, concealed in the ink on the page.

The thought of the library closing, and what would be lost, seemed, in those early hours when the starlings sing, incomprehensible. There could be no other place for her, Rosa and Bobby to be together, she knew that, and that was what she found herself missing even before it had ended. Togetherness—the creation of something new, something bigger than the sum parts of its people. She was sure that her daughter, who she often knew better than she knew herself, was awake in the next room, struggling with the same giant loss.

Bobby felt it more keenly still. He didn't want the summer

to end, but this news had sounded its death knell. He dreamed of closing himself inside the mobile library and bolting shut the doors. He could see in the darkness. There were no windows, yet there were thousands of windows, in every book on every shelf.

Despite the many ways his imagination had been opened up by the mobile library, he could not imagine wanting to be anywhere else, with anyone else. The mere thought of it filled his bones with the inexorable ache of yearning. It felt like being ill, so badly that it crossed his mind he might die. If it weren't for Sunny being back at school with him, he was sure that he definitely would.

"I don't want to go back to school," he said to Val as they sat on the steps of the mobile library late one night. "I want you to teach me with Rosa in the library. That way you can be a teacher and I don't have to go anywhere. We both get what we want." The separate swaths of her makeup—pink across her cheeks, blue across her eyes, red across her lips—conspired to resemble the showy belly of an exotic bird, circling overhead.

"You have to go back," she said, with evident displeasure. "It can't be summer forever." But Bobby was sure that somewhere, in a book he hadn't yet read, it could.

CHAPTER SIX

THE MOTHER

Only if the photograph of Bobby's mother was carefully examined would anyone spot the slight rotundity of her belly, cupped by shadow in her floral summer dress. The bump would be Bobby's brother or sister one day.

In the photograph, she held Bobby in her arms. Suitcases full of their holiday clothes lay beside them on the curb.

When he returned from Val and Rosa's house, Bobby often felt wistful and lonely in his bedroom. He'd been too young when it was taken to remember it, three, maybe four he guessed, but he found that looking at the photograph transported him into a memory he'd since built, where everything and nothing was real. There, on his back, holding the photograph above his face and with his feet on the radiator for warmth, he could still feel the faint pressure of her hands beneath his buttocks, and smell Mentho-lyptus sweets on her tongue where she kissed him, regardless of whether she ate them or not.

It was the first morning of the new term, another school year beginning. Bobby placed the photograph in the front pocket of his schoolbag with a lock of his mother's hair bound neatly by thread, two broken pencils and a chocolate biscuit that had melted and reset. This was the day he'd see Sunny as a cyborg for the first time—Jules Clay might not have been able to stop her son from injuring himself, but she always made damned sure he never missed a day of school. Bobby would tell Sunny what Amir and the two Kevins had done to his new friend Rosa, and have his vengeance wreaked. Then he'd never have to worry about crossing the park again. Though nervous, Bobby could barely wait. He took a wrench, a pair of pliers and a pocket screwdriver from his father's toolbox in case Sunny needed any urgent repairs. When his father found out he would be angry, but by then he'd have a fully functional cyborg bodyguard who could crush his skull and make a beach from the dust of his bones.

Bobby waited until the last possible moment before leaving the house and arrived at the school just as the last of the stragglers filed through it. Bodies flocked around the playground, swooping and diving, this way and that. New uniforms were noisily compared. The collar of last year's shirt pinched the skin on Bobby's neck, the cloth round his thighs strangled the flesh. Familiar faces, newly licked with suntans, kept an eye on the far side tennis courts, on the incline where new pupils instinctively herded. The school loomed over them with a sense of foreboding only institutional buildings can inspire. Bobby felt a pang in his stomach when he looked up toward the roof.

He checked behind the thornbushes by the art department where Sunny's tunnel was now a faint gray smudge on the brickwork. This was where they usually met, but Sunny was not there. Instead he found two older pupils locked in a long sloppy kiss, undisturbed even by the sounding of the bell.

Mr. Oats had been peculiarly shaped by years of overindulgence in pastry and whisky. His hair was flat at the sides and on the top. A frosting of toothpaste had settled on the uneventful thinness of his top lip, which had somehow forged a right angle from nothing. He held the register out in front of him and leaned forward, as if he was going to preach.

"Penny Abrahams," he said. Penny's arm shot up into the air. She had spent the summer changing, new curves carved into her tumbling silhouette. Mr. Oats took a second to gather himself before proceeding, but in that simple thrusting of her hand upward and the extension of a natural line—this larval transformation of womanhood—she'd sucked the wind right out of him.

"Thomas Allen." Thomas Allen, who hadn't changed at all over the summer, limply made himself known.

Mr. Oats read the entire register without saying the name *Sunny Clay*.

"Sunny Clay," Bobby said. "You missed out Sunny Clay." The

chair in front of his, where Sunny always sat, was empty. Bobby refused to look at it.

"Sit down, Bobby," Mr. Oats said. He slipped the register inside the drawer of his desk and slammed it shut. Thomas Allen whimpered.

"But you've left somebody out. How can it be a register if you missed out Sunny Clay?" Bobby heard his name being whispered behind him, carelessly churned in the mouths of others. He became flustered and unable to think clearly. Nobody in the room would have guessed that it was born of a fear that his protector was not there.

"I said sit down, Bobby. When you're a teacher it will be your turn to stand up in front of the class and say whatever you like. That day is not today."

"Just because he's turned into a cyborg, it doesn't mean he isn't part of the class anymore." Other children began to snicker.

"What on earth are you talking about?"

"Sunny is a cyborg now, and when he comes he'll smash your skeleton to smithereens!" Everybody gasped. Bobby was sure he felt the air move around him. He kicked over his desk. The cheap wood splintered, scattering sharp needles across the freshly shined floor. Penny Abrahams screamed, a far fuller scream than she'd have managed just a few precious months before. Mr. Oats took Bobby by the arm and walked him out of the classroom. Once they were in the corridor with the door shut behind them, the laughter grew loud enough to rattle the glass.

Mr. Oats pushed Bobby against the wall. He could feel anger vibrating in his twisted arthritic hands.

"I suggest you calm down," he said, though he himself was not calm. That wave had already broken, and the foam of its pungent wash gathered in the corners of his mouth.

"Fuck you," Bobby said, pretty sure that it would be impossible to be in any deeper trouble than he already was. Mr. Oats had known all manner of profanity hurled at him in his forty years teaching. These days he hardly noticed. He drew slowly onward like a hearse, ignoring their insults, the flowers flung at it. Nobody knew what an exemplary teacher he had been in the beginning. He barely remembered himself.

Bobby sat outside the headmistresses' room for the rest of the morning copying equations from a math textbook. When Mr. Oats arrived with Mrs. Pound beside him they talked quietly, then summoned Bobby into her office. A plant on her desk had died over the summer. Cigarette smoke tinged the blinds. Everything was a sickly, terminal yellow.

Mrs. Pound sifted through a stack of papers, occasionally circling lines with a thick red pen. Despite stern features, everybody said that she was a kind woman and so Bobby was not scared, especially when she talked in her gentle, dripping lilt.

"How are things at home, Bobby?"

"Fine," he said.

"I guess what I mean is that we know things haven't been easy for you. So, as it's a new term, I wanted to see how you were doing." Mr. Oats had declined a seat and was cramming himself into a small space between the door and a filing cabinet. Conversing with children was hard enough, but a child and woman in a position of authority stretched him beyond his meager means. He yearned for the tobacco-spiced sanctity of the pub darts team, the order with which they approached drinking beer, the strange solace they found in the smell of each other's farts. He hadn't always been this miserable. Bobby could see it in his eyes, a look he recognized from his father.

They had never had a holiday before. Bobby's mother showed him a picture postcard of the sea and he didn't even recognize it as being water, rather a mass of blue crystal baking in the sun.

"What's that?" he asked, pointing to a long, waggling stripe of white.

"Chalk," she said, "a cliff face."

He sat on the bed and watched her pack. She folded the clothes into neat squares, then stacked small towers of them atop one another. She assembled the towers into columns, until there was a grid of clothing layered by material. Wools at the bottom, silks at the top, cotton a soft filling in the middle. Then she deconstructed her work and rebuilt it inside the case. Afterward she had Bobby jump up and down on top of it so that the buckle came together with the strap. She strained and pulled until finally the metal prong slid through the eyelet, then explained what they'd find when they got there.

"Giant cliffs," she said, "the very edge of the country."

"What do you mean the very edge? The end?"

"The end. There is no more. It's like flicking through a story-book and running out of pages."

"What happens if you fall off the country? Can you get back on again?"

"No one ever falls off the country. It's impossible."

"What if the edge of the country moves until it's not underneath your feet anymore?"

"For that to happen you'd need to stand in the same place for millions of years."

"We'd move, though, wouldn't we?"

"Yes, baby," she said, "we would move." She closed the bedroom door and fixed Bobby with her most serious stare. "Now I need you to listen to me."

"Uh-huh."

"I mean really listen to me."

"Okay."

"When we get there we're going to do something very special."

"What is it?"

"We're going to run away." His mother lifted him off the packed suitcase and held him in her arms. "Together, just you and I."

"To where?"

"It doesn't matter. We'll be gone."

"How?"

"When we get to the beach . . ."

"By the cliffs?"

"Yes, by the cliffs, I'll ask your father to go and get an ice cream, and when he's gone we'll walk away, just like that." Bobby toyed with the shiny buckle on the case.

"He won't like that."

"No, I don't expect he will."

Gee Nusku laughed, delicately, like bubbles bursting on water. She pushed her hair (long, silken, its texture an innate obsession of Bobby's even then) behind her ears and stood, looking down at her feet. It had been so long since she'd worn heels. Bobby's father didn't like them. He said they made her too tall, but by that he meant taller than him. Gee stashed her highest pair inside a beach bag, wrapped up inside a threadbare towel.

"All you have to do is keep a secret," she said.

"About your shoes?"

"Well, yes, about my shoes. But also about us running away. Your daddy cannot know."

Bobby nodded. "Okay."

"You promise?"

"I promise more than all of the other promises added together forever."

"Good boy." She lifted Bobby up from the bed and placed him on the floor. He wound himself tighter, arms hooped around her legs, head pressed against the mound between them, her pregnant belly above him, the impeccable correlation of mother and son.

"You promise you won't go without me?" he said.

"Like I've always taught you. Never hurt anyone. Never lie to anyone. Of course I wouldn't lie to you."

"We're going to lie to Daddy."

Gee sighed. "No, we're just not going to tell him anything. There's a difference."

"So promise."

"I promise more than all of the other promises added together forever. Now get some sleep. In the morning we go on holiday for a very, very long time."

When Bruce got home he was covered in paint. He painted other people's houses for a living. In his own house there were many bare walls of cold plaster, so the air always had a chill in it, a sense of loss that gave Bobby goose pimples. He didn't talk much, and when he did it was mostly about the everyday ins and outs of his solitary profession.

Bruce never worked without a bottle of denatured alcohol tucked into the pocket of his tool belt. He liked its ruthless functionality, how it was the shark of the ethanols. He had spent his entire adult life painting and decorating, and in doing so he had used denatured alcohol as a weapon against almost all of his professional banes. Not just paint, but ink and dust. Even mealybugs, which had overrun the solarium of a florist whose skirting boards he had painted. He had used denatured alcohol to disinfect the cracked skin on his heels before draining an angry-looking blister. He had employed it as a germicide by rubbing it into a persistent cold sore that clung to his top lip like a baby koala. He had even poured it into the glistening wound left when he severed the little finger on his left hand by trapping it in the metal hinge of a foldaway ladder. The surgeons did not commend his efforts when he arrived at the hospital carrying his finger in a beakerful of it. By then it had killed the skin cells, serving fine as an antiseptic for the wound but destroying what had once been there. Still, they were impressed that he had driven himself to Accident and Emergency.

What he liked best about denatured alcohol was that, despite its potency—or rather because of it—its manufacturers still had to put something in it to stop people from drinking it. It was called denatonium benzoate and was the bitterest known chemical compound. Unpalatable to humans, they used it in animal repellents and nail-biting preventatives. Without denatonium, people would drink denatured alcohol even though they knew that it could make them blind or even kill them. Some people still did. What a thing, that you could still love it no matter what ruin it brought. Bruce respected that about it, and deep down hoped the same principle could be applied to him.

"You know this is a waste of time," he said. "The beach will be cold and strewn with dog shit. Everywhere will be packed with tourists. You won't even be able to see the view for the clouds." He pointed at Bobby. "And he'll be wanting everything he sees in every shop. We'll be dragging a screaming child down the seafront in the wind. I don't consider that a holiday."

"It'll be a holiday from this," she said.

They didn't speak again until the next morning as the cases were being loaded into the car, when she tried to soften him up with her special buttery diction. She asked him to take a photograph of her and Bobby leaning on the hood. She held her son in her arms. It took a long time for the flash to go off. Bobby could feel the bump inside her belly. Even though she was changing she was always the perfect shape for him.

Bruce agreed to put the radio on but the air-conditioning was broken, so the windows were open and the wind whipping at their ears meant they couldn't hear the music. Bobby amused himself by picking leather from the back of his father's seat, rolling it up into little balls and making tiny pyramids that collapsed in his hand whenever they hit a bend. His mother had taught him that counting was a good way to make the voice in his head louder than their arguments, so he counted the balls, then the dials on the dashboard, then the bugs' bodies splashed across the windscreen.

After two hours they pulled into a service station forecourt. Bruce got out, slammed the door and walked away sucking on a cigarette. The smoke made pretty designs in the air. He headed to a bar inside a hotel that catered to lonely traveling salesmen and truckers who had decided to stay parked up for the night, rather than face another mile of the road's endless trundle, a sight seared into their every waking minute. Bruce ordered a glass of port, which the barman found in a bottle on a dusty top shelf. Rarely did he drink port, but it seemed to call to him in that moment, bottled promise.

Bobby's mother opened the back passenger side door, unbuckled his seat belt and carried him to a small children's play area, where she pumped coins into a motorized car that suddenly began blinking light and making noise. Strapped in, Bobby went round and round while she watched. She bit divots into the hardened skin on her lips. She didn't like to get upset in front of him, which was why he always went to his room when she asked, as quickly and as quietly as he could.

When they got back to the car, his father was waiting. He hadn't calmed, if anything he seemed angrier, rubbing the stump where his finger once was.

"Hurry up," he said, in a low and bloated grumble. Gee lowered her son into the back of the car and kissed him.

Lips, soft, a cherry freshly plucked.

Bruce turned and stared. No matter how hard she fought the urge, she started to rush, as if he were in charge of how fast she moved. She clipped the seat belt in but it didn't catch and quickly came undone. Flustered, she sat down in the passenger seat and removed her coat.

Once they were moving again, Bobby's father began drumming against the steering wheel. Five fingers and then four, a curious rhythm, always cut abruptly short. Softly at first, so that you could barely hear the tap of it on the plastic, but then louder, and louder still. His mother slipped her fingers free of her rings and her wrists free of her bracelets, then handed the whole trove over to Bobby.

"Here," she said, "count these." So he did. One two three four five six seven. One two three four five six seven. One two three four five six seven. Every time he got to seven he had to start again as quickly as he could, without stopping for breath, so that he couldn't hear his father's voice through the space left, and he couldn't hear his mother's crying.

He did hear the crash and the crumple of the metal, the smashing of his head through the windscreen, the landing of his body on the car stopped in front. He heard that perfectly.

Afterward, their sandwiches lay strewn across the road. And their socks, forty-two, some balled together, some limp and alone. And their underwear. Twenty-one pairs, in different styles and sizes.

He remembered being glad that they were not dirty. He remembered feeling absolutely fine, not hurt at all, bar a mild dizziness that quickly passed. And he remembered knowing that there would only be three of them now. No baby. Just them, as they were in the wreckage, on the road.

"Mum," he said.

Bobby's bottom lip shook. Mrs. Pound shooed Mr. Oats from the room. Relieved, he shut the door behind him, scowling at Bobby through the glass.

"Would you like me to call your father?" she asked.

"Why?" Bobby said.

"You can take the afternoon off if you wish. Come back tomorrow. Start afresh."

"Can you call someone else?"

"A relative?"

"A friend."

"They would need authority from your father, Bobby." He looked at her shoes. They were black and shiny, small, like a doll's, but charmless, like a soldier's.

"It's okay," he said. "I'd rather be here with you."

Mrs. Pound let Bobby work for the rest of the day in the nook outside her office. It was the perfect spying tower over the schoolyard. Bobby wished that he had brought his father's binoculars, which his father had used only once, the wrong way round, to see how far away the television appeared through the lenses.

The yard was a thin concrete corridor with tall walls on either side. Pupils clogged the artery of the thoroughfare that led to the school's humongous heart, the hall where they convened for assembly.

Bobby had prepared mental maps of the area. It was a total of three hundred and eighty-four steps across the playground. The far gate, locked during lesson time, was only twice Bobby's height and so could be climbed with relative ease. There were twelve doors along the route that it was possible teachers could emerge from, but on the whole they liked to stay in the staff room, tarring their tongues with black coffee.

He waited for Mrs. Pound to leave her office, packed his belongings into a plastic bag and left through the side door of the administration building. It was lunchtime and the yard was busy. He put his back to the wall, crouched down low and began shuffling toward the drain. His plan was to circumnavigate the entire school unseen and at the far end make a dash for the bushes beside the basketball court. From there he could get to the gate undetected. The drain was blocked with leaves and mud, so he gave it a wider berth than he had anticipated, but no one noticed him by the time he got to the basketball court, where he paused to breathe and tighten his shoelaces.

Bobby reached the gate to find three figures climbing over it, coming in his direction. Though they were still some distance away, he immediately recognized them as Amir, Big Kevin and Little Kevin. Suddenly he became aware that the moves he wanted to make weren't those he was actually making. Instead of turning and running, he found himself frozen in an awkward squatting position. Their laughter sounded tinny. Bobby wondered if he was shrinking, and whether his heart would soon outgrow his chest, which he could feel happening already. He closed his eyes and wrapped his arms around his face. Warm droplets of piss spotted his crotch, cooling as they slithered down his thigh. The three boys approached as the piss forced itself through the polyester. He wondered what would happen if they were in a book.

Sunny the cyborg sliced the gate in two with the red-hot lasers blasting from his eyes. The steel in his feet crushed the stones and left imprints of his might in the ground. A charging sound, electricity gathering in the chamber of his enormous metal engine, then the titanium cannons reconfiguring, the robotic buzz of the gun barrel forming, the whir and click and fire. The smell of flesh, their skin and hair burning to vapor. Chinese lanterns—scorched hearts inside a charred rib cage—rocking. A metal arm clasped Bobby's shoulders, and a high-powered headlamp cut a pathway through the smoke.

When Bobby opened his eyes, all of them, or those that had existed, were gone. He plucked a leaf from the bushes and wiped his groin, but it did little to mop the stain. He waited for his hands to stop shaking, then climbed over the gate, catching his shirt on the spike and tearing a gash in the cotton.

A stitch needled his ribs by the time he arrived on the corner of Sunny's street. There was no sign of his mother's car parked outside. After rapping three times on the door, he hid around the side of the house. Nobody came. He tried again, harder this time, in case Sunny had already had his entire head replaced with metal but not had a chance to have his ears tuned to the correct frequency. Still nobody came. He used the secret hole in the fence to access the back garden. It had grown since he was last there and he sank ankle deep into the plush rug of the grass.

He tried the back door but it was locked. At the rear of the house the kitchen window still comprised only a plastic sheet. He peeled the tape away from the corner and peered inside. The kitchen was bare. Not just of food, of everything. The table. The chairs. Even the sink. Grease framed the space where the oven had been.

Bobby climbed in through the hole and entered the living room. A clean square of carpet in the shape of an armchair. A patch free of dust that was once the television. Walls with faint outlines remembered the pictures they held, the pictures of Sunny when his smile had worked, and Jules, in those long blissful summers when she was still able to protect her boy from harm.

Back in the garden, beside the shed, Bobby dug to find the shiny black stone that looked nothing like the others around it. This was the rock on which they'd both wiped their blood on the day they had agreed to be brothers. Sunny had said that it was binding for life. Beneath it was a small tin that once contained peeled plum tomatoes. Though Sunny had washed it twice, it still had a pulpy residue clinging to its rim. Bobby emptied the dirt from it and found a small plastic bag inside. In that, a scrap piece of card.

Dear Bobby Nusku. They have taken me away. Find me so that I can keep you safe. Sunny.

At the bottom was an address. He was gone. Bobby lay back on the lawn, his breath painfully trapped.

Whenever he heard people—teachers, mostly—talk about hope, it was as if it was something that people only had in times of despair. Bobby didn't think this was true. He knew, for instance, that his mother would return. This was hope. Hope is a constant, a pilot light in the soul. It never flickers, never dies. Though they may not realize it, people warm their hands on the flame every day. It gets them out of bed. It makes them leave the house. It powers them through life. Regardless, he felt bereft of it now.

CHAPTER SEVEN

THE OGRE

Dusting the ornaments, wiping the sill, Val endeavored to pass the time of day. In her own way, so did Rosa, ignoring the home-school work Val set for her to instead write his name again and again in her notebook, until the blackness blocked out the white of the page. Neither explicitly realized they were missing Bobby Nusku. Both were too concerned with the vague and sickly sense of longing bringing them low, which they couldn't quite place and mistook for hunger. This is how missing somebody disguises itself, so that those it inflicts are not driven to madness by want.

When Bobby knocked on the door, Val was surprised to see him, but not as surprised as she was delighted. Neither mentioned the fact that he should be in school. She invited him inside and noticed the greenish dock-leaf hue of his trousers. Tears filled his eyes as she put her arms around him, running her fingers up and down the harp of his spine.

"Sunny has been taken away because he's a cyborg and they're scared of what he might do," he said.

"To where?" she said. He showed her the address. "Oh my. That's on the south coast."

"How far away is it?"

"We're right in the center of England. This is a long way," she said, "a very long way indeed."

Val made tea and shortbread, then left Rosa and Bobby watching television while she filled the bathtub with water and bubbles.

Bobby's father didn't let him take baths. He claimed that the water was too expensive to heat. This was a shame because the bathroom was Bobby's favorite part of the house, even though nothing really worked properly. The extractor fan was broken. Steam had curled the edges of the lino and the ends of each individual slat on the blinds. The walls were mottled with damp and the pipes shrieked whenever he turned on the taps. The shower, despite the promise of its futuristic nozzle, was a constant disappointment, piddling no more forcefully than a toddler. The room's imperfections were everywhere, but they were constant. That's why it reminded Bobby of his mother, and all of the times he sat on the toilet watching her try to put her eyeliner on straight. It had not changed since she left.

Occasionally when Bruce came home covered in paint he took a bath with the door wide open, and Bobby would wait patiently outside for him to finish. Afterward, when Bruce stood up, the water was tepid and the tub ringed with murk. Water clouded with the paint and streaked down the sides of his face. It ran down his neck and chest and over the deadweight of his paunch. Only by leaning forward at the waist or sticking out his groin could he see his penis, gnarled, with an uneven rhythm to its creases, looking much like the finger he had lost.

Bobby took off his clothes and climbed into the tub while his father dried himself. As this was no more expensive, it was allowed. He strapped on his goggles, held his breath, submerged his head and gathered samples for his files. Toenail clippings and sock fluff, the softened floating shells of old blisters. One day, Bobby thought, he would have enough material to build a new father from the pieces. He had already decided that when the day came he wouldn't bother.

Val's bathtub was far more luxurious than the one at Bobby's house. Foam expanded and spilled from the sides, billowing out onto the floor. Heat rolled upward over his body and steam squeezed open his mouth. He let the water fill him until he was a part of it, a crouton in the hot soup. Val sat beside the tub and rubbed a bar of soap against the soles of his feet in ticklish decreasing circles.

"Does that feel better?" she asked.

"Yes," he said, his foam beard torn apart in clouds. She washed his hair with strawberry shampoo, the scent of it bringing Bert to an inquisitive halt at the bathroom door. Val filled a plastic jug with water and slowly poured it over Bobby's head. The suds cascaded down his back, which she traced with the nub of her thumb. He made a birthday cake from bubbles that exploded when he blew out the candle. She handed him a towel, cream-colored and marshmallow soft.

When she had gone he stood in the center of the room letting the water drip onto the floor. His piss-stained trousers sulked in the corner, surrounded by rose-tinted flannels, serums and softeners, floral-patterned linen and sweet-smelling salts. He realized what was missing from Val's house. The dirty water. The skin in the tub. The stink that made the scent of flowers all the sweeter. A man.

He found her sitting on the edge of her bed and was struck by the scarcity of her belongings. A bed with a bra hooked over the headboard and a box that contained the sum of her clothes, torn down one edge. The room was as functional as a corkscrew. He held her. They were briefly of the same faultless contour.

Bert's bark woke Bobby, but not Val. It became a growl and then a throaty mixture of the two. Val didn't stir until Rosa started shouting her name from the bottom of the stairs. Something in the sound of the knocking on the front door, in its force, its speed or both, untethered Bobby's heart from its post in his chest and readied it to gallop from his mouth.

Val straightened her dressing gown. Bobby followed her downstairs. Just as the door handle stopped shaking, the knocking started again.

"Who is it?" she said into the wood.

"Open up," the voice said, and Bobby froze.

Val, still extracting the shrapnel of a dream from the day,

clipped the chain on to the latch and opened the door a few inches. Rays of sunlight thrust through the gap, illuminating two worlds Bobby kept separate with the same stark and unforgiving gleam.

"Where is my son?" Bruce Nusku said.

"Your son?"

"*My* son."

Bobby's father wrapped a giant, lopsided hand around the chain and yanked it, screws and all, from the frame, pushing the door open until they all stood before him. "You," he said to Bobby, "care to tell me why the headmistress of your school is calling to inform me that you've run away?" Bobby was unable to look his father in the eye, for it might have confirmed he was real, that this wasn't a jolt in a nightmare into which he was locked, upstairs on the bed in Val's arms. Instead he concentrated on the area just above his father's head, where the light played with his baldness, finding funny angles in the dips of his skull. He thought about slamming the door, but Bruce had what remained of his fingers inside it. When the opportunity to hurt his father arose he couldn't take it.

"I'm sorry. I didn't mean to do it."

"What good is that now you've done it?"

"No good."

"Exactly. No fucking good at all."

"Mr. Nusku," Val said, "if you could refrain from swearing. There are children here other than your own." Bruce peered over her shoulder at Rosa, who was cross-legged on the floor with her arms tightly wound around Bobby's knee. He stepped into the house, blocking out the light. Bobby had read in an astrology book for children he had found in the mobile library about how ancient civilizations believed an eclipse signaled the end of something significant.

"My girlfriend said she saw you in town with my boy," Bruce said to Val.

"I took him shopping," Val said.

"For bathwear?" he said, nodding toward Bobby who was still wrapped in a towel.

"No, of course not for bathwear."

"But you have an interest in bathing my son?"

The smell of his breath made her flinch. Reading the wrinkling of her nose, Bobby knew it too. Stale beer. Cigarettes. The awful deadness of the two combined. "He was dirty. I wanted to make him clean."

Bobby's father tapped his thigh to summon his son like a dog. Bobby didn't move, but for the muscle twitching beneath his left eye.

"You're coming home now."

"But I'm okay here," Bobby said.

"Not with a woman who likes to see other people's children naked you're not."

Bruce tightened a rough hand around the back of Bobby's neck and tried to pull him out the door, but Rosa clung tightly to his legs, and despite his strength he couldn't manage their combined weight. Rosa started grunting, a bronchial noise that coaxed a protective snarl through Bert's clenched teeth.

"Mr. Nusku, please," Val said.

"Woman," he said, "you will not tell me what to do with my son."

Bobby's father shook him until his towel was shed, then cast him over his shoulder. His bare buttocks, still hot from the tub, glowed a similar hue to his father's reddening face.

"You're in very, very big trouble," Bruce said, carrying Bobby all the way home with explosive speed. This temper had been passed down from his father, and his father in turn before that. Parents breed parrots. Only exceptional offspring grow their own bright plumage, capable of penetrating the dull gray down with which they are born covered.

By the time they arrived, he was as exhausted as Bobby was mortified, but not enough to stop him from chasing his son up the stairs.

Bobby counted to one hundred and thirty-four. One hundred and thirty-four was the number he had reached when it was safe to open his eyes again. It felt as if he had traveled for miles, but he was exactly where his father had put him down when he started. On his bed, in his room.

Underneath the bed was a basket full of his mother's old lotions. One of them was pearl-colored and cold to the touch, meant for softening the face, combating the effects of aging and fighting wrinkles. He read the bottle as carefully as he could but came across nothing to suggest he couldn't put it on his arse. He'd done so before and suffered no adverse side effects. In fact, it was probably to thank for how supple the skin on his buttocks actually was, and why he could so clearly make out the eyelets on the lash marks left by his father's belt.

Blisters quickly formed. It was too painful to wear trousers, so he put on one of his mother's old dressing gowns. The faintest recollection of her smell lingered on it. Worried that as it faded further she would get smaller in his mind, he set about trying to re-create the scent.

Using an empty glass vase as a mixing cauldron, he discovered that a combination of aquamarine setting lotion and her "frizz-free" conditioner formed a near-perfect base note. Adding half a tube of her favorite toothpaste and what was left of her perfume made it too minty, too watery. It didn't quite work. Bobby's mother's skin had a medicinal quality, a cure-all balm he could inhale to be fixed from the inside. He needed to replicate it as precisely as possible, so he mashed a stick of lip balm to a fine paste, then added that to his own serum of antiseptic lotion and mouth ulcer ointment and poured it into the vase. It wasn't perfect, but holding his nose and mouth over the opening and inhaling as deeply as he could, he was closer to her than he had been in a while. He was also high, and so found that all of his ideas were good ones.

Bobby wrapped his arms around the pendulous bell of the vase, then liberally splashed its contents over every surface in the room. The bed. The walls. Cindy's many cases. It was time to prepare the welcome party. He wanted to be ready.

Finding old ribbon in his mother's craft box, he tore it into strips and hung them from the ceiling. Some of the strips were too springy, so he stole a handful of Cindy's hair rollers to weight them. He removed the white sheet from his bed and suspended it across the length of the far wall. Then he used Cindy's foundation and sponge to write *WELCOME HOME.* The words looked strange in the same salmon shading of his father's girlfriend's face.

When his mother left she didn't take her jewelry. Most of it was kept beneath his bed in a plastic tub. He shook it, delighting in the angelic clatter of the metals, which reminded him of her fingers moving up and down his back while she sang. He arranged the rings in a circle, silver on the left side and the gold on the right, positioning her bracelets in the center, the smaller ones inside the bigger ones, like the concentric ripples on a freshly skimmed pond.

Lacking any musical equipment, he quietly whistled her favorite songs, inventing melodies to replace those he couldn't quite recall. He was a blow whistler, not a suck whistler, and that's why he had to pause for a second as he lit the candle, because he only had two matches. Luckily he managed it on the first attempt and slipped the spare match into his pocket for use later. The tang of burnt sulfur had given him a winning idea for revenge that he dreamt about when he fell asleep on the rug, exhausted *not by the beating*, he told himself stoically, *by the counting*. When he woke the candle wax had crawled across the carpet toward him. He wished that it had covered him, entered him, thickened his skin. Any extra armor he could gather would be needed when he made the dream a vengeful reality.

His father told him he was not to return to school that week. Though he said that Mrs. Pound had granted him leave, Bobby knew that his father needed time for the bruises to fade. Under strict instructions not to leave the house, Bobby had plenty of opportunity to hone his idea, practicing the plan over and over in his head for seven whole nights, through which his passage was eased by fantasies of his mother's return.

Sitting in silence on the staircase, forbidden from showing his face and with his buttocks still stinging too much to disobey, he listened to the clack of the scissors as Cindy recounted to her customers how the woman who lived down the road had stripped him nude and bathed him. Each time she told the story it mutated into new and fathomless forms. By Friday it had changed beyond his recognition.

"She was in the bath with him, behind him," she said.

"How do you know?"

"Bruce found lipstick on his back."

On the morning of his return to school, Bobby, in his uniform and with his tie knotted tightly, found a woman in the hairdressing chair he'd seen there many times before. In her hand was a photograph of a famous American actress. Bobby didn't recognize the beautiful starlet, but he knew that the woman holding her picture had the profile of a bullfrog, and no graded mid-neck-length bob was going to disguise that.

"Here he is," Cindy said as he emerged from the door at the bottom of the stairs. The woman shook her head. "She stripped him and bathed him." A crunch of the scissors, then a clump of hair falling on to Bobby's mother's rug. The woman pushed a glob of saliva around her mouth with her tongue.

"Oh, you don't have to tell me," she said. "I've already heard. I think it's disgusting. Something should be done."

"I bathed myself," Bobby said. The woman turned her face, as if he had just secreted something disgusting from a hidden gland.

"She's my friend, and your hairs are on my mother's rug." Cindy put the scissors down on the arm of the couch and ushered him out of the room. He heard her apologizing to the woman on his behalf, which he'd have resented, had it not bought him enough time to go through his father's things.

He had to wrap the tool belt around his chest twice and tie it with a double knot to stop it from falling. Clanking against his midriff, the metals made him feel ready for war. He unplugged the telephone, then, for good measure, cut through the cable with the pliers.

Autumn had arrived but the day was bright and the wind only playful at best. Bobby got to school early, before the gate had been unlocked. Nobody noticed him behind the thornbushes as they assembled in the yard. New kids dragged their feet through mulched leaves. Bobby rehearsed the plan in his imagination. It would happen the same as it would in a book.

Since Val had given Bobby access to the mobile library, Bobby had become acutely aware of certain changes in his thinking. It was bigger somehow, wider, as if he were having dreams in the daytime while awake. He had read Roald Dahl's *Matilda*, and wondered if he too might have special powers. One night he spent three hours trying to move an apple across his bed by staring at it. It didn't work, but for the first time Bobby considered how, as he burst the apple's crisp peel in his mouth and wiped the juice from his chin, anything was possible, as long as you gave it enough thought. This was the mobile library's first gift to him, though he did not know yet how to use it.

There were two hundred and eighteen steps between the

thornbushes and the gate, giving him a window of around forty seconds, employing a brisk run and accounting for nerves. He removed Cindy's bronzer from his rucksack and smeared it over his face, neck and hands, until everything was a shade somewhere between the clay bricks and dead foliage. It would buy him the few extra seconds he'd need, if everything else went as planned.

The bell rang and the yard started to clear. Mr. Oats emerged to round up the stragglers and lock the gate, checking around the tennis court and behind the bike sheds. As he paused to rue another day's work, he looked directly toward where Bobby was standing. They held each other's gaze. Bobby fingered the loose ends of the knotted belt and prepared to untie it, but Mr. Oats moved on, leaving him behind unnoticed, another part of the scenery.

Relieved, Bobby took a last piss in the doorway. It crackled on the sullied ground and rose back up as steam. Conducting a final check on his equipment, he lay down in strike position, careful to avoid the puddle he'd just created. It was obvious to him now that without Sunny he would need to protect himself. That his plan would avenge Rosa's attack imbued it with a poetry he couldn't resist.

Amir and the two Kevins arrived twenty minutes later, clambering over the gate and sauntering across the yard in a slovenly three-pointed prong. Bobby remained still until they crossed the painted yellow line of the basketball court, then crouched, shutting his mouth tight to trap the hummingbird of his breath inside it. When they were in just the right place, he sprinted toward them, but the tool belt proved too cumbersome. He was not as quick as he had hoped.

Roused by the slap of Bobby's shoes on the ground, the three boys spun to face him. What a sight it was. The boy they had watched piss through his own trousers, caked in thick makeup, moving as deftly as a rusted tin man. Amir laughed, which permitted the others to join in. Bobby recognized him as the ringleader, hair shorn clumsily close to his skull, scalp dotted with dried bloody nicks. A thick brow hung over his eyes, so the light could not reach them to be reflected. Bobby slowed, then stopped, just a meter away.

"Hello again," Amir said. Bobby looked at the ground and mumbled, as if in prayer. He pulled up his sweater. Loosened by movement the tool belt rode down over his hips, but he caught it before it hit the floor. The larger of the boys bent over with his hands anchored to his knees and brought his face close enough to Bobby's that Bobby could smell chewing gum. He rubbed Bobby's cheek with his right forefinger and studied the brown smudge of makeup left on the tip.

Biting his tongue until it drew blood, Bobby plunged his hand into the front pocket of the tool belt and pulled out a bottle of denatured alcohol. He had pre-loosened the child lock. This was the benefit of planning. The cap spun off at the flick of his thumb. With a sharp stabbing motion he splashed half a bottle's worth into Amir Kindell's eyes.

They all held their breath, Bobby included, as if in mourning for a moment that had only just passed. They knew, in their flawed togetherness, that when they exhaled again it could never be undone. Amir dropped to the ground, clawing at his face, and screamed so loudly that Bobby was sure the entire school must have heard it. Without further thought, Bobby emptied the rest of the bottle in a large skyward arc into the wide-open targets of the other boys' mouths. They both fell to their knees at his feet.

He took the match from his pocket and saw how, with its shiny red hat, it looked like a soldier reporting for duty. Kneeling, he struck the match against the concrete floor. The three boys clambered around one another, eyes streaming, and Bobby held the lit match in the air above them. Amir grabbed at the hem of Bobby's trousers. He could not see what was in Bobby's hand, but he had sensed it. Fear, that cruel cramp of the soul. This, which the boy had given to Rosa in the mud, is what Bobby saw, and loved, on the twist of his face.

Running as fast as she could, Mrs. Pound's movement had a balletic quality, as if the small doll-like shoes she wore were mementoes from a past calling to dance. She snatched the match from Bobby's hand, extinguished it, and slapped the empty bottle from his grasp. It bounced five times and spun before stopping, a gelastic little dance of its own.

Bored but keen not to show it, the younger of the two police-men, standing in the corner of Mrs. Pound's office, cradled his hat in his hands. The older of the two had turned his chair to face Bobby's. Occasionally their legs touched and the static in his uniform rushed across his thighs. His own children had grown up years ago. Dealing with kids now seemed an alien task, one with which he was wholly uncomfortable, though his wife would have argued that little had changed.

"Son," he said. Thick black hairs hung from his nostrils, levers moving when he spoke. "You'd be advised to talk to me if you have any interest in fixing the situation you've found yourself in."

The plastic denatured alcohol bottle was perched on the edge of the desk, curving the sunlight inside it. Mrs. Pound squeezed a stress ball, the shape of a banana.

"I'd like to apologize on Bobby's behalf," she said.

"I'm not sure an apology will settle this," he said. "Those boys are in the hospital. What Bobby did was very serious."

Mrs. Pound walked around the desk and stopped behind Bobby, gently laying her hands on his shoulders. "Bobby," she said, "perhaps you'd like to wait outside."

Though they lowered their voices to a funereal hush, the smallness of the room and the glass panel in the door meant he could still hear every word they said, amplified, almost as if it was inside his head. All he could think about was a time in the near future when he was somewhere, anywhere, that wasn't here.

"Bobby is a pupil to whom we pay special attention," she said. "He's had a lot of trouble making friends, and the only friend he did have moved away over the summer."

"Mrs. Pound," the policeman said, "we're investigating what amounts to assault with a toxic substance. Amir Kindell might be lucky to keep his vision." Bobby pushed his ear more firmly against the wall, the spidery shadow cast by a plant in the corner climbing across his face.

"I appreciate that."

"Then you'll appreciate the importance of us getting his parents here as quickly as possible so that we might get the matter resolved."

"We've been trying, we can't get through."

"Then we'll go to them, if you'd kindly supply us with an address. You have that, don't you?"

"Well that's just what I'm getting to . . ."

With his knees bent, hoisting it first onto his lap, and then standing to let it rest against his chest so that he might net his fingers on its underside, Bobby picked up the plant pot, a hulking great thing fired in clay. Before he'd even exhaled he had it up to neck height, and from there, with every ounce of push his arms had left in them, he threw it through the glass panel of the door.

He could hear Mrs. Pound screaming as he ran down the corridor to the staircase, gliding along on the freshly polished floors.

Gleaming with sweat, beads on his neck stuck to the coldness of a fast-dampening collar, Bobby arrived at Val's house to find her standing outside, facing the front door so that she did not see him approach. He stood behind her, trying to make sense of what he was seeing. In her shabbiest clothes, and a tattered apron, Val scrubbed spray paint from the door's dark wood with a stiff-bristled shoe brush. Tinted pink water ran off the bottom, a mazy trail down the path to the drain. Hints of the letters, where the red paint was sprayed most thickly, still remained, a now indistinguishable and patently unwanted legend. Val had found it that morning as she'd stepped out into the street clutching another letter, the third that week, wondering who would have the gall or motive to pen such a blatantly hurtful untruth, and post it through her door. She was none of the things they accused her of being, but the more she read them, the more she felt as dirty as they made her out to be. At her most desperate she wanted to scrub herself with the brush, scrub until nothing but a shiny pile of bones remained. Perhaps that might satisfy them. All of the books in the mobile library could not have prepared her for words as unspeakable as these.

"What did it say?" Bobby asked. Val knocked over the lathery bucket and the wash hit his shoes, where it broke into two foamy arcs.

"You can't be here."

"I am here."

"But you can't be." Val looked one way down the street and then the other. "Quick," she said, "come inside."

In the light of the kitchen, Bobby could see paint-stained fingertip tracks trailed across Val's face. The glare of the bulb searched the sunken wells in her cheeks, shifting as she sobbed into her hands. "They're talking about us," she said.

"Who are?"

"Everyone. They're saying the most awful things."

"But nobody knows us."

"Yes. And that's the problem."

"Everything we make clean they will dirty." Clumps of tissue the size of snowballs built up on the table by her side. Bobby scooped them into the bin. "I got them for you," he said.

"Got who?" Her grip tightened around his arms.

"Those boys."

"What boys?"

"The boys who hurt Rosa."

Val paused. "What did you do?"

"I got them. That's all. They won't hurt her again." He could feel movement in his chest, as if his heart had become a bird and started beating its wings.

"Bobby," she said, weeping. "Go."

"What?"

"Go. You have to go."

"Why?"

"Go!" Val slammed her hand on the sink. Teacups trembled on the draining board. He buckled with the punch of it. She put her arms around the middle of his body and squeezed. He winced, not just with his face but with a shudder that traveled the length of his body and ended as a twinge in his toes. "Oh God," she said, "did I hurt you?"

"No," he said, his forehead creased with pain.

"I did. I know that I did." The rings around her eyes were dark but colorful, like cross-sections of strange fruit. She lifted his sweater and untucked his shirt. A bruise, much bluer than it had been, the lightness of a clement sky, curled from a third of the way down his back to the top of his waistband. On closer examination she could see the mark of his father's left hand. Val unbuttoned his trousers and rolled down his underpants. The bruise's persistent stain continued, breaking up on the bow of his buttocks. Three fingerprints and one thumbprint fading.

CHAPTER EIGHT

THE BRIDGE

Val didn't share Bobby's mother's approach to packing. Fumbling for the opening, she handed Rosa a bin liner.

"Rosa," she said, "cram as many of your clothes into this bag as you can." Bobby filled Rosa's rucksack with pens and paper.

"Thank you, Bobby Nusku," she said. Val instructed them to take all of the food they could find in the cupboards, including the stuff they didn't recognize or particularly like to eat. Bobby piled it all inside an empty sports bag, making sure to take a tin opener, then filled four side pockets with cans of dog food for Bert, adding the squeaky chew toy in the shape of a pork chop for which he had only ever shown a grumpy disdain. Val emptied a box of Rosa's old toys and packed it with toiletries. By the time they were finished the house looked as though it had been ransacked, which in a way it had.

"Where are we going?" Rosa asked. Val paused, though only briefly.

"We have our own mobile library, and there are many books to be delivered."

"Like the elephant and the donkey?"

"Exactly. Like the elephant and the donkey." Rosa and Bobby danced around one another. "Now hurry, we're going to need to leave soon." Dizzy, they leaned against the living room wall and waited for the floor to catch them up.

"We can go past my house on the way," Bobby said. Val pulled the zip on the bag so hard it almost came loose in her hand.

"No we can't," she said.

"But we have too. I need to pick up my files."

"I'm afraid you're missing the point, Bobby. If your father finds out we're going he won't let you come with us." Outside it was early evening, but dark clouds already gave the illusion of night. He picked up a kitchen knife, with a long blade as slender as it was sharp.

"It's okay," he said, "I have a plan."

Parked in its usual space, vinyl stickers displaying his name and number peeling from the rust on the side, Bruce's van was a sorry wart on a hog-faced street. The rubber on the tires was worn, so the knife glided through them with ease, just like it had in the movies Bobby had seen in Sunny's attic. They hissed a final, desultory wheeze.

Bobby lifted the flap of the letterbox and put his ear to the slot. He heard his father and Cindy laugh at the television, and the tinny speakers on the box rattled by a blown bass channel. Bobby slipped the knife into his sock, then slid the key into the hole as quietly as possible.

Taking extra care not to let the front door slam behind him, he tiptoed into the hallway. At the end was a small wooden box containing trip switches, meters and dials he was forbidden to touch, now they were urgent and irresistible. He gripped the handle of the knife, held it above his shoulder as if about to throw a spear, and rammed it into the center of the box. A brief flurry of sparks glowed and then perished as the house was cast in darkness with a thump.

Between the entrance to the lounge and the bottom of the stairs were seventeen mini steps, taken in a half crescent to circumnavigate the sofa. Bobby moved through the room in night mode, undetected, as Bruce and Cindy argued over which of them should find their way to the fuse box. Losing, Bruce leapt up, knocking over the hairdressing chair and smashing it into the television with a loud crash. Bobby was close enough to feel the hot, angry spray of his father's spittle fall like drizzle onto his cheek. He was close enough to let his fingers hover over his father's shirt where his heart was meant to be as he stumbled around, glass crunching underfoot, yelping every time he moved. He identified a quiver in his father's voice. A peculiar, jittery cadence, it was one he'd heard already today. Fear. His father was scared. To be lost inside his own home was a terrible discombobulation with which his wife might once have sympathized. Bobby hoped that it would swallow his father whole and change him forever, just as it had her.

He savored it for a few more seconds, then took two stairs at a time without stumbling and entered the bedroom. The smell had faded. It was still his mother's, but from a distance, carried on the wind. Sidestepping along the near wall he approached the head of the bed, where he felt for the large box in which Cindy stored handbags she never used. He tipped them out and filled the empty box with his files. The jars of hair, the notes, everything. The complete sum of his work. He packed it as well as his mother taught him to.

Downstairs, Bruce was still trying to make his way to the fuse box. He banged his knee on the coffee table, and fell again when he stubbed his toe on the armchair.

"I can't see!" he shouted, unaware that his son was passing right by his side.

Bobby walked thirteen steps across the room to the far corner, ducking halfway to avoid the lampshade. He remained there for a moment as his father flailed through the dark, before creeping up behind him, just an inch from his ear.

"Boo!"

Blind and terrified, Bruce dived to the floor, shrieking as he hit the shelf where a picture of Bobby's mother had once taken pride of place. He landed on Cindy's hairdressing scissors, implanted in the soft flesh of his thigh, the sound of a melon being spliced. Bobby stepped over his father's prone body and left the house unseen. He was followed by screams into the night.

Val, Rosa and Bobby loaded the suitcases and boxes into a dented wheelbarrow from the garden. Rosa carried Bert, Val locked the door, and they made it to the mobile library without seeing a single other person. As quickly as they could they stacked everything into the back of the truck. Bobby ditched the wheelbarrow in an adjacent allotment, stealing some earthy potatoes and a fistful of carrots in case they came in handy.

He had never been in the mobile library's cab before, and was surprised by how big it was on the inside. It even had a bed, set back above the seats, and Bobby, outstretched, couldn't reach both ends at the same time. Val turned the key in the ignition and the dashboard lit up with a wave of tiny lights so that it looked like a city in the distance. Cracks webbed the leather seats, as gnarled as the skin on an old man's hands. Protruding from the center of the cab's floor was the swan's-neck bend of a silver gear stick. Val ran her fingers around the glossy black plastic coat of the steering wheel. It would test the full span of her arms to turn it. A furry green monster hung from the rearview mirror on a frayed elastic cord. Rosa gave it to Bert to chew.

"Okay," Val said to herself.

"Have you ever driven something this big?" Bobby asked.

"I haven't driven anything one-sixteenth this big."

Nothing could prepare them for the dragon belly roar of the engine firing when she pushed the button. Vibrations throbbed through the seats. Bert held his paws around his muzzle. Bread crumbs hopped along the dash. Val wrapped her fingers around the hand brake and exhaled.

"Are we ready?" she said, not having any idea what they should be ready for.

Bobby clipped Rosa's seat belt into its buckle, then took care of his own. A click, and the headlamps blasted the shadows in front of them. They moved out onto the road, as white as a blank page, and he watched in the wing mirror as the back of the mobile library tore the gate from its hinge, then ripped the fence from its joist and dragged it across the grass.

"Shit," Val said. Bobby covered Rosa's ears a second too late. He could see that Val was already beginning to sweat. She put the truck into reverse and it beeped a loud warning. Lights switched on in the windows of surrounding houses. A woman emerged, annoyed at having had her evening interrupted by this unexpected racket. Finding a better position to attempt the turning circle, Val edged the library forward and narrowly avoided crushing the woman's car. Newly applied, the woman's lime-green face pack set in surprise.

The metal fence was chewed by the tires and spat back out at the end of the road.

Then they were gone toward what they did not know, and until now had not dared even imagine, in their giant library on wheels. It felt like opening a book about which they knew nothing.

They drove the main street that ringed the town center. Val, still getting used to the truck's tremendous size, sideswiped the occasional parked car, leaving deep silver scratches in the metalwork. Rosa laughed whenever she accidentally pressed the horn.

"We should have an adventure," Bobby said.

"We're having an adventure," Val said.

"Will they look for us?"

"Yes. They'll look for us."

"Will we be in trouble?"

"Only bad people get in trouble." Rosa cheered.

The mobile library segued into the migratory pack of the motorway, mechanical buffalo charging down the plain. Rain on the windscreen blurred the lights into an endless cable of color.

Rosa fell asleep beside Bobby. He covered her with an old blanket he found behind the seat, and smoothed it down to ensure that she was tightly bundled. There was nothing in the glove box but a flashlight, a set of binoculars, a screwdriver and an old newspaper. Every few minutes he tore out a tiny strip, rolled it up and fed it through the gap in the window, where the wind dashed away with it. He hoped that his mother would be able to follow the trail he had left. It had worked for Hansel and Gretel.

A red light flashed beside the indicator.

"We need fuel," Val said. The mobile library's engine had begun to splutter. "And we need it fast."

She pulled into the next roadside petrol station, where neon signs bleached their skin exotic pinks. Bobby looked after Rosa and Bert while Val searched for the cap on the tank. Numbers rose on the counter clicker as she filled it, quickly becoming a figure higher than Bobby had ever seen before. Combined with the lighting and the nighttime, the petrol station, to a child's eyes, had the air of a flashy casino. Val came back to the cab to fetch her purse from her handbag and Bobby accompanied her into the shop to pay.

The man behind the counter leafed through a magazine about fishing, appearing constantly on the cusp of a gigantic yawn. Clusters of teenage acne had formed a glistening trail from his cheeks to his neck. Val and Bobby filled a basket with chocolate bars and treats.

"Let me do the talking," Val said to Bobby as they neared the counter.

"Midnight snacking?" the man said, running the packets across the winking red glow of the scanner. On his badge was the name *Bryan*. He had been awarded two silver stars, but it did not say what for.

"Something like that." Val counted the change in her palm.

"A little past your bedtime, isn't it, young man?" Bobby nonchalantly ruffled a display of salted peanuts and deepened his voice to little effect.

"No," he said, "sometimes I stay up all night." Val laughed, clutching her sides so that Bobby knew she was faking.

"I need to pay for some fuel as well," she said. "Pump number six." Bryan looked out of the window across the forecourt, then at Val, then again at the mobile library.

"That truck," he said, "it's yours?"

"Yes it is."

"A little big, isn't it?"

"For what?"

"For, uh . . ."

"For a woman?"

"Well, they're not my words. They're yours."

Val sighed. Bryan pretended to operate the till, pointlessly stroking its buttons.

"Actually, it's not technically a truck. It's a mobile library."

"And you take it out at night?"

"Of course," she said. "I'm a librarian. I wouldn't make much of a truck driver with these little, feminine arms, now would I?"

Bobby watched himself in the monitor on the wall, an inch-high column of gray and black pixels. From some angles he appeared taller than he was, and if he held his hair apart at his crown it looked a little like he was going bald. He wrongly concluded that manhood's first warning shots were being fired across his bow and silently punched the air in celebration. They were very welcome.

Val paid and they left the shop before Bryan could give them a receipt. She almost knocked over a petrol pump on the passenger side as they pulled out of the station. The checkout assistant banged balled fists on the glass, greasy skin smears smudging the pane. In the window, lent a faded glamour by the neon strobing of the signage, he looked like a showgirl seeing Vegas from a taxi cab.

Nectar-colored streetlights trapped the stillness of entire towns in amber. The high-pressure squeeze of hydraulic brakes cut the air and set off car alarms passing by. Occasionally pedestrians stopped in their tracks at the sight of the mobile library sailing through the night. And it did feel like sailing when they built up speed, as though nothing but an iceberg could stop them. Bobby wound down the window and let the wind explore the back of his mouth. It made his teeth ache but he didn't stop. He wanted to make his insides feel as new as his outsides did.

They came to a crossroads. Freshly painted white lines sliced through the oily black of new tar on the surface. It was quiet enough that Bobby could hear the mechanics of the traffic lights buzzing, the gentle tick between red and green, as a police car pulled up beside them.

"Oh God," Val said, "close the window." Bobby could tell that she was annoyed because her voice lingered on that uneven middle ground between a whisper and the volume of everyday conversation. "I said close the window, Bobby. Close the window right now." Bobby tore off another bit of newspaper and slipped it out of the gap. It fluttered through the air and landed on the hood of the police car. The policewoman inside it looked up at Bobby and smiled. He smiled back. When the lights changed, they both pulled away in opposite directions. She'd no reason to suspect he was anything other than a child whose librarian parents didn't mind him getting tired enough to be in a stinking mood all day tomorrow.

Bruce Nusku was too busy sobering up in the emergency department of the local hospital to notice that his son had gone missing. The gauze Cindy had wrapped around his thigh was now soaked in blood, and all he really wanted was another drink.

Had the lady who lived opposite the mobile library been more community-spirited, perhaps she'd have phoned the police. Instead she sliced up a cucumber and laid slivers of it across her eyes, before reclining on the sofa and falling asleep. She had never used the mobile library. To her it was just an eyesore parked across the street.

Bryan often met unusual people while working the night shift at the petrol station, and had been supplementing his wages by skimming notes from the till for six months. Having the police sniff around was the last thing on his agenda. Besides, for all he knew she *was* a librarian, even if her working hours were peculiar. He didn't know any librarians.

The policewoman's radio would crackle into life eventually, but not until the sun had long laid claim to the day. An amateur gardener had noticed two things about his allotment. First, it was missing some potatoes and carrots. Second, it was catching a whole lot more of the morning light than it had in the weeks previously. Having only just recovered from an operation to remove double cataracts, he assumed his eyes were to blame. Only later did he peer through the fence to find that the mobile library had disappeared. If the council had found money enough to fund it again, then he was pleased, for he often whiled away entire mornings with his granddaughter over a book or two. But he hadn't heard any news of that. He made himself a mug of peppermint tea, dwelled on it for a while, then picked up the telephone, wondering if these were the first few glimmerings of senility.

"Hello," he said, "now, I'm sorry if I'm wasting your time . . ."

Nobody had missed Val and Rosa enough to alert anyone to their disappearance. To miss someone you must notice they have gone.

Four hours of steering had made Val's arms ache from her shoulders to her wrists. It was time to get off the road. She assigned Bobby the task of looking out for somewhere to stop for what remained of the night. The adrenaline had faded now, doubt had set in, and she quietly resigned herself to their being caught at any moment.

They drove down a thin country lane, a tight seam through a patchwork of barley fields, to where Bobby spotted a copse atop a hill. Val slowed the truck and pulled into a small, pretty clearing. Caught by the headlights, bluebells twinkled with a faint morning frost. The mobile library could not be seen from the road, even when the entire plot was lit by the unforgiving full beam of a passing car. The branches bathed in the red of the brake lights looked like blood trickling across the moon. Nothing keeps a secret like the trees.

They set up camp in the back of the truck, sleeping on the carpet by the shelves of children's books. Val, Rosa and then Bobby, facing the same direction, curled into the shape of a C. With the door closed they could have been anywhere, not just in the real world, but beyond it. The walls were lined with escape routes and exits, to deserts, space and oceans and to stranger places still.

"Read to us," Bobby said. He chose the biggest, oldest-looking book he could see, one that would seem to suit the scale of events that had unfolded. He handed Val a heavy hardback copy of *Moby-Dick* by Herman Melville, with dog-eared burgundy trim.

Bobby listened to the words. They were not coming from her mouth, but from somewhere in the middle of her body. Rosa and Bobby put their ears to her chest, rising and falling to the rhythm of her lungs. Neither of them spoke until she stopped reading, exhausted, just as Starbuck exhorts Ahab one last time to desist from chasing the whale through the sea.

"Moby Dick seeks thee not. It is thou, thou, that madly seekest him!"

"Does this story have a happy ending?" Bobby asked.

"There is no such thing as an ending," she said. "Good things come out of bad things and bad things come out of good things, but it always continues. It's as in life. Books are life. There is just the part you read. They start before that. They finish after it. Everything carries on forever. You are only in it for those pages, for a tiny window of time."

The metal walls of the mobile library stored the morning heat. Outside, they cleaned their teeth with mineral water. Val cooked breakfast on a small gas stove she had bought years before, part of an unrealized dream to take Rosa camping. Hot fat bubbles burst on burnt sausage skin.

"Are we going to live here now?" Bobby asked.

"I don't know," Val said.

"I'd like it if we did."

Bobby fetched the binoculars from the glove box in the cab and lay in the long grass on his back with Rosa flopped across his belly. They tried to catch golden leaves as they fell and made Bert snuffle out chestnuts from the undergrowth. Val strung up the conkers with old bootlaces that they spun around their heads, pretending to be helicopters. They played chase until they were out of breath, then teased a beetle that had wandered into their path, until it disappeared in the dirt. By dinnertime Bobby had pronounced it "probably the best day of my life." When Val lit a fire and they read each other stories, he was sure. He studied the lines beside her eyes as they wriggled in the flicker of the flame, and wished that he had his own so that Val might think him wise.

"How old are you?" he asked.

"You should never ask a woman her age," Val said, "but seeing as it's you I'll make an exception. I am forty years old."

"That's kind of ancient."

"I'm a museum piece all right." The heat of the flames had made her woozy.

"How come you're not in love?"

Val toasted another marshmallow. Hot white goo dripped down the stick. She had never had these conversations with her daughter. On more than one occasion this fact had broken her heart.

"How do you know that I'm not?"

"Are you?"

"Yes, I am."

"Who with?"

"With Rosa." Rosa draped herself around her mother's shoulders, assuming her outline as readily as silk.

"But I mean with someone else." The brittle wood in the fire cracked like small animal bones.

"I guess it just didn't turn out that way."

"Why not?"

"Who knows?"

"You must know, you're forty."

"Age does not wisdom bring."

"You sound like you're talking backward."

Val blew on the marshmallow and tested its heat with the tip of her tongue. "Were you in love with Rosa's dad?" Bobby asked.

"We were in love with each other, when we married."

"You were married?"

"I had a ring and everything."

"Wow."

"Yeah. A whole other life ago. I told you, the story starts long before you get there. It will go on a long time after you've gone." Bobby considered the comment.

"You must have been a grown-up for a very long time."

"You could say that," Val said. She snapped a fallen branch across her knee and tossed into the flames the end that Bert didn't walk away with. The fire belly-danced across the ash. "When he met Rosa he decided that loving a little girl like her would be too much work for a man like him. Even though Rosa gives love unconditionally. When someone thinks that way, well . . ." It seemed as though she might say something else, but she was content to listen to the owls, as if they would finish sentences on her grateful behalf.

"I think you're wise," Bobby said.

"Then maybe I am," she said.

"I think you're wise too, Val," Rosa said.

"Then I definitely must be!"

Rosa combed Bert so that his coat reflected the moonlight. They read ghost stories with torches under their chins, throwing the shadows of their noses over their foreheads. When they heard noises coming from the woods, they scared each other with talk of wolves and hungry bears, but nobody believed that they were really there. Outside of the three of them the world didn't exist anymore, and neither did the monsters in it.

CHAPTER NINE

THE CAVEMAN

Morning hours vanished somewhere inside the books. Bobby read *The Little Prince* by Antoine de Saint-Exupéry, amazed that a man whose name he couldn't pronounce might write a story that seemed like it was written just for him. Like the young prince, he too found the adult world strange. He too saw very few certainties in it. Afterward, Val shaved Bobby's head. The blade tickled as she pulled it over his scalp.

"Stop fidgeting," she said, "or I might slip and cut your ear off." Thick brown locks fluttered to the ground, in keeping with the seasons.

"Are we all going to shave our heads?" he asked.

"In terms of us hiding in plain sight, I'm not sure how effective it would be."

"But there is no one here to hide from."

"We're going to need to go and get supplies. I think the sooner we do that, the better."

She and Rosa put on floppy hats that concealed most of their faces. Bert, though invited, opted to spend his time sleeping beneath the mobile library, hiding from the high-hung mist.

The three walked down the long country road, which dipped and twisted at the seam of the fields. A postman idled by. Gray plumes of smoke rose from a lone collapsing chimney. This quaint caricature of English country life reminded Rosa of the Enid Blyton books Val had read to her in the mobile library. She put her arms around Bobby's shoulders with a sisterly affection, but Val couldn't help wonder whether people would be more convinced they were siblings had they fought with bared teeth.

The elderly woman in the grocery shop complimented Val and Rosa on their hats.

"Don't see many people with them in the village," she said, as if they'd just ridden into town on the back of a mammoth. Val spotted a small thatch of loose hair on Bobby's collar and plucked it off before the woman noticed. They bought milk, orange juice and three luscious apples. The woman gave Rosa and Bobby each a lemon-flavored lollipop, the reason why her shop had long been a fixture for the children in the village.

As they were leaving, Bobby spotted an image he recognized on the front of the newspaper. It wasn't the main story, which featured a photograph of a familiar face, Detective Jimmy Samas (he appeared even younger than he had before, if that were possible). Instead it was tucked two-thirds of the way down the page in a slim column on the right-hand side. A picture of him.

The box had been labeled "Miscellaneous" by his father, but the contents were actually united by a theme—they belonged to his mother—and so were anything but. This was Bobby's favorite box of things in the whole world, and formed the centerpiece of his files. To anybody else it was just an umbrella, a hair dryer, a camera . . . life's accrued detritus. But he knew that it contained parts of her, as fundamental to her being as arms, legs, teeth and eyelashes. The umbrella. She carried it even in the sunshine so that Bobby's neck would never burn. This was her soul. The hair dryer. She would train it on him in the mornings, warming up the air when it was too cold to get out of bed. This was her heart. And the camera. It still had film in the back of it, pictures she'd taken, memories she'd wanted to keep. This was her mind. Sorting through it after she'd gone, he realized that he could rebuild her out of this. He could make her all over again.

There were four photographs left on the roll before it could be developed. A few weekends after first meeting, Sunny and Bobby took it to the The Ponds. His mother would have liked Sunny, especially when she saw how he protected her son, so Bobby took a photograph of him stirring the pea-green algae of the ponds with a stick. He took another photograph of the flowers that grew in the damp ground. She had cherished their delicate audience when they stole away together for a picnic.

Sunny took a photograph of Bobby trying to shimmy up the trunk of the tallest tree he could find, but he slipped at the vital moment and landed on his arse in the mud. Both were convinced the results would be too blurry, and so needed to ensure that the final photograph was one Bobby's mother would want to keep forever when she returned. A memory indelibly written in love's stubborn ink.

They walked to Bull Rock. Nobody else called it Bull Rock. That was a name they had given it. From a certain angle, on the far end of the lake, two smaller shelves of stone rose like a bullock's thick horns. When the water's reflection bounced off the surface, it looked, when they tried extra hard to see it, like the hoop of metal puncturing a bullock's nose. Sunny and Bobby climbed to the top. They could see the far clouds dyed rose by the sundown, and a chevron of geese swinging over the treetops. They could see the dull fog that hung over the town, and the mist made of midges that moved across the water. They could see their entire world from the spot where Bobby once sat with his mother and watched it, planning their escape. A photograph of her favorite view, with Bobby all grown up standing in front of it, would make a perfect addition to his files.

"Left a bit," Sunny said. "Right a bit. Now crouch down so that we can see the lake and the town behind you at the same time." Bobby knelt in position on the cold rock, his ears lit up by the sun. "Ready? One, two, three."

There was a click and a whir as the film wound back, but the whiteness of the flash remained in Bobby's eyes. If he'd known that one day this photograph would be on the front of a newspaper, he might have cleaned the mud from the arse of his jeans and washed his hands in the water of the lake.

Less than a year later Cindy had relegated the photograph to a small frame atop the fridge, where it couldn't be seen. That was where the police had taken it from—the most recent photograph of Bobby in existence.

Bobby, Val and Rosa walked around the village for a while. Crumbled ruins of a castle wall braced against the wind where a farmer tended two horses. One of them was pregnant, the oak-colored barrel of her belly swinging as she ate.

A cottage where a famous poet was born had been turned into a museum of her life. They shadowed a group of tourists, mostly older couples. Bobby imagined that he and Val were married, though he was unsure exactly what this meant and it made him feel a little odd. All he really wanted to be was the kind of man who could repair anything she asked him to. On Rosa's insistence they bought pens from the gift shop and decided to make their way back to the mobile library while the afternoon sun was still approaching its peak.

"Here," Rosa said, coming to a standstill outside an old tearoom. The cupcakes in the window had been arranged around a display stand in the shape of a helter-skelter. She pushed her fingers against the glass like she could reach through the surface and take one. "I want a cake."

"I'm afraid you can't have one," Val said.

"Yes I can." Rosa clenched her fists and rubbed the back of

them against her forehead. She made a strange chuntering noise, as if incanting a temper.

"Come on," Val said.

"No." Rosa ground her teeth, punched herself in the chest, and then in the face, fighting something inside her angrily waking from hibernation. Val had warned Bobby about Rosa's tantrums, but he was never prepared for the ferocity with which they arrived. Her face flushed a violent crimson. She slammed a hand against the window and shouted, but the words were clumped together to form one long and indistinguishable roar. Val made a grab for Rosa's wrist, but Rosa swatted her away.

A woman emerged from the shop, shocked to find Rosa standing there in distress.

"What on earth's going on?" she said. Rosa swung her foot, narrowly missing the woman's shins, and kicked a hole in the rotten wood at the bottom of the door frame. She smacked the glass again. It wobbled, and Val could hear it, like the chime in the air after a gong is struck. Inside, the tearoom was busy with tourists. Val could see them watching through the window.

Another woman joined the first in the doorway. She said something, but she couldn't quite summon from her tiny frame a noise that could compete with Rosa, now shouting at the top of her voice. Rosa barged past the two women, almost knocking them to the ground, clambered into the window display and kicked the cake stand to pieces. Outside, Val, Bobby and the two women watched thick dollops of cream drip down the glass. Val, scattering the confetti of apologies behind her, chased Rosa into the shop, leaving the two women staring at Bobby with their mouths wide open. Across the street hung linen flapped on a breeze that never made it to his skin.

"You," the first woman said, "I've seen you."

"You haven't," he said, "I'm not from around here."

"You must be," she said, before turning to her friend, "musn't he?" Bobby thought about the mobile library, imagining it rearing up behind him like a trusty steed. Of the hundred stories he now knew, the only one that popped into his head at this very moment was the one he'd read most recently. There were others more believable, less fantastical, more fitting, but under pressure of the scenes unfolding they had vanished, as if they'd never been written at all.

"No," he said. "I am not. This is not even my home planet. My home planet is tiny. It is an asteroid the size of a house. I have been exploring the galaxy. I've met a king with no subjects, a man who believed himself to be the most admirable on his planet even though he lived there by himself, a drunk who drank to forget the shame of being a drunkard, a businessman who said he owned the stars, a lamplighter who lit the same lamp every minute and an elderly map maker who had never explored the world he claimed to have mapped."

The more Bobby talked, the more he felt like the Little Prince, even posing as if a crown was perched proudly on his head.

"Oh . . ." said the woman, but Bobby didn't let her finish.

"He's the one who told me to come here, to your teashop in a village on Earth. And now I have met you." Val emerged from the shop, dragging Rosa—plastered with cake—behind her. "Now if you'll excuse me."

The two women watched them walk all the way up the street in the wrong direction. Once out of sight they waited in a dank alleyway beside a pub, then climbed over a fence and cut across five freshly churned fields. Soon their socks were moist with mud.

"What did you tell them?" Val asked.

"That I was the Little Prince," Bobby said. He expected Val to be angry, but she laughed, embraced him, and landed a kiss on the soft flesh of his earlobe. By the time they arrived back at the mobile library Rosa's tantrum had evaporated. But for the cherry squashed into the fabric of her coat, no one would have known anything unusual had happened.

"And that's how it goes," Val said. "The story carries on."

Bert was nowhere to be seen. Val checked the mobile library. Rosa searched the cab. Bobby crawled beneath the truck and around the tires, finding nothing but a half-eaten biscuit and the shape of Bert's profile in the grass. They stood at the edge of the woods and called his name. Rosa rattled a tin full of his favorite snacks. All that came back was the buzzing of insects, heard but not seen, as though the leaves themselves were humming.

Seeing Val upset, Bobby swapped his shoes for wellingtons and wandered further into the trees. He tapped a stick against trunks and rustled bushes as he passed, actions that he thought a man might do.

"Bert!" An echo carried his voice away with it. When he'd walked so far that he could no longer see the mobile library, he mournfully returned without the dog.

Val made a fire as the night drew in. She held Rosa, and no one spoke of anything much.

Expecting the wail of sirens to bomb into the clearing at any moment, to fill it with red and blue, Val wished they could all disappear into the woods like Bert. Until this excursion she'd not strayed far from home, and had certainly never broken the law. At camp, when her school friends had taken boys back to their bunks, she had faked an asthma attack and slept in the medical bay. She'd remained a virgin until she met Rosa's father—someone special—whose specialness had drained from him with startling speed, the lights still off, the sheets still damp.

Val had never been late paying the electricity bill. She barely even swore. Only recently, once Rosa had become slightly less dependent, had she found time to examine opportunities not taken. And there were many. Meeting Bobby had marked a sea change in her thinking. What better motive to rebel than granting this boy a reprieve from a rotten start in life, even if it did turn out to be fleeting. She felt a tremendous, soaring sense of freedom that not having a job exacerbated, but it was intermittently disrupted by the same six words rolling around inside her head. *Where has that bloody dog gone?*

Close to midnight, Bert casually sauntered out of the darkness and sat down next to Rosa, who hugged him so hard he dropped what had been in his mouth—a dirty pair of rolled-up green army socks. Val asked him where he had been, and whose laundry basket he had pilfered, like he might draw her a map of the area. Bert yawned and padded up the steps of the mobile library, reminding them all that it was way past their bedtime.

•   •   •

The next morning, nestled in the nook of the cab, Bobby read *Stig of the Dump* by Clive King while Val washed their clothes—and the new socks—in a bucket of water, hanging the dripping goods from the bough of a tree.

Bobby kept his files clean and organized, and started to design for his mother the most comfortable bed imaginable, made from the ripped-up pages of the mathematics textbooks and an intricate bedstead woven from twigs.

"Look," Rosa said, pointing. Bert waddled once more toward the woods. He was old and slow, so they caught him up easily, leaping over roots and slinking under brambles. Bert didn't seem to mind that they were following him, but paid no attention when Val tried to make him stop. At a brook they presumed he might give up, but he jumped its width without breaking stride.

They walked until the canopy of the trees was thick enough that the daylight only dripped through, where they came to a storm drain. Beside it was a pile of sodden rags and a collapsed tent, teased by the wind, opening and closing like an unhealthy lung.

Bert sat down next to a large mound of leaves, whipped up and dumped by the wind.

"I think Bert might be going a little senile," Val said.

"What does that mean, Val?" Rosa asked.

"Silly. Because he's old. Like your mother."

Val tugged on his tail to try to make him stand up but

he jammed his snout into the undergrowth and pushed mud around with his nose. "Bert, come on," she said, "it's time to go home."

"Yeah, Bert," Rosa said, throwing a stick in his general direction, "stop being senile, it's time to go home."

Suddenly Val screamed, stumbled backward, tripped over a cluster of toadstools and landed on her behind. Bobby moved to help her.

"No, Bobby, get back!" she said. The mound of leaves next to Bert shifted, the ground beneath them rising, and underneath he saw it—a dirty human hand, with grubby fingernails, black as the hair on a skunk.

"Run!" Val said, but Bobby found he was stuck, his feet rooted as deeply as the trees. The hand became an arm, pushing upward from the earth, and then the filthy face of a man. His long blond hair was greasy and bedraggled. There was mud on his teeth and his beard was knotted, disgusting old rope.

"Don't be frightened," he said, his voice deep and driven through gravel. He got up slowly and they saw that he had been hidden inside a hole in the ground not much bigger than a coffin. The hole was lined with wooden panels to stop it caving in, and fitted with a wooden lid. Inside it was a bag of the man's belongings—a jug for fetching water, sheets of tarpaulin, string, knives and a first-aid kit in an olive green box.

"It's just for the cold nights," he said, "warmer than the tent, and less chance of . . ."

"Bears?" Rosa said.

"Ha. Yes, bears." Val shushed Rosa with her fingers to her lips as she got to her feet. Bobby put himself between the man and her, picking up the biggest stick he could find in the mud.

"Who are you?" he said.

"My name is Joe." Bert traitorously rubbed his head against the man's leg, and Joe bent down to pet him. Clearly they knew each other well.

"What are you doing in the woods?"

"Well, actually, I live here. Temporarily, I mean. I'm traveling to Scotland. But I'm resting here a while. Fresh water and shelter. All of that good stuff."

"How do I know you're not a caveman?" Bobby asked, half a mind still on the Stig.

"How do I know *you're* not a caveman." He laughed like Bobby was meant to join in, forgetting that it was Bobby's joke in the first place, even though it wasn't meant as a joke at all.

"Because I have my own mobile library."

"Bobby!" Val said. She clasped her hands across his chest. "I think we should leave the man alone now to get on with his camping." She didn't usually speak to Bobby like he was a child.

"I don't mean to scare your kids," Joe said.

"I'm her friend," Bobby said.

"Well, all the same."

"Not at all," Val said, "we were just out for a walk. *We* didn't meant to disturb *you*."

"You didn't." The man picked Bert up, holding him in a sort of headlock and rummaging around inside his ear with a knuckle. Bert's tongue lolled out of his mouth and flapped around, rippling with an intense pleasure humans shall never experience. "Is this your dog?"

"His name is Bert," Rosa said.

"Bert's a nice name for a dog. Is your name Bert too?" Rosa rewarded him with her warmest, most affectionate giggle. Bobby wanted to cuff her around the back of the head.

"My name is Rosa. Rosa Reed," she said, pulling her notepad from her pocket and writing down the stranger's name next to her own.

"And is Bert your dog?"

"Yes. Bert Reed. And this is Val Reed and this is my best friend Bobby Nusku." The man extended to his full height, slowly, and was approaching twice the size any of them had imagined him to be when he was still sitting in the hole.

"Val, huh?" he said.

"That's right," Val said. A pause, nothing but the trickle of water.

Joe, suddenly aware that his size might intimidate the woman and the two children, folded slightly at the belly. It had been a long time since he had seen another person, let alone looked them in the eye, and he had forgotten his own considerable dimensions, or even what he looked like. He pictured the clean-shaven army lines and buzz-cut hair, the standard-issue licks with which he knew himself best. Only the scratching of his beard against his chest, or now, meeting others, seeing the way they flinched when he moved, reminded him with a jolt that the truth was very different.

"Val," Joe said, "I think your dog might have eaten my socks."

"No," Val said, "they're in one piece. Actually, better than that, I've washed them." Joe's evident delight showed it had been some time since he had worn clean socks. To Bobby this seemed like another reason not to trust him. Bobby hadn't met a man he trusted immediately or fully in his entire life.

"That's very kind of you," Joe said. "If I'd have known Bert was a laundry dog, I might have given him a whole bag of my clothes." Val laughed.

"Well, again, I'm sorry if we disturbed you. We should let you have some peace." She held out her arms and Joe passed Bert to her. A low grumble and the lazy kick of an errant hind leg let his discontent be known.

"And the socks?"

"I'll have Bert bring them to you."

"Let him keep them," he said. "It'd be an honor."

"Goodbye," Rosa said.

"Goodbye."

They walked back through the woods in silence to the mobile library, where Bert went and sulked in Romantic Fiction. Even a chocolate bone couldn't tempt him to join the others on the rug.

"Nobody ever lives in the woods," Bobby said.

"We live in the woods," Val said.

"We live in the mobile library. It's different."

"The man is traveling. Some people are travelers. That's what they do."

"Like who?"

"Alice from *Alice in Wonderland*. She's a traveler. And Gulliver from *Gulliver's Travels*. I told you. In every book is a clue about life." Bobby sighed.

"We should move," he said.

"I don't think we can move at the moment. You know that

there will be people looking for us? Hunting for us? Your father. The school. The police."

"We could go to Sunny's house. He's a cyborg. He can take care of us."

"It's too far," she said.

"No," Bobby said, "I don't think it is. Not so long as we're all together."

CHAPTER TEN

THE HUNTER'S HOUND

A ringing hung in the air like the distant buzz of insects. The sound was far enough away that at first Bobby thought it an effect conjured in his brain by the words in the book he was reading. Sometimes, when characters he adored got scared, he could hear their hearts flutter. When they made a joke, their laughter came from his mouth. They moved with his hands, walked with his legs and saw with his eyes. He experienced their stories not with them, but for them, their fortune in that moment his own. Today he was Jonathan Swift's Gulliver, prisoner of the citizens of Lilliput. Their tiny knives and spears nicked his belly open. Bobby clutched the wound, raised a bloody hand and together he and Gulliver begged for their freedom.

It sounded like a bell. Not a big bell from the clock tower in the village, a small bell, elfin, fragile, Lilliputian. Roused, he placed his book back on the shelf and searched the library. Nobody else was there. Val was sleeping in the cab. Outside, Rosa was trying to persuade Bert to roll over with the offer of a biscuit, which he'd decided he'd get to eat eventually whether he performed for her or not.

Again Bobby heard the sound, but slightly louder this time, and for longer, as if the bell's clapper had come loose inside its chamber. He looked up to the tops of the trees and briefly searched the long grass.

That's when he realized what was coming. Or rather, who. His mother.

She had worn a bell-shaped pendant. Nestled at the apex of her bosom, jingling as she moved, he remembered it now. It was there, in the photograph of them standing by the car, him toying with it, the bell, precious in his hand, its mellow gold reflection on her skin.

He ran back into the library and hunted through his files, slipping the bottle of her hair down the front of his trousers and sliding as many of her rings onto his fingers as would fit. Her bracelets fell from his wrists too easily, so he threaded his feet through and yanked them up his ankles. He filled his pockets with the slivers of material cut from her dresses, and stuffed the clippings from her pictures deep into his sleeves. Finally, he sprayed himself with her perfume so that it followed him around as a sweet sticky mist.

Leaving the clearing, Bobby skipped through the veil of trees to the edge of the woods by the road. Here the sound of the bell was much louder than before. She was close. The road bent in both directions, and because of the wind he could not ascertain from which end the sound was coming. He climbed the tree closest to the path for a better view. Halfway up its aged trunk, brittle bark breaking to the touch, a swarm of thick black flies dangled in midair. Bobby held his breath as they bumped against his ears and nostrils. He climbed until they stopped, then shimmied out onto a sturdy branch and scanned the horizon with his binoculars. There, set against the green of dormant fields and the undulating yellow rapeseed, he spied a figure in a bright red coat.

Woolen, soft, he remembered it now. She had been wearing it in the photograph too. Parallel columns of brass-colored buttons and pockets almost elbow deep into which he would bury his hands. It had been her favorite coat, one she'd always hung carefully to stave off the creases.

Such was the feeling swelling in his chest, he had to cling extra tight to the branch in case his heart thumped hard enough to launch him into the sky. He wanted to shout her name but there wasn't the air. He breathed deeply and as best he could twisted the lens into focus. When he saw the figure clearly his heart cramped.

The man in the red windcheater beckoned his dog, the bell on its collar tinkling.

The rush of excitement dancing down Bobby's back quickly turned to pins and needles. The man and the dog were walking in his direction. He had to warn Val, to protect her.

Bobby slid down the trunk through the swarm, forgetting to close his mouth. Flies thick as raisins rode his tongue. Halfway down, where they gathered, he lost his grip and fell, landing on the bottle tucked into his waistband, which smashed on impact. Glass fragments scored his belly. Blood stuck his mother's hair to his skin and pooled in the cradle of his underpants. There was no time to stop, or to let the pain sneak in. Pinching his tongue between his teeth, Bobby made it back to the clearing and banged on the door of the cab. Val peered out of the window, one eye crusted with sleep. Blood roses bloomed on Bobby's shirt. He pulled his jacket closed to hide them. The wounds began to burn. He did not wince. This, he reasoned, is what a man would do.

"Someone is coming," he said. Panicking, Val ushered Rosa and Bert into the back of the mobile library and told them to be as quiet as they could. Rosa buried her head beneath a pillow and gave Bert the remainder of the biscuit, as a reward for his obedience, making him believe he'd been right all along.

Bobby followed Val to the clearing's edge where they lay down behind a brush of golden Alison on a mound of dirt, somewhere they wouldn't be easily spotted. They were just in time. The man was close enough for them to see the vinegar-colored patches of sun-bleached skin on his arms. The dog, a chestnut Irish setter, had waded through the flowers and was sitting on the mound above them, nostrils quivering at the scent of Bobby's blood.

"Shoo," Val said. "Shoo!"

"Come along, Lola," the man said in an accent that sounded clear and rich, no more than ten feet away. Had he deigned to look up for more than a second he'd have noticed them there, Val and Bobby, lying in the grass like guilty lovers. The dog offered a derisive snort, somehow in on the joke.

"What will we do if he comes this way?" Bobby asked.

"I have no idea," she said.

"Well, don't worry. I'll protect you." She gripped his hand.

The man toyed with the bluish glow of the mobile phone he was holding. This far outside the village he couldn't get a signal. Doubting that anyone was trying to reach him, he still felt compelled to return to a place where bars appeared on the phone's display, as if he were a whale who needed to break the ocean's surface now and again to breathe.

"Come along," he said once more, causing the dog to moan and then retreat.

Bobby and Val waited until they couldn't hear the bell any longer. Then, pain besting him, Bobby groaned and rolled over onto his back. When Val saw the blood on his shirt she put her hand to her mouth and grimaced as if she'd taken a bite of a rotten apple.

"What happened?" she asked.

"I cut myself," he said, "by accident." She unbuttoned his shirt. Glass and grit twinkled in the wounds, his chest smothered in whorls of hair and deep red. Val jumped to her feet. Guilt consumed her in an instant. She felt no more capable of protecting Bobby from harm than his father had been. It was writ large in blood on his skin. She did not know that reaction to suffering, not wont to mete it out—is how good people are defined.

Bobby tried to stand but felt faint and faltered. Val carried him back to the mobile library. He reclined on the steps while she frantically searched the drawers beneath the desk. Rosa, seeing the blood, started to cry.

"Don't worry," Bobby said, the loss now enough to fade the color in his vision.

"I have nothing," Val said, "I have nothing." She poured water across his stomach. As soon as the wounds were flushed they filled again, a hundred bloody smiles. She pressed a towel down on the skin but it soaked up the red and made room for more. "We will have to clean you up properly," she said, "we have to get you help."

"No," he said, "I'm fine." She pulled one of his mother's hairs from a cut that ran around the top half of his navel. Dirt dangled from the end.

"They'll get infected and you'll have to go to hospital."

"I won't," he said.

"And the doctors and the nurses will know who you are. They will send you home." Bobby would rather have had a lifetime of open wounds than let Val speak to Joe without him there to protect her.

"I'll be fine. Please," he said, but she was gone before he could say it twice.

Gasping for breath, her lungs rusty springs, Val collapsed onto the ground outside the mobile library. Joe followed behind her, the first-aid kit a toy in his enormous arms, this giant for whom Swift might have invented the word Brobdingnagian. He knelt down beside Bobby, who took one look at the mud covering Joe's hands and saw an opportunity to assert some authority.

"You'll need to wash them first," he said, despite the biting pain in his innards. He closed his eyes and pictured Lilliputians, stabbing their spears deeper, tightening the ropes around his waist until they cut through the flesh.

Rosa fetched a bar of soap and a bottle of water and Joe

washed his hands. Now white, they seemed even bigger against
his dirty fatigues.

"Relax," Joe said. He doused clumps of cotton wool in antiseptic lotion, then cleaned and dressed the cuts with a tenderness
neither Val nor Bobby had expected, leaving his midriff a patchwork of plasters, bandages and tape.

"Good job," Val said.

"I'm trained," he said, "by the army. They teach you to save
people, after you've tried to kill them."

Bobby thanked him, making sure reluctance registered in his
voice.

"Will you let me fix you a snack to say thank you?" Val asked.

"Sure," Joe said, "I'd appreciate it."

Val took Rosa into the mobile library, while Bert jumped onto
Joe's lap and fell asleep almost instantly.

"You really do have a mobile library, huh?" he said.

"Yeah," Bobby said. "And I'm in charge of it."

Joe laughed. "I don't doubt that for a second." He took a
packet of tobacco and a cigarette paper from his pocket, both
miraculously bone dry. "Wanna see a trick?"

Bobby disappointed himself by agreeing so readily, but as
it was just the two of them, him cut to ribbons, he figured it
couldn't hurt.

"I can roll a cigarette anywhere. I've rolled them in a mon-
soon. I've rolled them in a gale. I've rolled them in the darkness of the desert at night, and that's a real darkness too. Not like
nighttime here, with all this light pollution and residual glow. In
the desert the darkness is a thick black everywhere that feels like

never." Bobby had never heard someone talk this way before, with measured pace and poetry.

"Why would you want to do that?"

"When you're in the army, no one is gonna stop for you. Learning to do anything anywhere at anytime without help is a pretty useful skill to have."

"I mean smoking. It turns your lungs to cancer and they go black and crispy and then you die before you even get old. We learned about it at school. Did you not go to school?"

Joe had grown up in the foster care system, so had been surrounded by children more than most, but was alarmed to realize he'd forgotten how wonderfully direct they could be. "I didn't go to school enough."

"Well," Bobby said, "what's the trick?"

"I bet I can roll one with my hands underground." He wrung dust from his beard while Bobby considered the stakes.

"Totally underground? So we can't even see them?"

"Yes, totally underground so we can't even see them."

"You're on."

"What do you bet?" Even though Joe was dirty, with dried mud matted in his hair, Bobby couldn't think of one thing he had to offer him beside books, which he was pretty sure Joe wouldn't be able to read. He preferred to think that the mobile library, and everything in it, were for Rosa, Val and him alone.

He shrugged.

"You're already getting some food. We need everything else. I have nothing to bet you."

"How about a wash in your mobile library?"

"I don't think you should go in there. The books are clean and so is the carpet. You'll only mess everything up. Some people make everything dirty, so there is always something to clean."

"That so? Then I'll stay out here. Just bring me some more water and soap. And maybe a mirror so I can shave. I won't even ask for a towel." Joe sensed Bobby softening. "Shake on it?"

"Okay." They shook, Joe's hand swallowing Bobby's whole. Joe licked the narrow strip of gum on the paper, then held it on his open palms with a generous pinch of tobacco. He balled his hands around the precious inventory with his fingers contorting inside it. When he felt sure it was airtight he dropped to his knees and thrust them both under the dry layer of topsoil on the ground, which he had piled high in preparation.

"You look stupid," Bobby said. Joe's lips twisted into strange shapes as he concentrated.

"I don't care."

"This bet should have a time limit."

"No need," Joe said, "I'm done." He pulled his hands to his chest, soil cascading down, and slowly opened them up. "Ta-da!" There it was, a cigarette. A little messy, but a cigarette all the same. He popped it in his mouth, took a match from the box and lit it in a single fluid motion. It smoked. Sure, there was a lot of dirt in it, now collecting round his tonsils, but not enough that he was about to choke. He sucked it right down to the stub, two big lungfuls that made his chest whistle, then slapped Bobby on the shoulder. Bobby was impressed enough to let the feeling drip slowly down his back.

Just then Val emerged from the library with a tin of glistening peach segments and a mug of strong coffee.

"Joe," Rosa said, "what is your last name?"

"Joe," he said.

"So your name is Joe Joe?"

"Yeah, that's right. Joe Joe." Rosa immediately accepted his answer and began shaping the letters in her notepad. Bobby barely tried to disguise his suspicion.

Scrubbed, washed and dried, Joe assumed a different color altogether. His skin a soft, babyish pink; his hair fluffy and blond, like stuffing protruding from the head of a teddy bear. Val gave him her oversize dressing gown to wear, and he made a fire five times faster than she had managed to all week. Bobby fetched a pile of books from the library, pretended that he was going to read them to Rosa, and built a dividing wall between Joe and everyone else, except the traitor Bert.

"So this is your library?"

"I'm the librarian, yes," Val said.

"They let you live in it?"

"I'm just driving it to its next home and we thought we'd make a little camping trip of it. Much like yourself, I guess." Part of Val didn't like to lie, especially not to a man who had been as kind as Joe. He cleaned up well, and though clearly into his thirties she could still sense the roguish, youthful glint he'd honed in the dormitories where he'd come of age. A pinkish rash, cast in the shape of strangler's hands, appeared around Val's neck, disappearing under the collar of her shirt. This always happened whenever she found someone attractive, though it had been a while. She rubbed the skin as if chasing it away.

"Seems strange is all," he said.

"They were closing it down," she said. "They're closing them all down. You must have read about it in the papers?"

"I don't read the papers much."

"No," she said, "me neither these days." They both smiled. "The long and short of it is that the mobile library would only have gathered dust. Books are nothing until they're opened. Stories aren't stories unless they're told. Characters might be good or bad, but until you have known them they are neither, and that's worse."

Joe rolled another cigarette. "You're the librarian," he said. "Who am I to argue?" Rosa closed her book with a thud.

"We're camping," she said, "because we ran away from home."

"Rosa!"

"We all run away from time to time," Joe said. For a second, Val and Joe shared a look that told him whatever it was she was up to, she didn't want to be caught, not yet. That was enough. The children seemed happy enough to him. He didn't want them to be caught either. It was a desire he didn't just share. It was one he completely understood.

The broad plates of his forearms were covered in dark green tattoos, twisting like Japanese knotweed up to his shoulders. There were anchors, wizards and snakes wound round shields, swords, scrolls and hollow-eyed skulls. Words bled out. Bobby inched closer to see but the dressing on his belly came unstuck.

"What about you?" Val said. "What are you running away from?"

"Who said I was running away?" Smoke rolled over Joe's top lip and disappeared into his nose.

"You're living in the woods."

"Staying in the woods."

"Why?"

"Because I have nowhere else to go. I'm just one of those people, I suppose," he said, letting the flames warm his legs.

"Nowhere?" Bobby asked.

"Uh-huh. Been in the army since I was old enough. I quit, so that's over, and I guess I'm just a traveler now."

"Why did you join the army?"

Joe thought for a while. "To stay out of trouble, I guess."

"By going to war?"

Joe laughed. "Huh. By going to war."

"Well, you needn't sleep rough tonight," Val said. "You can stay in the cab if you like."

"I wouldn't want to make a nuisance of myself."

"It's no nuisance. The children and I sleep in the truck. It's fine."

"I'm not a child," Bobby said. Rosa copied the way he'd shaken his head.

"I'm not a child either," she said.

"Well," Val said, "okay. But you know what I mean."

They talked about nothing, both intent on not probing too deeply into each other's lives. Come dusk, tired by the events of the day, they decided to call it an early night. Val showed Joe how to wind down the sun blinds on the windows and lock the doors. When he wasn't looking, Bobby removed the keys from the ignition and hid them beneath the front wheels. Once Val and Rosa were asleep, Bobby stayed up until morning—only the owls for company—with his vision turned to night mode and trained on the cab's door just in case.

CHAPTER ELEVEN

THE BOY

Gargantuan and apparently endless, Joe's appetite saw the mobile library's stocks diminish speedily. After that first night he stuck around and became a steady fixture, or, as Bobby saw it, a black hole for food. In return he serviced the engine (he had been responsible for the upkeep of Warrior armored vehicles during his time in the forces) and helped out with everyday chores, most of which Bobby was happy to shirk so long as Val didn't notice. He had a sore belly and his files to maintain, which since he'd smashed the hair jar were in a state of disarray.

He had begun mapping the area around the mobile library. There were thirty-seven lunges across the clearing. Two routes through the woods were passable at night, one via the brook, another by the thicket. The road by the clearing averaged three cars an hour in the daytime (one, at most, by night) and beneath the mobile library there were four gaps above the wheel arches that would make decent hiding places should they ever be needed, though Joe would never fit. Bobby marked that down as a victory of sorts.

"Come on," Joe said one morning a few days later, as he leaned against the untouched shelves of books in the self-help section.

"What?" Bobby jumped, dropping the battered volume in his hand. He had been engrossed in John Steinbeck's *Of Mice and Men*, which he'd found crammed behind two intimidating hardbacks under Classics. He found it dense, too dense for his tender years, but the old-fashioned language lured him in to where the sentences spiraled around one another, and that was how he found himself entranced by the relationship between George Milton and Lennie Small. How different they were. George was small, uneducated but as smart as any teacher Bobby had ever known, while Lennie, lumbering Lennie, was big as a rock and twice as dumb. Yet despite their differences, or because of them, their friendship thrived. George kept Lennie calm. Lennie protected George from harm. They had become dependent upon one another in so many different and wonderful ways. It filled Bobby with warmth, as if they existed right there, talked their talk beside his ear.

"We need food," Joe said. "I'm going to teach you how to forage."

"You mean seeds and berries?"

Joe shook his head. "No. Much better than that."

"What then?"

"Come on. It'll be an adventure."

Seeing it as a good excuse to get Joe away from Val and the mobile library for a while, Bobby agreed. Val made them promise not to go too far, but Bobby didn't want Joe to watch her mothering him that way. He made sure he rolled his eyes so that Joe could see the whites, then put on his wellingtons and raincoat and they headed out together, promising to return with supplies.

"Where will you get supplies?" Val asked, before deciding it might be best if she didn't hear the answer.

Tractor-dug trenches had made moats around the fields. Banks of mud collapsed beneath their feet. Bobby got stuck and Joe had to heave him out by his armpits, then sling him over his shoulder and free his boots from the slop holes.

"This was a stupid idea," Bobby said, pointing at the clouds swilled with inky darkness.

"Means there will be less people around," Joe said. "Means we will leave less tracks. Trust me. If the army taught me one thing it is how to disappear. Rain should always be welcomed by outcasts like you and I."

"I'm not an outcast."

"Whatever you say."

Joe removed a small set of bolt cutters from inside his jacket and snipped through a barbed wire fence. Bobby skulked nervously behind him, keeping his fists balled so that Joe didn't see his fingers quaking. They stalked the back lot of a farm, hiding between plastic water barrels when the farmhouse curtains twitched. The rain wouldn't let the cowpats settle so the air was thick with the smell of shit. They ran behind the hay bales that blocked the back entrance to the stables, then dipped down low to reach the chicken coop beneath the farmer's kitchen window. Joe reached inside and picked up six white eggs in one enormous hand. He carefully lowered them into Bobby's pockets.

"Close your eyes," Joe said. Bobby didn't trust him completely, but when he saw Joe wrap his hand around the neck of a chicken he shut them tight. He heard what he guessed was the cracking of a tiny bone, then the gossipy jabber of a final cluck, and he nervously braced himself for blood to splatter his face. It didn't come.

"You can open them now." Joe lifted the chicken's body, inviting Bobby to prod its downy bloat. "See," he said, "it's okay." It was so warm to the touch that Bobby felt jealous when Joe put it in his jacket. He fantasized that he too could take a chicken's life with such virtuoso control of brute strength, and reveled in a mischief that reminded him, happily, of Sunny Clay.

They hiked down a waterlogged rambler's path to the outskirts of the village. At the back of a bakery was a small tower of boxes containing unsold stock. Joe hid behind a fence and watched the baker take a cigarette break. When he'd finished, Joe reached over and took a box from the top of the stack. They went back out into the fields to survey their bounty.

"If we get caught stealing we'll be in big trouble," Bobby said. He bit into a doughnut. Custard oozed from the end.

"You never read *Robin Hood*?" Joe said. "Surely they have that in your mobile library."

"Yeah, I read it."

"I'm sure the merry men stole from time to time."

"They didn't steal almond croissants."

"Hungry's hungry. And hungry is what we're all gonna be very soon unless you and I act like men and do something about it, merry or otherwise."

Joe had eaten five doughnuts to Bobby's one when the clouds cleared and a rainbow watermarked the sky. Their clothes dried quickly in the sun and were soon stiff and uncomfortable, Bobby's T-shirt chafing the tender flesh on his tummy. As they walked Joe plucked the chicken and flung feather darts at the horizon. Bobby snapped a pink rose from a bush and put it in his pocket for pressing later.

"You're a florist now?"

"It's for my mother. I'm going to put it in my files."

Joe had observed Bobby working on his files. He recognized the boy's longing. With hard-skinned palms impervious to thorns, Joe tore out another handful of roses and put them in his coat with the chicken.

"Then you might as well have a whole bunch."

From the meadow they could see the rows of gardens at the rear of the village. An old lady hung the washing while her husband dutifully carried the basket.

"Bingo," Joe said, "disguises."

"Disguises?"

"We're thieves now. On the run." Bobby thought of George and Lennie, traipsing across the outskirts of a California plantation like brothers, watching each other's backs. When the couple had gone, Bobby kept lookout while Joe took every last item from the line, underwear included, and carried the heavy wet stack out into the barley fields. Bulky and worn, the jacket fitted him neatly. Bobby wore the old man's flat clap and a threadbare cotton shirt so big his hands barely made it past the elbows. Joe held a turquoise patterned dress up to his body and swished it around like a tango partner.

"What do you think?" he said.

"Not your color."

"Not for me, smart ass. For Val. A gift."

Until now it hadn't occurred to Bobby that Joe might have some romantic affinity with Val. The thought brought him out in prickly heat. "She hates turquoise. Reminds her of the Caribbean Sea."

"What's wrong with being reminded of the Caribbean Sea?"

"She nearly drowned in it," he lied.

Joe tossed the dress to the floor and Bobby made a mental note of its exact whereabouts—twenty-eight paces from the tree, perpendicular to the electricity pylon—so that he could collect it come nightfall.

Joe put on a pair of the old man's gray pinstripe trousers, tying the waist with string, then smoothed his hair to the side. "What do you think," he asked Bobby, "disguised?"

"Kind of."

Joe rummaged through his pockets.

"Then maybe I've got a better idea." He was holding a switchblade inches from Bobby's face, close enough that he could feel the metal's coldness reflected on his skin. "How about you give me a trim?" Joe handed Bobby the knife and squatted down beside him. The pump of an artery throbbed in Joe's neck, tender, slit-able. Shaking, Bobby wound the mane around his hand and shaped it into a ponytail.

"Get a move on, will you? I don't want a perm," Joe said, "slice it off. We can tidy it up back at the ranch." The blade hit the column of hair with force enough, but the angle was skewed, so Bobby sawed through it with the corrugated edge. Eventually the golden rope of hair came free in his hand, and the knife felt more like a sword.

"Good boy," Joe said, tidier, the two buds of his ears now visible and making him instantly more human. Bobby instinctively stuffed the hair into his pocket.

They walked back the long way, over fields and out toward the bypass, where factories, warehouses and a homeware depot formed a small, depressing-looking business park. Reject piles of broken furniture and dented paint cans littered the yard. They made their way back to the mobile library, declaring their booty enough.

Joe stripped and gutted the chicken, tossing the liver and heart to Bert. They cooked it over the fire, slathered in what was left of the barbecue sauce, and ate it with doughnuts for dessert. The night froze their words in mist, so they put on as many of the stolen clothes as they could and took it in turns to read stories to each other. Rosa rocked in the warmth of the flame.

Bobby picked up *Of Mice and Men* and read the last few pages. Though he was sad that George had shot Lennie, he knew that it had been for the greater good, so that Lennie didn't suffer. He wondered if he could kill Joe should he need to, and tried to remember into which of his pockets Joe had put the knife.

"It's your turn, Joe Joe," Rosa said.

Joe's tongue curled a mouthful of smoke into an S-bend. "I'm not one for stories," he said.

"Come on," Val said. "Rosa will pick one for you." He shook his head. Bobby envied the authority he mustered.

"I told you," he said, "not for me."

"Then tell us what's in Scotland."

"Huh?"

"Scotland. When we found you, that's where you said you were headed." Joe flicked the cigarette's clubfoot into the embers.

"A house."

"A house?"

"*The* house. More of a mansion, if I'm honest."

Bobby wolf-whistled. Unable to copy him, Rosa said "Switz-swoo" in a pitch that sent Bert scuttling around the camp.

"Saw it when I was a child," Joe said. "Never forgot it. Right beside a dam, and the clearest blue loch you'll ever see, I swear. Damn thing's a mirror made of water."

"Who lives there?" Rosa asked.

Joe lit another smoke. "That's the thing. I doubt nobody lives there anymore. Whole place is empty, I reckon. Some decrepit country pile, falling down to nothing. Needs a lot of love. Whole tanker full of paint, ten thousand nails and all the time in the world, but I could fix it up all right. Then it'd be total privacy. No one goes that far into the wilds for a crumbling old wreck of a house like that."

"What do you mean you saw it?"

"Moved around a lot as a boy. Different homes, different families. Went hiking in the mountains one time. Just came across the place, standing up in the fog like a castle or something. Always promised myself I'd make it back there one day." Rosa smiled. "Want to know the best bit? Whoever lived there had their own private zoo on the grounds. I swear, on a still day when the wind wasn't screaming havoc in the hills, you used to be able to hear the lions roaring, and the parrots squawking and the . . ."

"Bears growling?" Rosa said.

"Exactly. Grrrr. Heard them all from the other side of the wall. Always wanted to find out for myself where all those animals lived."

Val blushed. It had been a long time since she'd seen another adult talk to Rosa in a way that made her respond in kind, or even really talk to her like a fellow human being, but there she was, rolling around at the feet of the man from the woods, dressed in stolen clothes. What did it matter if Joe was spinning a yarn? They had come this far. To hell with the truth. Lit by only the flicker of a fire, everything is the same, more or less.

A jangle, far away, grew nearer.

"Shh . . ." Bobby said. Val and Rosa stopped talking and soon they could hear it too, the familiar sound of the dog collar bell coming up the hill from the village. It got closer this time, moving on the other side of the thick oaks, then without warning the dog burst into the clearing and headed for the chicken carcass.

"Lola!" Her owner was still some distance away, but nearing, and worse, searching. Bert growled. Val wrapped a hand around his muzzle.

Joe baby-stepped toward Lola, hands out by his sides, and tentatively shepherded her back up the track to the trees. At the final moment, defeat in her nose, she swooped beneath his grasp, snatched the chicken and savaged it, showering Joe in splintered bone and flecks of cold meat.

"Lola," the man said, closer still. Joe kicked out at the dog in panic, missed, and thrown from balance fell over the grassy verge they had been using as a platform from which to piss. Angry and embarrassed, he climbed back up and reached into the pocket where he kept the switchblade. Anger overtook him. With one smooth jab Joe could slit the dog's throat, let the threat bleed silently onto the mulch. He was ready to kill it—but that would give them all away—and Bobby was the only one thinking clearly enough to realize it.

"Lola," the man said again, now at the cloak of the trees, close enough to hear. The dog walked toward Joe and passed underneath his legs. Joe reached down and grabbed his tail. Bobby launched himself at Joe with all the force he could muster, causing him to topple over the dog, almost crushing it, and land on his back on the grass. With all his strength, Bobby tried to wrestle the knife from his grip. In Joe's hands Bobby's arm was a twig, brittle and small. Joe let go before he broke it. Bobby stood over him, the knife in his hand, the blade exposed. Lola dropped the chicken and its spine shattered on the ground. Bobby lifted the blade above his head. He thought of George and Lennie. He thought of the greater good.

He slashed the knife down through Joe's bootlaces, yanked them from his feet and quickly removed his socks. With one hand, as swiftly as Joe had ever rolled a cigarette, he balled the socks and dangled them in front of Lola's eyes. Enraptured, she licked the salty liquorice-blackness of her lips, as, exalted, Bobby launched the socks high into the sky. They sailed to the top of the tree line and disappeared out of sight, with Lola in rapid pursuit.

"There you are," the man said, jangling the bell as he clipped her lead to its collar. "Where the hell did you find these dirty old things?" The dog sneezed. "Come on, let's get you home." The ringing faded until all that was left was their breathing as one.

Bobby ran to where Val and Rosa were standing and they threw their arms around him. Joe flung the tattered remnants of his laces into the woods. As he walked over to join the embrace, his boots slipped free from his feet.

Bobby, finally, felt like a man, or at least, the glue in which others are caught. The two, he decided, were one and the same.

They went into the mobile library together.

"Joe," Val said, "I think it's time we told you who we are . . ."

CHAPTER TWELVE

THE HUNTER

The trees were black paper pasted on the sky. Mirror-eyed rabbits bounced back the moonlight. Inside the mobile library, Bobby and Joe lay on the carpet together, the files spread out before them. Bobby had never showed them to anyone before. Neatly arranged like this, they made him tremble with pride.

"And these are parts I cut out of her clothes," he said, "so that she remembers what dresses she had and can buy the same ones again. If she's still the same size." What he could rescue of his mother's hair from the pine needles he kept pressed inside an atlas, beside the roses, now flat and crisp. In an envelope were the locks of it congealed with blood that he'd salvaged from the flesh wounds on his stomach. Joe didn't recognize his own blond tresses tangled in the mix. He held the photograph of Bobby's mother, rubbed his thumb over the pregnant hump of her dress and had an idea of sudden and stunning clarity.

"A family!" he said, to Val, who was reading *The Lion, the Witch and the Wardrobe* to Rosa, reclining on a bean bag in the corner by Travel.

"What?"

"They're looking for a woman and two children in a stolen mobile library."

"And a dog," Rosa said.

"Right, and a dog. But they're not looking for a family. So we become one. The disguise we need is each other." Joe, just like any other soldier, had been schooled in camouflage when he joined the army. He appreciated it not just as a necessity in combat, but as a discipline that could be twisted into everyday life.

"You think we can just walk out of here?" Val said.

"Uh-huh."

"Then you're crazy. Or stupid." Val ran a finger around her collarbone, as if making a wineglass sing.

"There's only one way to find out. You're going to have to trust me on this."

"Trust you?" she said, as though she found the suggestion confounding, but in truth she already trusted him completely.

Working from a book entitled *Teach Yourself Face Painting* and using Rosa's paints, Val turned Bobby into a lion and Rosa into a witch. These had been Rosa's C. S. Lewis–inspired suggestions and, sensing a tantrum brewing, everyone agreed.

"Okay," Joe said, "let's put it to the test."

They walked to the village, Val, Joe and Rosa arm in arm, Bobby sprinkling the road behind them with a torn-up paper trail. It was a cool night and the chimneys belched blackness into it. The village pub was a squat ugly building made of damp gray stone and the front door was small, as though it had been made for a time when people were much shorter. But when they stepped through it the room opened into a space that was big, golden and magical, with candles on tables nestled in coves, and a smell of damp fur that made Rosa think of Narnia. Three men stood at the bar, and she checked their legs for faun's hooves.

Val, Rosa and Bobby took the table closest to the fireplace. Bobby worried that his face paint would melt in the heat. Joe approached the barman. Snaking gold chains lurked in his chest hair. He ordered two lemonades and a bottle of red wine, paying with the money Val had given him before they arrived.

"Been to the fair?" the barman asked. Joe shrugged. The barman pointed to Rosa and Bobby. "The fair in the next village. Aslan and, er, the . . ."

"Oh, yeah. The witch," Joe said.

"Win anything?"

"Just some books." Val removed two from her bag and placed them open on the table.

Rosa and Bobby invented words to fill the melodies sung by the jukebox. Val and Joe challenged each other to remember the real lyrics. Bobby half expected that particular menace he associated with the smell of the grape. But nothing changed. They almost fitted together.

This was the normalcy Val had craved. She wondered if she had subconsciously willed it into being. She had agreed they try disguises. It was she who allowed for them all to go to the pub, though she knew they might be caught. Why would she take such risks? Had she meant all along to create this, the world's strangest first date?

Joe had also secretly longed for something of this happy ordinariness. He sloppily rolled a cigarette too plump in the middle. It had been a long time since he'd consumed alcohol, and was surprised how quickly he'd managed to get drunk. Eased into a groggy stupor, he declined another glass.

"Suit yourself," Val said, draining hers and pouring another, her arms a soft elastic that made Bobby want to tie them in knots around himself.

"I've an idea," Joe said.

"Of course you do, this is our second bottle of wine. You're a philosopher by now. Let's get another bottle. You'll be Aristotle."

"A bottle of Aristotle," Rosa said.

"Precisely, Rosa. A whole damn bottle of delicious Aristotle."

Rosa laughed, leaning back, her stool on two legs so that Joe had to catch her before she fell.

"No, I'm serious," he said. "You should come to Scotland with me. To the house. It's big enough for all of us, and no one will find you there." Bobby sucked up the last of his lemonade with a slurp.

"All the way to Scotland?" Val said.

"Yeah. Why not?"

"You think we'd make it those hundreds of miles without being seen?"

"Right now we're sitting in a pub with other people. I'm just suggesting that it's no more improbable than that."

"Right now we're not sitting in a mobile library, with the words *mobile library* painted in huge letters on the side, whilst loads of people are looking for a big old mobile library."

"Now that," Joe said, changing his mind about having another glass of wine, "is a point worth making."

Val couldn't help but find Joe's idea thrilling—if unworkable—but Bobby, rolling an ice cube around in his mouth, would not be so easily persuaded. Scotland sounded like an awful long way to leave his paper trail, and in the opposite direction from where Sunny Clay was waiting to protect him.

Uncut nails clacked on the cold stone floor. Joe looked up to find Lola on the lead of the man who must have been her owner. Sniffing up the dust, she followed a scent around the room that ended at Joe's feet.

"Lola," said the man, pulling on the lead, but she stayed put, even when Joe nudged her with his shoe. The man came to the table.

"I apologize," he said. His nose was misshapen and red, over whisky-stained teeth and the bruised chin of a drinker who falls asleep at the table.

"No need," Joe said.

Again the man tugged on the lead but Lola refused to budge. "She doesn't normally do this," he said.

"It's fine, honestly. She can stay there if she wants." Lola rubbed her flank against Joe's ankle and the man stumbled over to the bar, looking back at the dog as if it had been replaced with one that wasn't his.

They stayed late, dreading the shrill wind outside. Besides them and the barman, who slept in an armchair by the kegs, Lola's owner was the only person left inside the pub. He twice tried and failed to slot his hand inside a glove, then woke the dog to stop its legs pumping rhythmically to the jazz beat of a dream. They found themselves leaving at the same time, into the cold.

"Again," he said, "sorry about earlier."

"Huh?" Joe said, memory sodden with wine.

"About the dog. Seems she's a little obsessed with you or something."

"Oh, please, it's genuinely not a problem. She probably smells a little of my own dog on there. You know how they get."

"Yeah, I know how they get," the man said. "New to the village?" Val hooked an arm through Joe's and tried to pull him along, but he was too big and heavy to so subtly persuade.

"Oh no, just visiting. Getting some good clean country air." The old man smiled approvingly, and they started up the hill. Val felt relieved that the wind was forcing the illusion of sobriety on her.

"Without a car?"

"Huh?"

"Without a car!?" The old man was shouting over the bluster. "It's a hell of a walk up the road that way this time of night. If you haven't got a car, I mean."

"It's okay," Val said.

"The next village is twelve miles. I'm not sure I'd try it, let alone in the dark, what with kids in tow and a storm coming in." Lola whined, smoothed her ears back against her head and crept toward Joe as if approaching a shrine. Val pushed Rosa and Bobby in the direction of the mobile library, her cackling and him roaring, neither dropping out of character. "I could give you all a lift?"

"It's fine," Joe said, "honestly."

"Okay then. If you're sure. But if it's"—the man brought a cupped hand to his mouth and jiggled it around—"you're worried about then don't be, all I've had is a couple of whiskies and I know these roads like the back of my hand." He hiccupped.

"Thank you. That's very kind. But really, it's absolutely fine. Good night." Joe gave Lola a firm shove and she slunk away, unrequited love raking her heart.

He had almost caught Val up when he heard the man yell, "Hey, wait a minute, where'd you get that coat?" but he chose not to turn around.

Fifteen minutes' walk away the mobile library lurked in the raggedy shadows of the branches thrown across the clearing. Val and Joe were too agitated to give Bert the fuss he'd hoped for, so Rosa and Bobby chased him around the bookshelves.

"It's a matter of time before he comes up here with that dog again, and you'll be caught for sure," Joe said, stroking the coarse run of his stubble. "You have to go. Even if you have to leave the library."

"We can't leave the library."

"But you'll be caught."

"And you?"

"I guess I'll go back into the woods. I'll be fine."

A melancholy wedged in Val's chest. "On your own?"

"I'll be fine."

She swallowed. "Then let's all go. To Scotland, together. Like you said, they're not searching for a family."

Bobby was sure this was a bad idea, but he recognized the look on Joe's face, to have been blessed by her affection. The pinch of jealousy followed, and remained, until she held Bobby's head against her side, where in that infinite mellowness she made, no such thing could exist. He thought of Sunny, and how much he missed him. He wondered whether cyborgs miss people too.

Rosa wrote their names down, the five of them, unsullied by punctuation, one after another. *Rosa Reed Val Reed Bobby Nusku Joe Joe Bert.* That's when Bobby had an idea of his own. He grabbed Rosa by the hand and they ran to the back of the library, tumbling over the pillows left piled on the floor. They found it, thumbed enough that the pages were thinning, and scurried back to Val and Joe with it held above their heads, a children's book they loved to read together, *The Big Orange Splot* by Daniel Manus Pinkwater.

Rosa opened the book at the end, her favorite page, where Mr. Plumbean has persuaded the neighbors that their houses can look however they want them to look, can be painted however they wish, that a home, like a family, is what's inside it. They read the words together.

"Our street is us and we are it. Our street is where we like to be, and it looks like all our dreams."

"We paint our house," Bobby said.

"With what? Rosa's face paints?" Joe said.

"No. We're going to go on an adventure. Let me teach you how to forage."

Joe and Bobby crossed the fields. Bobby counted two thousand three hundred and fifty-three steps across flat land, on the one-mile walk to the business park. Night birds circled, hunting mice on the black blanket of ground. He saw the white brush of a badger flit by, fur caught on thorns and fluttered by the breeze. Climbing mud swells and craters burned in their thighs, but they hiked without once complaining of the cold.

On the opposite side of the bypass stood three warehouses surrounded by flickering security lights. They waited for a gap in the traffic, then crossed, to a wire fence that Joe used his bolt cutters to cut open with ease. They ran to the back of the homeware depot, a monolithic building made from a material neither of them could confidently name, then hid behind a stack of pallets while a lone forklift truck drove across the court.

"Stay behind me," Joe said.

The depot's loading bay was open awaiting night deliveries. They crawled on hands and knees past the watchman's office, his snore blunting the finer details of the radio play that had sent him to sleep.

Inside the vast warehouse they heard the wind beating on the corrugated tin façade, sending ghoulish howls around the roof. Strip bulbs crisscrossed the aisles, robbing shelf-stackers of shadows as they slowly replenished the stock. It was neither daylight nor nighttime, but a suspension of the bleary minute when the two bleed into one another.

They edged thirty-nine crab-steps along the back wall until it got too dark in the corner.

"I can't see," Joe said.

"Then you had better stay behind me," Bobby said.

In night mode he led Joe to the far end, through another door and into a secluded area of the yard littered with crowns of broken glass and battered boxes. A tall black trash compactor stood redundant in the center. Beyond that, a pile of paint tins three times Bobby's height, dented and unsellable. They loaded two trolleys with all the shades of white they could find, magnolia, Isabelline, ivory, seashell and Bobby's favorite, cosmic latte, two terms he enjoyed for the way they pawed at each other on his tongue as the lid came loose and he dropped a tin of it over his feet.

They wheeled the trolleys back through the depot to the exit, stopping to seize an armful of rollers, past the snoozing security detail, through the fence and over the road to the mud, where the ghostly paint trail of Bobby's footprints finally disappeared into brown.

Dragging such heavy loads through the fields doubled the twenty-minute walk back, but they arrived with time to spare before dawn. When they did, Val woke and heated water over a fire to wash the paint from Bobby's hands. Smoke rose into the crisp air, the way it does in the aftermath of battle.

Val tussled with the notion that she was now a woman who was complicit in the theft of eighteen liters of paint. What version of her had it been? One drunk and bedeviled, one Joe had awoken. She sat down before she fell over. Excitement always made her light-headed.

Though exhausted, they immediately set about painting the mobile library, haphazardly merging white shades together to chase down the remainder of the green. Bobby sat on Joe's shoulders, the concert of them making short work of the task. Soon the words *Mobile Library*, once proudly emblazoned on the vehicle's side, had vanished completely. Rosa raised her arms aloft, victorious.

"Our street is us and we are it," she said. "Our street is where we like to be, and it looks like all our dreams." Together they admired their handiwork, in a row, the four of them now seamlessly stitched.

"The trick to a good disguise is not just camouflage, but to also hide your tracks," Joe said. Bert followed him into the woods where he made sure no sign of his old camp existed, tramping down the swirls of disturbed mud, collapsing the wooden hoardings of his hole and stuffing his tent deep into the water outlet, where it would never be found.

Val filled the fire hole with fresh soil and threw the empty paint cans into the thick undergrowth. Bobby climbed the fly tree and listened to the whispered applause of the leaves on the canopy, as close a sound to peace as he knew. He had never prayed before. But up there, where the sky started, above the branches so his one wish couldn't snag, he asked aloud for his mother to find him, wherever that may be.

After she had gone, when the doorbell stopped ringing, and the neighbors' interest in cooking for them waned—in the short time before Cindy arrived—Bobby had spent long evenings wondering how to talk to his father. It was far simpler for them both to not speak at all, a decision they came to mutually, and, fittingly, in silence.

Bobby's father heated soup, a lot of it, so much that the kitchen walls sweated blush tomato vapor. One day he burned the plastic kitchen counter with the underside of a hot metal pan. This was how Bobby's files began, with a scraping of the charred laminate, so that he might show his mother how awful his father's cooking was in comparison to her own. They soaked the soup up with thickly sliced bread slathered in salty butter; most nights his father would eat three-quarters of a loaf. His belly would distend, a mottled hairy boulder wedged between the sofa cushions. Bobby would lie across it, lifting and falling, listening to the gurgling springs of acid inside and enjoying the way he stroked his hair— gently, and with nine fingers. If Bobby stayed extra still and quiet his father would put his arm around him, and he could smell the undercarriage of it, as squishy on his neck as blancmange.

This tenderness made Bruce feel awkward. It didn't last.

When there was no soup they had sandwiches. Bruce was bad at making sandwiches. Torn by the knife, the bread fell apart, half the crust clinging on as an afterthought. The soft white top deck bore the imprint of his hands. Limp squares of processed cheese and tinned meat fillings smelled of swimming pool skin. They made Bobby's stomach ache well into the night.

Both found it difficult to sleep. Bobby double-plumped his pillows, hung one foot from the mattress and even made a blind-fold from an old sport's sock, but nothing seemed to work. One night he nibbled the tiniest grain from a sleeping tablet he'd found amongst his mother's things, but got so scared that he wouldn't wake up when she came home that he ran to the bathroom and made himself sick. He prayed that night, too.

"Come down, Bobby," Val said, peering up into the treetops, "it's time for us to go." Morning was coming and the chirrup of the insects slowed, but the woods remained alive in silhouette.

The mobile library was packed up and ready. Val held the keys in the ignition.

"Ready?"

"Ready!" Rosa said.

But they were too late. Bert cocked his head, splashing drool against the window. He'd heard what they all had, the jangle of the bell on Lola's collar once more.

The man had woken on the rug beside the fireplace, Lola's wet tongue taking the shape of his inner ear. His hangover was sturdy, thick-footed, and would be difficult to topple, certainly more robust than any in the previous fortnight. Turning to his usual emergency cure (reserved for instances of this severity), he made himself a sugary bowl of porridge laced with the tartest lime pickle available to man. Then, as was customary, he sipped a mug of hot chamomile tea, listened to the news on the radio and tried to piece together exactly what had happened the night before. He remembered drinking all afternoon, starting on home brew in his garage and moving on to rum before supper. He recalled going to the pub, where, as usual, he'd been roundly ignored by the other locals, most of whom his drunkenness had irked in the past.

And that was it. It had been an evening like almost all of the others.

No matter what form his hangover took—sometimes they hid from him as a niggling headache, only to bloom into a lobe-splitting migraine around lunchtime—he always walked the dog. Lola was his only real friend, and the least he could do was reward her undying loyalty with a saunter up the hill. That it was still dark outside made the prospect more appealing than it would be later on, when the hangover came on strongest. He'd hate for his inevitable nausea to blossom in the sun. He was still drunk, and so felt artificially magnificent.

He checked his phone—no calls or messages. It was while putting on his worn leather boots that he noticed them in the corner. Green socks, balled up like a hand grenade, glistening with slobber. Then he recalled a conversation with a large man, whose feet Lola had been obsessed with. He had a wife and two children, their faces painted as animals that right now he couldn't place. They were walking up the hill to the next village. In that weather. At that time of night. He'd offered them a lift. *Good job they hadn't accepted*, he thought. Last time he went out that drunk he'd left his trailer upturned in a ditch. But the man, neck wide as a beech, had been wearing a coat he recognized. Not from sight, from its description. A shaggy donkey jacket, torn at the lapel, faded mauve color and worn epaulettes. The coat that an old man from the village had described having stolen from his washing line in a conversation he'd overheard at the store.

"Joe, wait . . ." Val said, but he had already opened the door, climbed out of the cab and was gone. Rosa, Bobby and Val sat in silence for ten minutes as the wind rose, branches shaking like angry fists. He did not return. Somewhere in the woods the bell kept ringing.

"Should I switch on the headlights?" Val asked.

"No," Bobby said, thinking of the blade in Joe's pocket. "I'll go and find him."

"Don't get out," she said, but Bobby was already outside, nettles lapping his calves.

Following the sound of the bell on Lola's collar, it was fifty-three side steps to the edge of the clearing's rough grass. Seven long hops made it over the bank, an eighth skirted the brook where it petered to nothing. Sticky mud took the shape of the tread on his soles, but he skipped through it. The bell got louder. Bobby placed it behind where the trees were most dense. A thirty-second jog around the stone track, one short skip to the foot of an old oak and twenty long strides across the forest floor where the fallen leaves were sheltered from the wind, so the ground was spongy and no movement could be heard. That's where Bobby spotted Joe.

The old man was crouched at Joe's feet wearing his shirt as a blindfold. Joe's balled-up socks, which the man had carried with him so that Lola could follow the scent, had been crammed into his mouth. Lola cantered around the clearing, driven delirious by her owner's whimpering.

Joe knew this feeling of numbed clarity well. Aware of what he was doing, but incapable of stopping it, he had experienced it a thousand times since he was a boy, the bad hawk of rage that swooped down and took him in sharp talons. Gliding in the air above himself, watching powerless as the unrecognizable figure tied the old man's wrists with rope. It always happened for the same reason. Because he was scared. Here, now, he was scared to lose Val, Rosa and Bobby, this slapdash family, the closest to one he'd ever known. All that stood between them, in that moment, was the man, fright flushing all traces of hangover from his shivering system. Something had to be done.

Joe held the torch in his mouth while he rummaged through his pockets for the knife, and the wandering spotlight picked out Bobby in the trees.

"What are you doing?" Bobby said. The man jumped but his begging was muffled. Joe suddenly became aware of time, of place, of the man sobbing by his feet and the boy watching, just as scared as he was. He couldn't answer. He didn't know.

Bobby unclipped Lola's collar and threw the bell into the undergrowth, then knelt down close to the man's ear while untying him. "Sorry," he said. "Go home." The man clambered to his feet. Lola followed him to the road. They walked together down the hill, the soberest he'd been in a very long time, remembering the boy's final words.

"Tell them we're on an adventure." *By God*, the man thought, *do I need a drink*. He knew that no one would believe him.

Bobby led Joe back to the mobile library.

"Will you tell Val?" Joe asked. Bobby didn't answer. Joe hung his head and closed his eyes. He didn't need to see the path. Bobby had it all taken care of.

CHAPTER THIRTEEN

THE ZOO

With full beams dipped to oncoming traffic, the mobile library snaked slowly down the lanes that sliced the country up. Joe drove. He had barely spoken since the incident in the woods.

"You're a professional," Val said of his driving.

"My other car's a tank," he said.

She let her hand settle on his thigh. The lean, solid muscle dried her mouth instantly, reducing her voice to a squeak. Joe relaxed and pondered his tremendous good fortune, but a tightening in his lower back made him wonder if it could last.

Rosa rested her head on Bobby's shoulder. He read to her, *Treasure Island* by Robert Louis Stevenson. Rosa squawked at every appearance of the parrot, Flint, who always perched on Long John Silver's shoulder, and shrieked as Flint's pirate master revealed his

ruthless violent side, murdering a member of the crew as part of
his plan to escape with the treasure.

"Do only baddies have parrots?" Rosa asked. Bobby thought
about it. The stiff beak. The beady eye. Hooked nail claws for
tearing the skin.

"Probably," he said.

"Then why don't they fly away?"

"I don't know," Bobby said, "I don't know." Together they
sang "that old sea song."

"Fifteen men on the dead man's chest—yo ho ho and a bottle
of rum!" He read until they reached the light strip of the motorway, where the cars sped small around them, fish swimming in the
slipstream of a shark.

Before midday, Joe turned the mobile library in at a service
station forecourt and parked in the area reserved for long-haul
vehicles. When he switched off the engine there was an abrupt-
ness to the way the silence arrived.

Tired-looking men came and went, but despite the days and
weeks of radio news coverage, the amount of times they'd heard
those names as they retuned for a traffic update, the chats they'd
had with other drivers ("How the hell could a forty-four-ton
truck disappear just like that?"; "What kind of amateurs do they
employ as policemen these days anyway?" and "Bet she's rolled
the thing. They'll find them against a tree in a field somewhere,
that poor little bastard she kidnapped was probably dead a long
time ago . . . might as well give up the search"), none of them sus-
pected that the most sought-after vehicle in Britain was the one
they'd pulled up next to. Or that in the back was the infamous

Joseph Sebastian Wiles, with Rosa sleeping beside him, as she had taken to insisting on doing. He didn't mind. In fact he adored the way she used his arm as a pillow, and he didn't even move it when it went dead.

Morning, afternoon, evening and night become vague terms for how light the sky was and nothing more. They slept when they could and drove when they couldn't, never staying in a single place long enough for anyone to get more than one look at them. They cut back and forth across the country, detouring to avoid towns, taking any minor road the mobile library would fit down and trying some it resolutely wouldn't. Joe made Val cut her bank cards in half with his knife and they spent what remained of the cash as slowly as possible. They split into unsought twos, mother and son, father and daughter, and bought provisions from rural mini markets. Roadside vendors sold them freshly picked fruit and vegetables. Farm shops filled plastic tubs with cheaply priced milk. When the sun was high enough they stopped in fields to eat and rest, then picked spiky yellow seedlings from the fur on Bert's back. They played cards and built half-finished dens they knew they'd soon abandon. Joe kept the truck in order, Val made the meals, Rosa tidied books away and Bobby fetched clean water from streams in a rusting tin bucket. They moved by night.

Every day had a different view. Cloud-thronged snow peaks on mountains in the north. Valleys in the west, green, lush and wet with mist. Lochs stiller than death and entire meadows that bowed to the wind.

Bobby read voraciously. He consumed stacks of classics Val had recommended. He discovered new books for himself, based

on little more than a feeling he got when he held them and read
the back cover, an itch that would not abate until it had been
scratched.

Rosa listened. As Bobby gave voice to the characters, she
found that a hundred friends lived inside her greatest friend of all.

Just over the Scottish border they parked the mobile library
behind a disused crematorium, put on their disguises and went
to a fun fair on the lip of a national park. Val and Bobby rode
the bumper cars, where the first crash shunted his face into the
candy floss and left his forehead sticky for the rest of the night. Joe
claimed a prize of two helium balloons in an apple-bobbing competition. He gave them both to Rosa. They walked home—and it
was home—along a rambler's path surrounded by sheep, balloons
tussling for position in the sky.

Everywhere they went they left a book. Sometimes they buried them, or hid them beneath a rock. Sometimes they left them
on show so that they could easily be found. One was left in the
center of a hilltop fort. Rosa left another in the cave walk of a
gorge. Bobby gave an illustrated book about birds to a crying
girl at a market, and a copy of Fyodor Dostoevsky's *The Brothers
Karamazov* (Val's idea—he hadn't read it) to a grumpy-faced boy
whose father wouldn't let him have a plastic ray gun from a toy
shop.

"It's about patricide," Val said, "he might get a kick out of it in
a few years' time."

"Patricide?" Bobby asked. It sounded to him like a drink.
"What's that?"

"Something you'll never need to worry about."

When needed they bought cheap clothes from charity shops. In a tourist-friendly village where the air carried the odor of compost, Bobby chose for Rosa a purple velvet cape that might once have been a curtain, and she picked for him a hat with corks dangling from it, the same as a kangaroo might wear in a cartoon.

"What a darling family you have," the lady behind the counter said to Val. Her makeup was white and patchy, like sea wash breaking on sand.

"We're on an adventure," Bobby said, and Rosa repeated.

"We're on an adventure."

"I bet you are!" Her eyes thinned. She recognized the girl, but why? It wouldn't crystalize.

"You do *such* a good job. I bet it can't be easy," the lady said to Val.

Val smiled. So many people had said this to her in the past, as if her daughter were a machine she had to operate. Such a peculiarly hurtful thing to say. They left before the lady could piece the memory together, and it went to the graveyard of thoughts that are never fully formed.

"That's the key to good camouflage," Joe said as they wound down the mobile library's metal steps. "People only ever see what they are looking for. And if we look like a family, if we behave like a family, then we become a family, we *are* a family."

And that's exactly what they did. Val and Joe held hands. Warmed though she was by the tandem of it, Rosa was unable to spot the signs of two people falling in love. She had never seen or even heard of it. Love, for her, was constant. It didn't come or go, grow or subside. You didn't fall into it, you didn't fall out. It was the nook of her mother's armpit, cheese melting on a hot baked potato and the way Bert guarded her meals without ever snatching from the plate. It was how she felt about Bobby Nusku. It didn't develop, it was there and now, with no past or future at all. It just was.

Val was experiencing it very differently. Feelings she'd suppressed for years were rising up, seeping through her pores, sitting there in puddles like surface oil on a south Californian rock. Bobby had noticed. Val, as she changed her underwear behind the shelving marked Biology, uplit only by the desk lamp, was ravishing. She had a smile on her face. She was a puzzle solved. He decided not to tell her what he'd seen take place between Joe and the man. His overriding urge, for her to be happy, remained paramount. He could keep Joe in check. He could protect her if he needed to.

They drove for days, Joe searching for a hint of a landscape he recognized, anything that hadn't changed in the two decades that had passed since he was last in rural Scotland. Fields collapsed into shores lapped by solemn stretches of water. Soon they stopped seeing people, or even lights on distant houses that they mistook for low stars.

"It's near here, I swear it," Joe said, in bursts of confidence spurred by a bend in the road, or the gulp as they drove across a humpback bridge. Occasionally he'd stop the truck, stand in the road and scan the view through the box of his fingers. Then he'd shake his head and they would keep on going, Joe scouring every turn, braking and checking every lane. "I promise you, it can't be far."

It was the end of a long day, one that began before the first blasts of orange combed the sky. There was damp in the air and everything was as moist as a cucumber heart. They were near the sea and far north, but unsure exactly where. In the stormy center of a tantrum, Rosa had thrown the atlas from a bridge into a fast-running river, so there was no way of knowing.

"Oh no," Val said, tapping the red flashing light in the shape of a petrol can blinking behind the steering wheel. They parked. The white sides of the library were splattered with mud and Rosa's cape was already tatty at the trim.

"What do we do now?" Bobby asked. Val moved four copper coins around in her hand.

They climbed down from the cab. Bert idly watched a rabbit hop inside a hollow log, then licked sea-salty wetness from the bark.

"We don't do anything," Joe said, pointing through the trees to a flat gray dam, creaking with the weight of water pushing. He wiggled his finger to show that he meant for them to look beyond the fog, where they could just about see a large structure atop the steep incline of a hill. "We're here."

"A castle!" Rosa said, loud enough to make Bert scuttle back inside the library.

"Almost," Joe said, snapping his fingers. Bobby had thrown so much paper out of the window that there were no pages left between the covers of the physics textbook on his lap. His trail had lasted just long enough.

They waited by the roadside while Val reversed the library down a thin winding trail into the pines. Joe wove leaves and branches through the grille to disguise it, but there were no tracks there, just unblemished earth where nothing came nor went. Bert dug with his snout and found the bones of a bird. Even he had sense to leave them undisturbed, that there were some places people—or dogs—just didn't belong.

Joe carried Rosa up the steep side of the dam and then they walked across the top hand in hand. On one side was the lake, on the other a drop into nothingness. An uneasy thinness comprised the line between two fates.

At the gateway to the towering country pile, its crumbling brickwork, wild garden and holey roof, they stood and stared. It was just as Joe had described. They shimmied over the outer wall to find a long gravel driveway writhing toward the door. A grandiloquent expanse of oak, it would have been impressive even if it were not set into the foreboding gothic archway, disappearing on either side into the mist. Bobby had never seen a bigger building. Its intricate corners hid magic in shadow. He was relatively sure they'd stumbled across Hogwarts.

In the center of the door was a large brass knocker carved into the shape of a bat. Rosa slammed it down on the wood three times, then hid behind her mother.

Joe pushed the door ajar. "Hello!" he said. An echo scurried away from him.

The entrance hall was long enough to cast the back wall in darkness. Faded portraits of long-dead men had tired of never being looked at. Now the paint was brittle and chipped. Vines grew through the cracks around the windowpanes and leaves blown in rotted on the dirty floor. It was difficult to know where the outside ended and the inside began. Rosa and Bobby yelled at the top of their voices, but the words were returned in ever quieter echoes. Clocks showed time that never passed.

Rosa opened a cupboard and climbed inside.

"We can live here, Val," she said.

They stalked rooms lined with dusty furniture, sticking together in case they got lost. Labyrinthine corridors curled around spiral staircases, and in the furthest corners the building was reclaimed by the grounds. Even the weather crept in, clouds somehow wafting between the rafters, condensing then dripping from the beams. Bobby let the cold drops fall into his mouth.

They passed through an impressive library. Almost all of the books were old, chocolate-box gold and green with covers thick and dusty, shelves too tall for even Joe to reach the top. It smelled different from the mobile library. The pages had broken down, and now gave off the scent of a good-quality vanilla absolute, giving Bert a ravenous desire for ice cream.

There were too many rooms to assign a unique name to each. Bobby passed through the filthy drawing room, with its curved chaise longue and green baize billiard table, to find that the next room was almost identical. Taxidermy gathered in packs, a deer with its own forest of antlers and snow foxes frozen mid-prowl. He ran his fingers across the sharp combs of their teeth. Their tongues were waxy purple, clammy to the touch. Above them an eagle stretched its wings to full span.

Into the next room, a kitchen, with a pantry bigger than any room in any house Val had ever lived in. There were enough tins of food to last a year or more, and a musty smell that made Bobby's lungs kick against his chest. Joe swiped a finger across the dining table then blew a thick layer of dust from the tip.

An hour later and they had still only searched the manor's east wing. Joe smashed apart an antique table and used its broad stanchions to seal the front door closed. With what wood remained he built a fire while Val blocked drafty windows using sandbags from an unfinished conservatory.

Bobby investigated the basement, guiding Rosa through the darker corridors in night mode. Piles of junk sagged with the onset of damp. Mold ate cardboard boxes and spiders scuttled by. They found engines and chains, batteries and belts, a dismantled vintage motorbike, each part stripped, painstakingly spread out on a dust sheet and then abandoned. Everywhere were mechanical items, none loved enough to work.

Another basement room, smaller this time, colder, had been painted pink a long time before. On the widest wall was a stencil of a girl holding two balloons and floating away into the sky, but being held down by a small dog pinching her sock in its teeth. In the middle of a room was a crib, cobwebs layered across it, collapsing under the weight of trapped lint. Then a rocking horse, its hollow chest now home to only insects and a bird's nest long deserted.

Rosa pulled a photo album from an expensive but unloved chest of drawers. Leafing through it, a story of strangers emerged, a man surrounded by exotic animals, but there was no beginning, middle or end to the story, just snapshots of an unknown narrative.

Joe appeared in the doorway.

"You shouldn't be down here," he said.

"Why not?" Bobby asked.

"It's too gloomy. These are someone else's memories—someone else's story. Not yours." He pulled from his pocket a large silver key. "I found this. Let's see if we can find what it unlocks."

The garden was vast and the grass had grown out the markings of what was once a perfect croquet lawn. A fountain over a pond in the middle was dry and caked with bird shit. Joe beat a track through the wild pasture and piggybacked Rosa over the sod—a sight Val found pleasing. She held Bobby's hand and they followed close behind. They reached the wall at the bottom of the grounds, alive with climbing plants and tall enough to mark the perimeter of a high-security prison. Above it, the steel sky of a Scottish evening.

"It must be here somewhere," Joe said, plunging his hand into the ivy to feel the rough scratchy surface of the wall.

"What are we looking for?" Rosa asked. Joe smiled.

"A door."

"Like in *The Secret Garden*?" She and Bobby had read *The Secret Garden* by Frances Hodgson Burnett together as the mobile library had rolled over the Scottish border. Though she hadn't been able to articulate it to Bobby, she imagined herself as the young Mary Lennox, the book's heroine unloved by her selfish wealthy father, who is healed by the gardens she finds one day while playing with her skipping rope. She was, for the first time, outside herself, and this new terrain, her imagination, was a secret garden of her own.

Joe looked to Val for an answer. She nodded.

"Exactly, like in *The Secret Garden*."

Bobby counted that they'd walked four hundred and eighty-three steps along the wall before Val stopped them in their tracks.

"Here," she said, pointing to an area behind the foliage that was not the raw-meat red of brick. She parted the ivy to reveal a green wooden entry. Joe hacked around the entrance with his knife, and the lock creaked as he turned the key. As soon as it had opened, Bert ran, faster than he had in many years, and disappeared into the acreage of a dilapidated private zoo. Val opened her eyes wide.

"I didn't believe you," she said to Joe.

"I can forgive you for that."

Astonished, Val sat down on a decrepit bench. In every direction, gothic wrought-iron cages taller than men, with signs above them, for lions, leopards, chimpanzees; hundreds of animals that existed behind thousands of bars. Now the cages were empty, gingered by rust. Doors swung in the breeze. There was a sense of sudden abandonment and the haunting that emptiness brings.

Rosa made animal sounds for every sign she could, growling at the tiger enclosure and arfing at the seal pen. Bobby kicked a stone along the main walkway and imagined the zoo's former splendor, filling the cages with the animals he had read about in the mobile library. What a grand sight it must have been. Past the reptile house, where rare iguanas had lamp-bathed on heated logs, and an alligator, who had only emerged from the man-made marsh for a taste of warm, living lamb. An aquarium, where he pictured dolphins sharing a tank with tropical coral, now had broken glass and spent crab shells strewn across the floor like bullet casings. Vacant cabinets housed nothing but sawdust, and a cold ditch where the rainwater collected overflowed with floating bilge.

Bobby set off in search of Bert. He checked the barren penguin pool, and an enormous cage that the sign promised was once the playground of a grizzly bear. He found a small clump of hair in there, and put it in his pocket for his files. His mother was bound to be impressed by genuine bear hair. He remembered a faux fur coat she had owned that his father had burned in a bucket in the yard.

Bert sat looking up at the spectacular and curious thing he'd been able to smell since he got out of the mobile library, now made flesh before his very eyes. He didn't necessarily want to eat it. It was more that he wanted to hold it in his mouth. Regardless, it was making him drool, and his tongue hung out like the inflatable ramp on an airplane. He'd never known a smell like it before. Artificially flavored dog food often strived to achieve it, but no scientific mind could re-create a scent like this for a nose as finely tuned as his. He wanted more than anything to be on the same side of the mesh as it. For Bert, a dog old enough to know that very little was worth his effort in the end, this was a desire of profound intensity. It was worth all the effort he could muster.

"There you are, Bert," Bobby said, entering the disused aviary. Only then did he see it, a glorious blue and yellow macaw. It had a curved, charismatic bill, strong legs and sharp-clawed zygodactyl feet. When it spread its wings, Bobby gasped.

"Visitors," the macaw said, a word it had learned from its mother before she'd died of psittacosis, the parrot fever that had eventually wiped out the inhabitants of every cage in sight, except for him.

Joe, Val and Rosa came running when they heard Bobby calling their names. No one could explain where the bird had come from or why it was there, but they were all mesmerized by the vivid punch of its colors. Joe rattled the rusted padlock, its metal far too thick to slice through with his bolt cutters.

"Well, I'll be damned . . ."

"Can we keep her?" Rosa said. She read out the macaw's name from the small brass sign on the wall. "Can we keep Captain?"

"I don't know," Joe said. Bobby noticed that he had paled and put it down to a fear of birds. He'd heard a girl in his class at school claim she had a phobia because a pigeon flew close to her face as a baby.

Val noticed the damaged feathers on Captain's underside, where he had scratched himself with his beak. At the back of the enclosure a hole had been smashed through the wall, so that the macaw could fly away, if it ever wanted to. It was in the cage as a matter of choice.

"I suppose we'll have to," she said. Rosa and Bobby embraced in cheer.

"Visitors! Visitors! Visitors!" Captain said, his head bobbing from side to side.

Joe finished barricading the unused doors of the house. Everywhere Bobby went he could hear the thumping of the hammer. He climbed a ladder into the attic and from there through a hole onto the roof. Still he could make out the faint pounding of metal on wood. He had presumed climbing the scaffold and leaping from the shed onto Sunny's leg would have prepared him for dealing with heights, but he'd been wrong. As the sky turned purple, he feared he'd be struck by lightning, or be close enough to thunder to then get scared to death.

He trod carefully, six steps, along the guttering, a dizzying drop beneath him (two and a half double-decker buses, his conservative estimate), recalling Sunny's tips for bravery. The tiles were wet, kissed by highland dusk, so he tied the rope around his waist to the chimney stack. From here he could see for miles around, north, east and west, across the ground, past the zoo, mountains in one direction and a moody blue sea in the other. There was no light but stars, and no voices besides Captain's in the distance, still talking to Bert, who had refused to leave her side.

Frosty wind spiked Bobby's ears, painful things to have so thoughtlessly tacked to his head in this weather. But it would be worth it. He strung together the swatches of his mother's dresses, bagged the hair and tied the lot together with twine. Then he decorated the roof as diligently as one might a Christmas tree, the strange bunting flapping, noisily slapping the slate. He saw the sweeping majesty of nature before him and knew, this time, he didn't need to pray. The land was prayer enough, miles of beauteous proof that someone must be listening.

Joe found a hoard of air pistols in a stand-alone cabinet and went grouse hunting in the gardens. His training as a sniper in Iraq was a time he mostly remembered for the spectacular states of boredom achievable when waiting for someone to kill. *Perhaps that was what drove the lieutenant crazy*, he thought, though he knew, deep down, that it had been the death, the danger and the loss that thronged them daily, that woke them from the deepest recesses of sleep. He quickly picked off two young birds. It felt good to shoot something, to feel anger and make a bedfellow of its much-needed release. Wasn't that why he'd come here? He picked up the carcasses and headed toward the house.

Dinner—grouse, tinned fruit and rice pudding before an open fireplace—was the best they'd had in weeks. Joe found a gramophone, its scratched brass neck protruding from a jumble of warped vinyl, and wired it to a battery he'd uncovered in the basement. He played records, swing numbers that convinced Bobby joy had been mechanically trapped in the plastic, and they danced. Rosa's frock puffed as Joe swiveled her around his hips, her body falling limp in his arms. Next he took Val, held her and swayed side to side, while Bobby, Rosa and Bert watched from a pudgy old sofa. Everything outside the room could have fallen away, into the molten center of the earth, and it would not have mattered. Not one of them had enjoyed this feeling previously. The perfect choreography of family.

Bobby's stomach gurgled, content. He closed his eyes. *If there is no such thing as a happy ending, then end the story now.*

Joe poured a double Scotch from a grubby bottle, surveying the fingerprints still impressed on the glass. The fumes of sickness filled his mouth, but in the fug of it he couldn't decide whether they were a result of the booze, or the question of whether these were the fingers of the person who had kept the macaw so gloriously alive. Surely not.

Another drink, and then another, just enough to drown the persistent inquisitor living inside the thick walls of his skull.

Bobby retired to his own enormous, secluded bedroom at the far end of the hall.

Rosa went to sleep in a charming room above where they had danced, the floor still warmed by the toasting of the fire. In the corner stood an exquisite handmade doll's house. Through each window scenes of everyday life were played out by wooden figurines, eating, sitting and reading. Joe was sure she would cherish it, much more than its previous owner.

Finally, Val fell asleep on the chesterfield sofa. Joe carried her, legs around his waist and head rested in the crook of his neck like an exhausted child, to the master bedroom. Decked in showy gold trim and with a purple muslin-draped four-poster freestanding in the center, it was a sight befitting the faded opulence of the manor. He laid her down on the dusty sheets, the mattress creaking, brought back to life.

"Where are you going?" Val asked. He grasped the shiny ball of the doorknob.

"To bed," he said. She rolled aside, opening up a space just his size beside her. He twisted the ball right until it was locked.

CHAPTER FOURTEEN

THE ZOOKEEPER

"Visitors! Visitors!" A yellow feather floating, spinning, kissing Bobby's cheek. Above him, Captain's wings at full stretch, beating, pumping air enough to lift the bedsheets. Bobby covered his face with a pillow, fearing the macaw's sharp talons clawing off his nose. More squawking, then quiet, covers settling like snow. He peered out with one bleary eye. Captain came to rest on an outstretched arm inside a shabby black overcoat, an atlas of stains on the front. Bobby sat up quickly and then froze.

"Don't worry," the man said, gruffly, "we're not going to hurt you, are we, Captain?" Captain clicked the black grub of her tongue, head tilting agreeably to the side. The man was tall and old, eyes set back in alcoves on the craggy cliff of his face. An unruly beard, once jet-black, now the silver of a stream's bed

under fresh water, fibrously descended to midway down his chest.
Bobby could tell that he had been muscular in his youth, but now
his sagging breasts rose and fell when he spoke. His teeth were
brown and his skin the tan of toffee pennies. Clearly the man had
preferred to spend his life outdoors where possible. He looked
like a part of it, a root or a trunk. Dirt collected in the deep fur-
rows that quartered his brow. Though he moved gently side to
side, there was a certain stillness to his presence, one that suited a
man so allured by the totality of solitude. Bobby was surprisingly
becalmed.

"My name is Baron," he said, "what is yours?"

"Harry. Harry Potter."

"Good." Baron let go of the air pistol he'd been hiding, allow-
ing it to slip deep down into his pocket. With lopsided arms he
limped around the bed, looking not unlike a pirate with Captain
on his shoulder.

It had been months since Baron had come to the east wing of
the house, much preferring his room in the west wing, far easier
to keep warm and containing everything he needed. Blankets. A
bed. A fireplace where he could toast bread and boil water. In
moments of introspection, their frequency increasing as winter set
inside his knees, Baron considered the possibility of never coming into this part of the house again. As depressing an idea as that
was—he'd lived his entire life there, inside this hollow heirloom—
he'd resigned himself to it. *Fuck it*, he thought, with the devilish
finality only a Scot could lend the words. *Let the ivy claim me too.*

What is death anyway? Not an ending. Death's a comma, a colon at best. Pity the poor scoundrel still alive when the full stop finally cometh.

But he was here now. That morning he had set out to feed Captain at dawn with a cluster of nuts held tight in his hand and discovered the bird to be flustered.

"Visitors! Visitors!" she had said. Baron had ambled out into the light and stood in the center of the zoo, between the cages that once kept the pumas and the jaguars apart, looking up to where the sun's first rays stroked the roof. He couldn't quite see its composite parts from that distance, the dangling bags of hair, cloth and junk that comprised Bobby's files, but he knew that whatever it was, it hadn't been there before. It was enough to convince him he'd need his air pistol, and he'd need it quick. Visitors. Visitors indeed.

"Baron is a funny name," Bobby said.

"Ach, never mind that. Care to tell me what you're doing here?"

"Living here, I think."

"Oh, you do now, do you?"

Amused but unwilling to show it, Baron opened his palm flat and let Captain choose a seed. "And where might you have come from, to be living here?"

Bobby suddenly felt very small. Perhaps it was the grandness of the building they were in, or that the man was a giant of Hagridian proportions.

"I'm a wizard living within the ordinary world of nonmagical people like yourself. I have been invited to attend a special school that will teach me how to refine my magical skills. And also to play quidditch."

"Quid-what?"

"Quidditch. It's a sport. You fly around on broomsticks to catch the golden snitch."

"Golden snitch?"

"I came here to practice because there is so much space. Less chance of hitting a tree."

"Is that so?"

"Yes."

"Sounds like quite an adventure."

"It was."

"Especially for a little boy alone."

Bobby pursed his lips and wished he had a spell up his sleeve.

Unused to company, particularly such young company, Baron gave Bobby a slap on the shoulder, attempting to reassure him that he'd not just dropped anybody else in trouble. After all, they were many miles away from the nearest outpost of civilization. There was no way the boy had gotten there alone, unless he had actually flown in on a broomstick, or whatever it was he had said. Baron had remained unconnected from the world for a long time, but felt pretty sure sport hadn't evolved in such stupendous bounds as the boy described.

Bobby wasn't hugely reassured by the slap, which had hurt, but he recognized Baron's kind intentions in the rambunctious gesture. All he feared now was how Joe might react to the interloper, based on previous form. He had visions of him garroting Baron, stringing him up until his feet left the floor. He knew that it was his job to calm him, like George had Lennie. For Val's sake, if no one else's.

They walked the corridors to the bedroom at the far end of the landing. Baron, wisely, Bobby thought, had agreed to let his young charge undertake the physical act of waking Joe and Val, and gave him the key that opened their bedroom door. They slept in S-shapes. Bobby saw that beneath the sheet they were naked. Joe's body, against hers, was so much hairier and bigger than his own, which was all awkward corners, a jigsaw of hip bones and ribs.

"Joe," he said, squeezing Joe's bicep.

"Huh?" Joe, still half-asleep, licked the dryness of his lips. "What do you want?"

"I want you to not freak out."

"To not freak out about what?" Joe opened his eyes and was quickly alert, a military response to waking that had been implanted deep within his psyche.

"Is it the police?" he asked.

"No," Bobby said. Val groaned, reluctant to relinquish her grip on the deepest sleep she'd had in years.

"Then what?"

"There's a man here, with a beard. It's his parrot . . ."

"Actually," Baron said, standing at the foot of the bed, Captain now balanced on his shoulder, "she's a macaw." Joe leapt up off the mattress and onto his feet, penis dangling from the mossy darkness crowning his groin. "Rest easy," Baron said. "How about we go and have breakfast."

•   •   •

Bobby, Joe, Val and Rosa sat at opposite sides of a wide dining table in the west wing kitchen, apparently the only part of the entire estate still supplied with electricity. Tall stacks of newspapers lined the walls, some soaking up the ceiling's incessant dripping when it rained. In one corner an armchair buried in blankets stank of the smoke belched by an open fire, its shape scorched into the hearth. This was where Baron burned toast in a griddle, using bread he had made fresh that morning. Captain flew about the rafters. Val was amazed she'd not been killed by the smoky fug in the air.

Baron unscrewed the lid from a jam jar.

"Got strawberry. Got raspberry. Made them myself. That, I'm afraid, is your lot." Bobby covered his toast with a combination of the two, disguising as best he could the bitter char. Val spun Baron a tale, about them camping, running out of fuel, leaving the car, being lost, finding the house, thinking it was empty.

"Which," she said, "I guess it mostly is."

"Aye, I suppose you're right."

"Have you been here a long time?"

"All my life."

"With only Captain for company?"

"Since my wife died, aye. And then the animals of course, one by one, by death or by sale. Captain is the last bird standing. Only one I never could bring myself to sell when the money ran dry."

"No children?"

"No."

"Do you have a television?" Joe said. He hadn't realized it, but he'd been jabbing a fork into the fleshy bulb of his thumb so hard that blood was rising to the skin.

"Me? Nah. Never. Waste of time. Don't need one. No signal up here anyhow."

"A radio?"

"No radio, no. Just be dead noise and shipping forecasts in this part of the world, right? I'm no fisherman."

"What about a telephone?"

"No cables up here. No aerials, no antennas, no satellites. No one to call."

"So how do you stay in touch with people?"

"Now," he said, "what point would there be in that?"

Captain swooped down and landed on the table. Bert watched her eat the crusts Rosa had set aside for him.

"Where's the bathroom?" Joe said, clutching his gut.

Baron pointed to the far end of the room, where two doors flashed in the strobe of a flickering lamplight. Joe approached the one on the left.

"The other one, on the right," Baron said, "unless you wanna piss in a store cupboard. If you do, there's a mop and a bucket at the back of it. Be sure to put them to use."

Joe stood at the bathroom sink, twisting the taps to fill the basin with icy-cold water. He removed his shirt, and observed himself in the full-length mirror hung beside a bathtub coated with grime. Shifting his head slowly from side to side he had to concede that, yes, in this light, from that angle, he did look a little like his father. But only a little, around the eyes, and the slight boomerang shape of the mouth. Clearly it was not enough for him to have noticed. How hard must the calluses around Baron's heart be, Joe wondered, to not only deny his existence, but then fail to recognize his son as he stood before him now.

Dunking his head beneath the water line, and holding it there until the cold spiked him with brain freeze, he wondered how old Baron must be. Ninety or more, perhaps, and enduring, alone, in the cold like a boulder on an unreachable stretch of the coast. At least, with no television, he wouldn't have heard about Val, Bobby and Rosa, or the missing mobile library, and so, for the moment, they were safe. That was Joe's number one priority, their welfare, and as he couldn't bear to be parted from them now, their continuing evasion of capture.

If Baron hadn't been privy to the news, and thus heard about Joe's escape from prison, there would have been no reason for him to expect a visit from his son. It had been twenty-two years since he left, after all. But on returning, it seemed to Joe like only yesterday that he had watched the maze burn down to the ground, knowing that he'd still feel the heat of the flames on his face well into the future. And he could, crawling up his cheeks. He splashed his face again.

Most amazing of all was the realization he was experiencing only now, that he had not wanted to find the house empty after all, or hoped for his father to be dead. He'd wanted him to be alive, withered and old but alive, so that he could kill him, with those giant damn hands they seemed to share.

Bert watched Captain bobbing on the sideboard, entranced by her curious tics.

"Dog!" Captain said. "Dog!" Rosa had only ever heard about two animals talking to each other, in Rudyard Kipling's *The Jungle Book*, and it had been nowhere near as funny as it was now that it was coming true.

"Amazing the things she keeps in that little old bird brain of hers," Baron said. Val finished her toast.

"If you can help us get ourselves some fuel, we can get out of your way," she said, "with our apologies of course, for breaking in here in the first place."

"Nonsense!" He rubbed his chest, which was sorer by the day. He was already convinced he'd soon be seeing his last Hogmanay. "You stay here as long as you need to, you hear? No point you all camping out there in the cold when I've got all these walls going unused. I'm sure Bert agrees with me, don't you Bert?"

"But Mr. Baron . . ." Val said.

"Just Baron."

"Baron, we wouldn't want to be any trouble."

"Please, missy. Nothing troubles me anymore."

Joe emerged from the bathroom, beads of cold water icing his forehead. He felt more relaxed, but not so much that he couldn't feel his temples throbbing like full-term pupae.

"Joe," Val said, "Baron kindly says we can stay a while." Joe lingered, half eaten by the shadows thrown from candlelight beneath the taxidermy.

"You don't need to . . ."

"Hush," Baron said, "I insist. Now, I know you've already been for a walk around the grounds, but how about an official tour from the northernmost ex-zookeeper in the land?"

•　　•　　•

Captain rode Baron's shoulder, her movements attuned to his as if she were another limb. He led them to the western edge of the property. Ashen clouds grumbled, dismal light sapping glimpses of purple from the thistles. Before them was an enormous hedgerow maze, once awe-inspiring, now overgrown and impenetrable. Had they gotten close enough they would have seen that the branches beneath the newer leaves were still blackened by fire and smoke.

Doglegging the maze was a lake, sidling round the zoo and running off into the distance, crumpling like tinfoil beneath the sky's moody gray. When the wind dropped they could hear ducks quacking, and if they listened extra hard, Baron's shallow breath.

Rosa stood beside him, examining the trowels of his palms. She took his right index finger in her grip. Baron flinched, but let it stay.

"There," he said, pointing to a bird of prey overhead that had unsettled Captain with its glare. "A falcon. Nests up on the cliff face out that way, by the sea. A decade or so ago, when I wasn't such an old man, I'd have climbed down there and taken its eggs. Tasty, with enough salt and pepper."

They walked down across the gardens, long since manicured pathways now formlessly unkempt, and turned through a side entrance Baron used to access the zoo. Bobby looked at Baron's face—beard, brow and burst capillaries—how it had weathered as wonderfully as the landscape around them.

"My name isn't really Harry Potter," he said. "He's a boy from a story. I'm just a boy."

"Right," Baron said, confused.

Val and Joe walked some distance behind the others, watching Rosa hold Baron's hardened fingertip.

"Stroke of luck, huh?" Val said.

"What?"

"Baron, being here. I mean, the guy's clearly as mad as his parrot, but seems we're safe with him at least."

Joe grunted, which Val mistook for his agreement.

"Largest private zoo in Europe," Baron said, rattling a stick between the bars of the orangutan cage. "Primates and big cats mostly. But sea life also, and insects. Oh, and birds of course." He tickled the bright plumage on the back of Captain's head.

"People could come in and see them though, surely?" Val asked.

"Oh no. Private meant private. For my eyes only."

"But why?" Bobby asked, his arms down by his sides.

"Some people collect stamps. Some people collect art. I collect animals. *Collected*, should I say." Baron paused beneath a dirty metal sign, swiping the middle of it clean with his sleeve.

"A western lowland gorilla," he said. "Beat his chest so loud it sounded like the footfall of a monster. And here, three macaques, lightning-fast little things, screaming for breakfast, screaming for dinner . . ."

"And in here?" Bobby said, leaning over the fence around a cutaway of pool with a tiled plinth in the center.

"Sea lions. An amazing creature the sea lion. Throw them a

ball, couple of fresh fish, happy all the damn day. They need no more than that. Much preferable to children, wouldn't you say, Valerie?" Val smiled politely, but said nothing more as they walked to the far end of the zoo and back.

"He wouldn't tell me why he's called Baron," Bobby said to Joe as they repaired to the east wing for the afternoon. Val and Rosa helped the old man, wheezing, up the hill.

"It's not a real name, like mine or yours," Joe said. "It's a title. A hereditary peerage. Like King. Or Duke. His father was a baron, and his before him and his before him. They passed it down from one to the other, right through centuries of male lineage, until, I guess, they got to this one, and he decided to keep it all for himself."

"Decided?"

"Yes, decided." Joe coughed.

"You don't have to become your father, do you?" Bobby asked, nearing the doors.

"No," Joe said. "No you don't."

CHAPTER FIFTEEN

THE FAMILY

The feast was Val's idea, a show of gratitude for Baron's hospitality. He protested. "Ach, please."

She insisted.

"Then if you really must. I'll bring what whisky I have, and Captain shall supply her own seeds." His laughter filled the drawing room.

Despite his best efforts, subtle though they were, Baron couldn't get any time to himself for the rest of the day. The children followed him around constantly, the boy with incessant talk of his mother and a ridiculous story about a cyborg he claimed to have built but not yet seen, the girl with a fascination the young reserve for that which they perceive to be ancient. Patience was a virtue Baron lacked. He had been on his own so long that this part of him was out of practice, and like an unused muscle it was weak. It took a concerted effort to smile and nod, pretending that company was something he enjoyed as a change, but really he was just biding his time until he could return to peace and quiet.

Bobby tended his files to make sure nothing had blown off the roof overnight. Bar a slight tear to the bag—a snag on a tile—they had come through largely intact.

In the early afternoon Joe and Bobby siphoned fuel from a spare tank Baron kept behind the stables for a dormant generator. They pushed it across the dam in a wheelbarrow, down to the mobile library, splashes of it staining Joe's boots.

Before sundown, Joe went grouse hunting again. The rustle of the reeds by the lakeside proved seductive, cathartic even. He sat down to smoke a cigarette. The hiss of the burning tobacco reminded him of the time he'd watched the maze burn to cinders. Same air. Same light. Same time of year.

Val and Bobby sat on the steps that meandered down the slope to a brook, ending in the cymbal rush of a waterfall. He laid his head down on her lap, the heat from her thighs on his neck.

"You and Joe could adopt me," Bobby said. "Then we'd be able to tell everyone who we were and we wouldn't need to hide anymore."

"I'm not sure they'd let me adopt you, Bobby. I'm technically a kidnapper, not to mention a large-vehicle thief."

"But you're my family." Val brought his wrist to her mouth and kissed it. A twist in her womb, a small blade cutting quickly, the pain of knowing that it was where he should have come to exist. Her child. This boy. A story started in the wrong place.

"Will they catch us?"

"No, they won't catch us. They only catch bad people." She didn't know if she was lying anymore. Rosa appeared and folded herself around them both. Family. A puzzle of people.

Comparatively speaking it was a feast indeed. Particularly for Baron, who had subsisted on a diet of homemade soups and overly salted preserves for more than twenty years. Any decent food he'd had delivered had been fed to the animals, too many of them, until the money had dwindled to near nothing. He had sold most of them, the rest perished, and that money had lasted this far. He only hoped Captain would die first. The thought of the bird grieving in the rafters brought on an unquenchable despair. He'd not experienced a relatable sadness for anything that didn't have paws or wings since the death of his wife.

Fresh vegetables from the grounds—potatoes, carrot, an errant leek—mixed with the grouse, and some aged stock Val discovered in the pantry, made for a nicely hearty stew. Baron baked more of his homemade bread, and they used that to wipe their plates clean. Bert reclined beneath the bench, eating the scraps Rosa dropped between her legs. Captain opted for her usual spot, occasionally scratching her side against the hard skin of Baron's ear.

"So you never see other people?" Bobby asked.

"Sometimes," Baron said, more taken with finishing his second helping than with chatting to the boy.

"When?"

"Twice a year. Once in the spring and then after the floods, before the snow, I might drive down to the village. About twenty miles if the roads are clear. Pick up provisions from the shop there, but the woman behind the counter knows I'm not one for talking."

"What happened to your wife?"

"Bobby," Val said, "that's a very personal question."

"It's fine," Baron said, "understandable. She died. That's all. People die. Nothing really ends. You just get on with it." He stared at his plate. Bobby had seen this look before, frozen on the face of his father. The diminishing ability to discern life, after there had been death in such close proximity.

As it became obvious to Baron that she would die, and the only fight that remained was to keep their unborn child alive, he had so badly wanted it to be a daughter. His wife's beautiful face, that he loved so deeply, would be replicated then, would grow and live on in this new form of her. But instead came a son, and her face was gone forever. That, to him, was an idea worth mourning, far more so than her body in the ground. After she died, not a single other human being had been worthy of his gaze. The only way he could replicate the wonder that swelled his soul whenever he saw her face was to spend his riches on rare and exotic creatures, examples of a beauty, like hers, that only nature could make.

To him, the boy, who grew quickly, lumbering without any of his mother's grace, had been little but a footnote on a masterpiece, a hindrance, certainly unworthy of the family title which law and tradition dictate he hand down. Where possible, he left the boy alone, and did not once let him enter the zoo to see the animals, where Baron spent most of his time. He waited for an excuse to rid himself of the boy, who was increasingly angry and volatile. It came with the striking of a match, when he was just eight years old.

"When she died, that's when I started collecting animals. First one was a snow leopard. Can you believe that? The northern tip of Scotland, a damn snow leopard! A marvelous creature it is too. Endangered, not many left. Pale green eyes, rosette-shaped spots on their body. Can look as serene and as approachable as you like, but there's that coldness, that violence in their eyes. The way they look, the way they seem, it's all a trick to pull you close enough and bite you up. Now that's something to stand back and admire."

Rosa growled. Baron smiled, poured himself a second triple whisky then tipped the bottle toward Joe.

"Drink?"

"No thank you."

"Oh come on. Can't come all this way to the highlands on a camping trip and not drink a little fire when it's offered."

Joe put his hand across the mouth of the glass. "I'm fine." Baron noticed a dimple creased in Joe's chin, same as his own.

"Tell me more about the animals," Bobby said.

Baron stared wistfully at the ceiling beams. "After the snow leopard I got more big cats. Lions, tigresses, a puma or two. Then monkeys. Then birds. Millions of pounds' worth. You have to pay for their upkeep of course. Didn't take long for the money to burn out. I was never good with money. This old place fell to pieces. Started selling my animals one by one, and it felt like giving a little part of me away every single time. Nothing left at all now. No money to speak of. Just me and Captain here. Can't sell the place, wouldn't want to. Been in the family forever. So I'll die. To hell with it afterward, the story goes on."

Bobby thought of Willy Wonka, handing his magnificent chocolate factory down to Charlie Bucket, the only boy who'd been good enough. He had read it to Rosa in the mobile library, her coiled up by his side, their breathing a blissful inverse synchronicity.

"A shame you never had a child you could give it to," Val said. Baron ran his fingers through his beard, nails snagging on the knots, crumbs falling free and bouncing on the tabletop.

"Aye," Baron said, "I suppose it is." Joe sprang to his feet, the veins around the cartilage in his neck moving, what felt like popping candy underneath the skin.

"I need to piss."

"Door on the right," Baron said, draining his Scotch so quickly that the ice cubes kept their corners. He poured another, deeper this time, and swilled it, a greasy amber rib cage climbing down the glass. With each sip he grew visibly more sullen, black sinkholes opening up, threatening to swallow both his eyes. It resonated through the room, a saddening that Bobby felt first in his toes, then rising, up his legs, in his core, down his arms and filling his head.

Joe returned, his face doused in cold water, goose pimples struck across his brow.

"I think I'll have that whisky now," he said.

"Good show!" Baron said, helping himself to another. Rosa and Val opened tins of rice pudding, which they warmed in a pot above the flame. They added brown sugar for flavor. Captain flew back and forth through the steam. They ate quickly, before the air could cool it. Val noticed the spoon shaking in Joe's hand, tapping against the rim of his empty metal bowl.

"You okay?" she asked.

"He's fine!" Baron said, his accent broadening as the volume built. Joe placed the spoon on the table, aimed in Baron's direction.

"Must be entire wings of this place you haven't been in for years," he said.

"Aye. Doubt I remember where all the rooms are these days."

"I saw the roof has caved in on some of it. And there's tree roots growing through the ground in the basement. There's a little nursery or something down there."

"That's right, never used. It's a grand old building, that's for sure. But, these things decay. What's history without ruins?"

Joe's knuckles whitened through the flesh on his hand, like teeth bared by a vicious dog. "You could fix it up. It's not too late."

"A pointless endeavor. I'll be dead soon. Can hardly take the old place with me, now can I?"

"But you've so much here. Seems a shame not to share it."

"I told you, I shared it, with my wife."

"But to not have children . . ."

Baron dropped his own spoon in the bowl with a clang that slowly bled out into silence. "Would you say it was greedy?" he said.

"Well, I . . ."

"Greed is a funny word, isn't it? One man's greed is another man's right. It's what the world's fueled by, greed, what makes it go round. More money, more land, more worth than your neighbor. Isn't that how the planet has always turned." Baron hovered two inches above his seat. "So what is greed?"

Joe flinched. He'd been frightened of his father as a boy. It came back to him now, though he tried to hide it, a sawing inside his chest. His size, his age, his strength meant nothing. He was a child again, contorting to fit into his father's shadow. "I don't know."

Val had never seen Joe this way.

"Please, gentlemen," she said, confused by the turn of their exchange. "Perhaps you've both had enough whisky for now, huh?" Baron ignored Val, and a little of what had scared Joe crept beneath her skin.

"I'll tell you," he said. "Greed is an intense and selfish desire for something that isn't yours." He was standing over Joe, leaning down to bring their faces close together, and Bobby saw the likeness. "But this house is mine. All of this, the land, the zoo, the food we now eat, is mine. So it can't be greed, can it, if I own it? Greed can only be felt by someone who wants what isn't theirs. Like this house, for instance." He coughed into his fist. "So tell me, Joseph, where is the greed now?"

Joe unshielded his eyes and peered into his father's, creased with rage. "You recognize me?" Val and Bobby froze. Baron ignored them.

"The moment I saw you."

"You didn't say anything."

"Of course not. Thought I'd give you the opportunity to apologize first."

"Apologize?"

"For your temper. Or don't you remember?"

If he had ever intensely and selfishly desired anything, it had been his father's affection. Locked outside the zoo alone, hearing the calls of animals whose majesty he could only imagine, lighting that match had seemed as good a way to get it as any. He had set light to the outer wall of the maze. The wind had run with it, burning down one hundred and fifty meters of hedgerow before there was no further to spread.

"I have nothing to apologize for," he said. Val wrapped her fingers around Joe's arm, but he began to unpick them.

"Then you're wanting me to apologize for sending you away? Is that it?"

"No . . ."

"For packing off an angry, unmanageable, unpredictable, dangerous little boy into the care of people who could help him, and care for him and keep him safe?"

"You didn't want me. You didn't want me to have this place. You didn't even want me to have your name."

"I was an old man even then, Joseph. What was I meant to do? That's what you want an apology for, is it?"

Joe stood, expanding to his full size. "I don't want an apology."

"Then it is as I thought. Greed, pure greed and nothing else. You've come to lay claim to the house and the grounds, haven't you? You've come because you want what you selfishly and

intensely desire to be yours. My name. Baron." He banged his fist
down on the tabletop, scattering the crumbs that had grouped
there as if waiting for a sermon.

"Please," Val said, her voice wavering, "you'll frighten the children."

"Ach, sit down, woman," Baron said. Bobby, the hairs on his
neck spiking like a layer of frost, saw spit twinkling in the wire of
Baron's moustache.

"Don't talk to her like that," he said.

"Come now," Baron said, flopping back into his chair and
slugging Scotch from the bottle, "Harry, Bobby, whatever your
name is. I don't think a child will be telling me what to do."

Joe scanned the table, the spoon, the bowl, the knife. He imagined ramming it into the old man's abdomen, his intestines spill-
ing forth. Red jellyfish wobbling on the floor, Bert ravenously
gobbling up the meat. His fists began to tremble, and the muscles
in his legs pulled taut as he prepared to launch himself across the
room, directly at the old man's throat.

Then out of the corner of his eye he saw Bobby, his head
shaking slowly from side to side, a blink that lingered closed, then
opened to reveal those deep brown eyes, that calmed Joe like no
one and nothing had managed to before.

"Well, let me tell you," Baron said, one hand beneath his cape,
drunkenly fumbling for the air pistol in his pocket, "you'll never
have what's mine. It belongs to a family you were never part of."
Joe saw how grief had wizened the old man. He almost felt sorry
for him, but only for a second. "You were never my son, Joseph.
Your connection to this family died with your mother."

Bobby bolted back from the table with a piercing yelp, his shirt soaked through with sweat, and sprinted from the room.

One two three four five six seven. One two three four five six seven. One two three four five six seven. The crash and crumple of the metal, the smashing of his head through the windscreen, the landing of his body on the car stopped right in front of them, he heard them perfectly.

Bobby sat up. He ran his palms down his arms, over his legs and through his hair. No cuts. Not even a scratch. He waited, concussed, for the taste of iron on his lips, blood filling his mouth, but it never came. The scene was tranquil. There is no greater serenity than that which exists in hell.

Fragments of glass scattered across the motorway, crumpled metal folded over burnt rubber. A hubcap rocking on the road. Bobby was elated by the petrol fumes. The car, where he had been just seconds before, had jackknifed. Sharp steel stabbed through the smoke.

Bruce Nusku climbed out of the twisted driver's side door, nose busted open by an airbag. Unsure as to exactly where he was, he coughed, once, twice, three times, then ambled to the concrete wall at the side of the motorway and sat down in the dent where they'd struck it. A bloody trail zigzagged at his feet.

Bobby felt a great rush of sympathy for his father, crimson soaking through his clothes. He wanted to hold him. He wanted to apologize for what they'd not yet done, so he did, right there on the road.

"I'm sorry, Dad."

"You're sorry?" Bruce said, blood burning at the root of his tongue. "For what?"

"We were going to run away at the beach. We were going to ask you to buy us an ice cream, and then we were going to run away so that you never saw us again." Bruce rubbed his head and spat a tooth across the white line.

"That's okay," he said, "that's okay."

Bobby walked around the car to the passenger door.

"Mum," he said through the metal, "I told him. Even though I promised more than all of the other promises added together forever, I told him." He pulled the handle. She slumped to the side, held in the chair by her belt. His mother was dead, and the baby inside her. But she looked alive still, and at peace, how he had never seen her before. He kissed her on the lips, soft, a cherry freshly plucked.

Night had fallen, stars blotted by clouds, and the grounds were lost in darkness. But Bobby could see. He ran shoeless through the long grass, hurdling nettles and stones. Fifteen seconds to the fountain in the center of the gardens, the waterfall heckling from a distance. Twelve hops up the twenty-four steps to the east wing's grandiose doorway. Seven strides along the hallway wall, stopping halfway to edge around the grandfather clock that tolled no longer. Through the drawing room, past the downward slope to the old servants' quarters, to the staircase that spiraled up through the floors. Six minutes, forty-three seconds to the loft, and out of the hole caved in the roof, to his files suspended from the thick hunk of the chimney stack by a length of sodden rope.

On the ground, Val, Rosa and Joe were frantically searching. They explored the zoo, Bert sniffing for Bobby's scent but thrown by the lingering odor of lion that permeated the bars. Rosa checked the reptile pen. Val scoured the insect house. Joe entered each and every cage, pulling rotting hay bales from the alcoves where the bears and apes once slept. There was no sign of the boy.

Joe started toward the entrance of the maze, until Rosa began cheering.

"Bobby Nusku! Bobby Nusku!" She pointed at the figure on the roof, neatly framed by the moon.

Bobby looked down at the ground, eyes round as an owl's. He could see everything as clearly as if it were day. He stood with his hands on his hips, legs apart, eighty feet or more in the air.

"Don't," Val said. "Wait for me." He saw her lips move and wanted to kiss them. To know how different from his mother's they might taste. She ran into the house, and Joe positioned himself to catch Bobby, just in case.

Val arrived on the rooftop out of breath.

"Bobby," she said, "come down from the edge."

"She's dead," he said. He raised his fist. In it was the rope tied around the bag, which he swung around his head like a propeller, the swoosh of it cutting up the air. He let go of the rope, and his files, hair, cloth and all, sailed off over the grounds, landing with a crash somewhere deep in the maze. The moon made glowworm trails of the tracks falling down his cheeks.

You must remember there is no such thing as an ending. Good things come out of bad things and bad things come out of good things, but it always continues.

Val stood behind him and he fell back into her. Her boy.

Below, Joe sighed, and let relief envelop him. Rosa held his hand.

"I love you," she said.

How differently he'd turned out from Baron. What had been poured into the mold of the boy had not emerged in the cast of the man. For the first time in as long as he could remember, Joe felt the snick of pride in his throat. Baron had been right. They were not family.

He would not kill him. There are fates far worse than that, and to be left here, alone, deprived of this love that he had now, was just one.

A glint caught his eye, somewhere up there, by the roof. He could not see Bobby's dark form any longer, but something had moved, just slightly, in the wind. He scanned for it again, and with the patience of a sniper eventually found it by the gutter.

"Up there," he said to Rosa, "do you see that?" Rosa followed the line of his arm to the tip of his finger.

"Yes," she said, squinting, "I see it."

"What is it? Is it that stupid bird?"

"I know what it is."

"So tell me."

"A wire." As quickly as that it came clear into view. A copper cable feeding into the building, and off in the other direction toward the flat plain of the horizon on the opposite side of the house, where Baron had not taken them on his tour. There, a moonlit metal spike in the distance, was a pylon, and another, carrying the voice of his father, through the cable, south toward where civilization had waited two decades for word from Baron, the northernmost ex-zookeeper in Britain. He had a telephone.

CHAPTER SIXTEEN

THE BIRD

By the time Joe and Rosa made it back to Baron's living quarters he had gone.

"We have to get out of here," he said, "and we have to do it right now." Rosa, in her silence, understood. She began gathering their things. When Val and Bobby joined them the four embraced, their heads pressed together. Joe knelt, straining to bring himself down to Bobby's height, his neck dipped to get there.

"Are you all right?" he asked. Bobby nodded, letting Joe ruffle his hair.

"Are you?" Joe rose, bigger now, as if more of him had come from deep within the ground.

"We need to get out of here. Gather everything that's ours. Anything that isn't, leave behind. We do not want it."

"He's your father?" Val said.

"I should have told you before." Val rested her head against Joe's chest and heard the boom box of his heart. "I've something else I need to tell you," he said.

Bert growled. He scampered to the door on the left at the rear of the room, and began scratching at the thin strip of light leaking from the bottom. The store cupboard, and from inside, a voice.

"Visitors!"

Though it was locked, Joe pulled it cleanly, screws and all, from the frame. Inside was a room twice as large as the one Baron had told them he called home.

"Visitors!" Captain scraped her claws along a wooden beam in the roof, shavings of it sprinkling through the gloom. Barely any of the floor was visible under stacks of old newspapers, pages yellowing and damp, bordering a thin path through the center. Bundles of cash were scattered about, notes and coins randomly dumped. At the far end was a huge television, tuned to a news channel, and a radio, gurgling, caked in thick dust.

"Come in!" Baron said, sitting back in a large leather armchair in the center of the room, the telephone balanced on his right thigh. "Hope the boy's calmed down a little. Does nobody any good to get themselves as flustered as that."

Val expected to see a picture of herself on the television screen, in the recording that Baron was scanning back and forth with a remote control. It had preyed on her mind how she was being portrayed, out there, in real life, rather than in this story she'd created. A child abductor. A pervert. A monster. And what picture had they used? Ten years before, when she'd had her passport photograph taken, the flash in the booth had misfired. Her face had been half lit, creating an oversize shadow on the wall behind her head. The resultant image was burdened with doom. Rosa's father had left her not long before, and she had wondered whether the camera had in fact captured her accurately, as a woman followed by darkness.

What she saw was not herself, but something she had never expected to see. Joe. Or, as the caption had it, *Joseph Sebastian Wiles*, loomed large on the monitor, speeded, slowed, reversed and paused. His hair was buzz-cut short, his stubble shorn clean. He too had been photographed against a wall, but his had height markers down one side. Six foot four. He felt even bigger than that, stood beside her now, saying over and over, "I meant to tell you before."

Val put her arms around Rosa and Bobby, brought them close to her, put herself between them and the man who, in the mug shot on screen, was dressed in full fatigues.

Intercut with the picture of his face (no sign of the smile she cherished, or the happy kiss-shaped eyes) was footage Bobby recognized, taken from a police helicopter of a barn in the countryside. Its spotlight circled the roof. After that came a farmer perturbed by the press attention, rubbing his forehead and fearing what was hiding on his grounds. And then Detective Jimmy Samas, who looked far too young for the job.

"Wiles, who escaped from military prison . . ."

Val gasped.

"You didn't know? Oh my, you *didn't* know!" Baron said, spinning in his chair. "That's quite the story you're holding back from your girlfriend there, Joseph. Though of course she comes with a story of her own. Quite the pairing. Quite a reward."

*"A troubled youth, in and out of foster homes and young offenders'
institutions . . ."*

"I think she deserves to be told about your little temper. Seems
you never were able to shake it. Such a shame, but I told them,
didn't I? When they came to collect you I told them, what breeze
is in the boy blows a gale in the man."

Joe pinched his temples between thumb and forefinger.

"What did you do?" Val said, clutching the children tighter.
Bobby puffed out his chest and emerged from behind Val, ready
to defend her, ready to strike.

"Pulped a man's brain," Baron said.

"It's not true." Joe found himself sitting on the stuffed shiny
body of a jaguar.

"Oh, I think you'll find it's very true. Not just any brain either.
His own lieutenant's, no less."

"You killed somebody?" Val said.

"No," Joe said.

Baron laughed. "Dishonorable discharge. Flown straight home
to military prison. Of course, when the news said you'd escaped I
knew you'd come for me. I'm just surprised it took you so long.
Such an angry, angry child, now an angry, angry man." Joe sighed.

"He's wrong. I didn't kill somebody. I saved somebody."

Lieutenant Brass, perversely, had been the closest thing to a father
figure Joe had ever known. Not that he'd provided affection, quite
the opposite—he was a stern, unpleasant man—but to his credit
he was stern and unpleasant consistently. If Joe's life in the foster

system had lacked anything up until he joined the army, it had been consistency. That was the reason he had signed up. It would be a place where he'd find discipline, with people who might be able to help him control his temper. And it had worked. Consistency was what the lieutenant provided in spades. On that final tour of Iraq, ten months of death and skull-clogging sand, the lieutenant had grown wilder. Until one day, on a Baghdad rooftop baked by a tyrannical summer sun, he had finally gone haywire, his brain as good as stewed by war's barbarous chug.

"He was trying to make me shoot a boy, screaming it into my ear, to pull the trigger. To execute him. A boy." Recalling it now, Joe could feel the press of the gun's stock on his shoulder, see the crosshairs splitting his vision, and past them, the wispy black fluff that bedecked the boy's top lip. "He was unarmed. So I refused. I wouldn't shoot. The lieutenant was angry that I had ignored him in front of all the other men. He attacked me."

Baron jetted a brown slug of sputum at the floor. "Lies. You're an animal who should be locked in a cage. You always were. No son of mine."

"Don't listen to him," Joe said to Val. "I'm telling you the truth."

The lieutenant beat Joe until the flesh around his eyes closed over. The other soldiers stood around in shock, powerless to help. He wrestled the rifle from Joe's grip and took aim at the boy himself.

The shot rang out, but Joe had shoved the barrel aside just in time. Furious, the lieutenant aimed the gun at Joe.

"I hit him. Just once. But that was enough," Joe said. The lieutenant dropped the gun and flopped limp across Joe's chest like a puppet whose strings had been snipped. Joe saw nothing in the shallow pools of his eyes.

The boy was spared. But the lieutenant was not. Joe felt like he had as he watched the maze burn, looking out upon a world that had changed in those few seconds, one that would never change back. He knew then that whatever specter followed him would do so for the whole of his life.

"You killed him?" Val asked.

"No," Joe said, his eyes wet and overflowing, "he's alive."

"Barely," Baron said. "The poor bastard is a cabbage. A vegetable in a chair eating slop through a straw."

"I saved the boy," Joe said, "I saved the boy." He began to weep. Val went to him, cradled his head and stroked her fingers down his neck with a lightness of touch he'd never experienced.

"I didn't mean to hurt anyone."

"I know," she said, "I know."

"Ach, woman, don't tell me you'll forgive him this. You're a bad man, Joseph, a violent man," Baron said. The pistol's metal chilled his thigh. "You're a wanted man. I knew that I was right to get rid of you. Never lost a moment's sleep over it." This was a lie. Guilt had corrupted Baron's slumber on many occasions, and it came again over him now, watching his son cry in Val's arms. He was jealous, and this irritated him far more than any child could.

"And you, woman, only a person like you could forgive a man like him."

"Shut up," Joe said.

"Kidnapping a wee boy away from his father . . ."

"I said shut up!" Joe could feel the tears giving way to anger again. Though it was cold in the room, sweat covered his face.

"Letting him carry a big jar with her hair in it. Not even telling the poor little bastard that his mother was dead."

"Shut up!" Joe rose to his feet. What joy it would be, to tear the tonsils from his father's throat. What a pleasure it would be, to feel Baron's blood on the soft skin between his fingers, to hear his breath ebb away.

"Kill me," Baron said.

"I will."

"You should, Joseph, you should. That's what you came all this way to do." Joe imagined the sound his fists would make as they smashed the bones beneath his father's flesh. He took him by the neck.

"Stop," Bobby said. Joe halted, grip tightening, and turned.

"Huh?" he said.

"Baron isn't your father, because you are nothing like him."

Joe looked at the boy, with Val beside him. He looked at Rosa, and Bert. The way they were stood, in that certain order, like a family portrait hung above a fireplace in an ornate frame. With space behind for him. It brought him to his knees.

"Let's go," Val said.

Baron was nauseous. Another whisky, but one he could barely swallow. He rose from his chair, took the air pistol from his pocket, and shuffled toward where the four of them were locked in embrace.

Rosa's tantrum had approached quietly. The argument had made her anxious, and she'd pinched circular bruises on the soft skin

around her hips. She had, for the first time in her life, consciously
tried to contain it, and largely succeeded, until what turned out
to be exactly the right moment. Seeing Baron approach Joe from
behind, the pistol aimed and cocked, she launched herself at his
midriff, sending him crashing into a mound of newspapers and
out-of-circulation coins.

Winded, clutching his ribs, Baron couldn't quite find the air
he needed to say Captain's name as he watched the bird swoop
down from the rafters, land on Joe's shoulder, and be carried out
of the room.

The police finally came forty minutes later, having passed no
vehicles, save for a white truck on the roads. Baron's mansion was
not an easy place to find. It took them a further thirty minutes
of searching the many rooms to locate him, where he'd been left,
looking at the ceiling.

"You're sure about this?" Detective Jimmy Samas said when
he arrived. Looking around, at the sad sight of the old man, he
couldn't quite believe this was the most concrete lead they had.
Baron refused to pretend he enjoyed being questioned by a whip-
persnapper.

"Of course I'm sure."

"And he was with others?"

"Yes. The woman and kids from the mobile library. Been plastered all over the news for weeks. You'd do well to pay attention
in your line of work." Detective Samas was used to condescension
from his elders. It had started to bore him. Being bored, patron-

ized, or both he could handle. What he didn't appreciate was being lied to.

"How could that be?"

"You tell me. You're the detective." Samas should have been at home, with his pregnant girlfriend, watching television, their legs beneath a goose-feather quilt.

"And you didn't see the mobile library?"

"No."

"So they're not even in it anymore?"

"Drove it into the dam for all I know. Wouldn't put it past that crazy bastard, to finish them all off, just because he couldn't beat me. Anger issues, you see. Trawl it, find out for yourselves."

Detective Samas closed his notepad and looked around the room. He couldn't wait to leave, and was thankful that he only had one final question.

"Mr. . . ."

"Baron, just Baron."

"Of course. Baron. Are you any relation to Joseph Sebastian Wiles?"

Baron mopped his rear molars with his tongue and found a crumb of moist, stale bread.

"No," he said, swallowing it.

CHAPTER SEVENTEEN

THE ROBOT, PART TWO

Joe drove south nonstop for twenty-four hours. The police would not be looking for a lone trucker, and if they were then they would need to separate him from the thousands of others clogging Britain's arteries. It gave him ample time to think about Baron, for whom, and for the first time in his life, he suddenly felt nothing. It wasn't as if the old man had died. It was as if he had never existed. He occupied the blank void. The more Joe peered into it, the less he saw. Love, hatred and everything therein could not endure.

His only communication with Val, Rosa and Bobby came through the CB radio linked to a receiver in the back of the library, where they hid and read.

Bert gazed up at Captain, who'd made a nest of books in the

shelves above Zoology. If Val hadn't known better, she'd have sworn the dog's appetite had waned.

"That's ridiculous," Joe said, his voice crackling through the radio, "dogs don't fall in love."

"That might be so, but it's true," she said, putting down her half-finished sandwich. The agonizing inevitability of their capture loomed. They would be parted just as soon as they had come into each other's lives. She wished that their story would end at this exact moment, with them together, in the mobile library, as one.

After finishing a book, Bobby would post it through the thin gap atop the window in the toilet, leaving it behind them on the road, a trail of tales leading back over the border into England. Val let him grieve for his mother, though it pained her to see him enter a process without end. Grief is a fixed point from which one can only move further away. It never disappears, there is not space in the world to get far away enough. But minute by minute, mile by mile, they were leaving it behind, until it was a speck on the horizon. Whenever they hit potholes, the mobile library's metal walls shook and books leapt from shelves like fledgling birds learning to fly.

It was Rosa who was first able to coax Bobby out of his solitude. She sat by his side with a ream of paper under her arm and a case full of crayons in her hand.

"Would you like to play?" she asked.

"No," he said. He reread the top paragraph of the page open on his lap. *Chitty-Chitty-Bang-Bang: The Magical Car* by Ian Fleming. Stuck in a traffic jam, Caractacus Potts's creation sprouts enormous mechanical wings and flies away from trouble. Bobby wished the mobile library could do the same. No one would catch them in the middle of the sky.

"Bobby Nusku, would you like to play?" she said. He turned to find that she'd written their names again, *Bobby Nusku Rosa Reed Val Reed Joe Joe Bert*, but her handwriting had markedly improved. Letters that hung below the line curled with neat flourish. They had been realized in an even track of sumptuous black ink. At certain points the words clung together, or piggybacked each other, as if for survival.

"What would you like to play?"

She didn't know. Rosa hadn't planned for what might happen next, she never did, and that was one of the many things he'd come to love about her. She reminded him that the adventure wasn't over just yet.

"I know where we can go," Bobby said. Val, who had been listening to Joe absentmindedly singing through the radio, switched off the transistor and turned to face him. His shape had changed since they first met, but she only noticed it now, a broadening, with sharp new angles in his outline.

"What did you say?"

"I know where we can go, where we'll be safe." Through the cracks she saw glorious first hints of the man that the boy would soon become.

"You do?"

"Yes," Bobby said, grinning. He thrust his hand into his back pocket and gave Val a torn piece of paper. They were so short of options that this seemed as good as any.

They arrived near the south coast of England at mid-afternoon, where clumsy gulls fought for scraps on rooftops. A new super-store had opened up on the edge of the town, forcing the closure of the independent shops on the high street, so the residents were unsurprised by the sight of enormous trucks making deliveries on their otherwise quiet streets. Joe parked the mobile library behind a row of disused garages off the main road.

The receiver beeped.

"We're here," he said wearily, falling asleep on the warm leatherette.

The mobile library's metal steps unfurled and out came Bobby, sun hurting his eyes.

"Wait for me here," he said to Val, "I won't be long." He walked the length of a pathway overgrown with weeds to the street and quickly found himself out in public, alone, for the first time in months. He crossed the road to a sorry-looking house bookending a drab terraced row. Missing slates made the roof a gap-toothed mouth, the wonky chimney a chewed cigar. He approached the door, then knocked in three short, nervous bursts.

When Sunny Clay answered, there was no movement in his face. It reminded Bobby of the features carved into a totem pole. But he could tell how happy Sunny was by the way his voice rose an octave, and how tightly they embraced.

"Holy shit!" he said, closing the door behind him so that his mother couldn't hear, then hushing his voice to a whisper. "Holy shit, Bobby Nusku. What are you doing here?"

"You told me to find you." Sunny peered one way down the street and then the other.

"Yeah, but back then you weren't the most famous kid in the world."

"I am?"

"One of them."

"I'm so happy to see you, Sunny."

"Me too."

"How much?" Bobby said.

"Let's not get into this now." Sunny pulled Bobby inside by his elbow. They scuttled upstairs to Sunny's bedroom, box-shaped with cold exposed brickwork. Posters hung lopsided on the wall. Broken action figures fought among themselves.

Bobby pulled a package from the back of his jeans and gave it to Sunny. He tore open the paper. Inside was a copy of *The Iron Man* by Ted Hughes.

"It's a present."

"For what?"

"For becoming a cyborg. I know it wasn't easy, but you did it. You did it."

For Sunny, it had been a lonely summer followed by a sullen autumn. He was friendless in a new town, and it had proved hard to ingratiate himself to his schoolmates without the ability to smile. He felt like a grub unable to burst from its cocoon. Worst of all, the results of his transformation had been inadequate at best. He had a constant dull headache, his arm was weak, his leg was sore. In recent months he had been forced to face facts. He wasn't a cyborg. He was a boy full of metal.

The most telling indicator of his failure came in the way he had missed Bobby. It had hurt every day, a pain that bore through him like a drill. Cyborgs didn't miss people. They were never programmed to yearn. But here was Bobby now, expecting a cyborg, and Sunny wasn't just his best friend, he was his bodyguard. He had promised, and was only as good as his word.

"Of course I did it," he said.

"How does it feel?"

"Good."

"Stronger?"

"Uh-huh."

"Do you even have to eat food anymore?"

"Sometimes. But only for emergency refueling." Bobby flexed his fingers until the joints cracked. He couldn't tell that Sunny was lying. There was no sign of it on his face.

"Good," he said, "I have a job for you." Sunny sat on the floor beside the bed, twisted the key in a wind-up robot figurine and watched it walk across the carpet to the door.

"You do? What?"

"I have some new friends and we need protecting."

"From who?"

"The police."

"They said you'd been kidnapped."

"I wasn't kidnapped. I went on an adventure."

"There are a lot of people looking for you."

Bobby sat down next to Sunny and put an arm around his

shoulder. Bobby was now the bigger of the two and suddenly had a sense of how much he'd grown. It felt strange, like being able to see back in time.

"I know." The hum of Sunny's mother's vacuum cleaner vibrated through the floorboards.

"So what happened?"

Bobby closed his eyes and started to tell Sunny what had happened in a way in which they'd both understand it. Stories did happen to people like him after all.

CHAPTER EIGHTEEN

A CHILDREN'S STORY, PART ONE

There was a Boy who was trying to cast a magic spell to bring his mother back to life. That's why, in his pockets, he had thirty locks of her hair, twelve splashes of her perfume and twenty-five cuttings of cloth that he took from her dresses.

His biggest problem wasn't doing the magic. The Boy lived in a small house on an island that he could only reach by crossing a rickety wooden bridge. Beneath the bridge lived the Ogre and his girlfriend. They didn't like the Boy, and were mean to him every day. The Ogre was so mean that he had killed the Boy's mother. If the Ogre found out about the magic the Boy was planning, he would be extremely angry. He had already killed the Boy's mother once. He didn't want to have to kill her again.

To protect himself from the Ogre, the Boy began building

himself a robot. It would be the strongest robot in the world. He started by making the legs, because without legs, a robot can't stand or walk. When the legs were finished he made the arms, because without arms a robot can't pick things up or carry them. The final part of the robot he needed to build was the head, because without a head a robot can't do anything at all.

Building a robot head is tricky. It involves lots of wires, switches and buttons. Because building a robot head is so tricky, the Boy got it a little bit wrong. When he put all of the parts together, the robot's eyes didn't flash like he'd wanted them to. It was while he was figuring out how to fix this particular problem that something else terrible happened.

His robot was stolen.

Now there would be no one to protect him from the Ogre. When you're sad and alone, a house you can only reach by crossing an ogre's bridge isn't a very nice place to live.

The Boy wandered the streets until there was nowhere else to go. He sat down beside an enormous green bush and ate some of the delicious berries that grew on its branches.

That's when he heard a noise he'd never heard before, the clip-clop of a horse's hooves. The horse stopped at the bush so that he too could eat some of the delicious berries. The Boy saw that it was being ridden by a Princess. She didn't wear a crown or have long tumbling hair so strong you could climb it. This Princess was different.

When the Princess was snarled at by a nasty three-headed dog, the Boy looked into her eyes and saw that she was scared too. She wasn't so different after all.

He took the Princess back to her castle, where he met her mother, the Queen. The Queen was the most beautiful woman the Boy had ever seen. She was caring and kind and most of all, she loved the Princess more than any one being has ever loved another.

The Queen was the owner of two animals. The first was a lazy pooch who ate nothing but chocolate. The second was a huge friendly dragon, which she let the Boy ride.

Pretty soon the Boy, the Queen and the Princess were sitting on the dragon's back every day, enjoying the sunshine and telling each other stories.

They escaped to a small forest atop a hill and decided to rest there, where they wouldn't be found. The Boy was beside himself with happiness. Now he'd get to spend all of his time with the Queen, the Princess, the pooch and the dragon without ever having to worry about the Ogre or three-headed dogs.

One day, they met a Caveman. The Caveman was kind to the Boy. The Queen decided to repay the Caveman's kindness by letting him sleep curled up beside the warmth of the dragon's belly.

When the Hunter came looking for the Caveman he panicked. They put on disguises and made off with the dragon into the night.

It was a long, long journey toward the mountains, but they got there without once being spotted, to a zoo that the Caveman remembered from his childhood. He hadn't been raised a caveman. He had become one. People become cavemen when they have a father like the Zookeeper.

The Zookeeper was a wicked old man. He had all of the

exotic animals in the world locked up inside his zoo, but he never let anyone in to see them. Instead, he kept the zoo for himself. He lived inside a huge palace beside the zoo, which had a million bedrooms, but he did not allow anyone inside that either. The worst thing about the Zookeeper was that he pretended not to recognize his own son, the Caveman, even when he stood right there in front of him.

The Caveman wanted to tie the Zookeeper up, but he didn't, because he realized something very important that the Boy had tried to teach him all along.

Family is where it's found.

Family doesn't have to be a father, a mother, a son or a daughter. Family is only where there is love enough. For them it was there, in that unlikeliest group of people . . . the Boy, the Queen, the Princess and the Caveman.

They left together on the back of the Dragon while the Zookeeper watched all of his animals escape—even his beloved bird. He was the loneliest man in the world.

They went as quickly as they could. They had a robot to find.

CHAPTER NINETEEN

THE ROBOT, PART THREE

Sunny ran his fingers down the side of the mobile library. It appeared far bigger than it had on the television news, and was a dirty white, not the green he remembered.

Weeks earlier, Detective Jimmy Samas had visited Sunny at his new home. Mrs. Pound had identified Sunny as Bobby's only school friend. His mother made the young-looking detective take three pieces of shortbread she had baked that morning. One was enough but he had been too polite to decline. By the time he'd finished the third he felt sleepy. While she explained why they had moved south—to be closer to her ailing parents—he had closed his eyes for a second too long and almost fallen asleep. When he opened them again she had finished talking.

"Huh?" he said.

"Oh, I was just saying, the move might be good for Sunny here, too. Been in the wars, haven't you, honey?" The detective looked at the boy. Nobody had warned him about Sunny's condition, and so he was faced with a child he just assumed to be extremely serious. Little unsettles like a serious child. To lighten the mood he made two jokes, neither of them particularly funny. Sunny would still have smiled if he could, if only to put the detective, to whom he'd taken an instant liking, at ease.

"Have you heard from Bobby Nusku?" the detective said.

"No, sir."

"Has he ever spoken to you about a lady named Valerie Reed?"

"No, sir."

"Or any boys at school that he might have had a problem with?"

"No, sir."

Flustered by the case, and by an argument earlier with his pregnant girlfriend about the amount of time he was spending away from home, the detective slapped his clipboard against his knee. It had been a gift from the man whose job he had taken over. Detective Samas didn't like using it. He thought it made him look like a politician, and thus, on some subconscious level, annoying and untrustworthy. In his line of work, having people assume such character traits exist isn't beneficial for getting results. He used it anyway, so as not to offend a man who wasn't even there.

"Do you have any idea why Bobby Nusku might have run away from home?" Sunny thought for a while, long enough that Detective Samas assumed another answer in the negative.

"Have you been to his house?" Sunny asked. Detective Samas looked up from his list of questions at the boy, who had chosen to sit on the rug by his feet.

"I'm sorry?"

"Have you been to Bobby Nusku's house?"

"Yes," the detective said, remembering the coldness of his room, the scorch over the hob and the hole in the plasterwork. Remembering his father, spiced booze vapor on his breath, a broken television. The size of his hands. The angry stump of a missing finger. Talking to him, he'd identified a tone in his father's voice that he hadn't been expecting to hear. Only later had he been able to identify it. Relief. Relief that the boy was gone.

"Then you already know the answer."

"I do?"

"Yes."

"And what is it?"

"He hasn't run away from home. You can't run away from what you don't have." The detective declined another piece of shortbread. He thanked Sunny's mother and locked his briefcase, deciding never to use the clipboard again.

"One last question," he said.

"Yes?"

"Could Bobby be headed here?"

Sunny shook his head, comfortably aware that no lies would show through the dead mask of his face.

"No," he said, "he doesn't even have my new address."

Bobby insisted Sunny press the button at the rear of the mobile library. He was suitably impressed as the mechanical steps wound out to greet him. Val appeared in the doorway. She also looked different from the way she had on the television. Soft, wholesome, good. She had her arms around him before he could speak.

"I've heard a lot about you," she said.

"Likewise," Sunny said. She had been all over the news. An attractive, white female criminal (a kidnapper to boot) overshadowed even the story of the escaped military convict, whom Sunny was baffled to see climb out of the cab, yawning. "This is Joe," Bobby said. Sunny thought of the story that Bobby had told him and shook the man's hand. He thought of the reward offered, and how it could never be enough.

Next he embraced Rosa, and a new sensation came over him. He hadn't expected it, or ever really known it before. At first he couldn't quite define what it was. She asked what his first name was and then wrote it down in her notebook. Watching her shape the letters, looking back at his face as if painting a portrait, he slowly pieced it together. Rosa hadn't noticed his palsy. She hadn't traced the fallen half moon of his mouth, or the heavy sack of his bottom lip. She had embraced the other, the inside, with a purity so tangible Sunny swore he could feel it pressed against his chest. It was lovely and warm, a bath at the end of a hard day. A tear seen by no one tumbled from his eye and down his cheek. He did not feel it.

Finally he was introduced to Bert and Captain. The patch of skin on Captain's underside was healing nicely.

"Visitors!" she said, dancing to a pop beat tapped out on the wood with the stiff bullet of her beak.

Sunny's neighbor, Mr. Munro, watched from the upstairs bathroom window of his home that backed on to the lot of garages. This was where he spent most of his time these days.

A pink evening sky struck out the day's crisp blue. Sunny waited until his mother had left for his grandparents' house before emptying the cupboards and fridge of food. He tipped the lot into an old sleeping bag, which he dragged across the road and down the path to where the mobile library hid behind the garages. If they rationed it sparingly, Val calculated that it would be enough food to last them for a week.

Sunny and Bobby crossed the petrol-stained gravel to the garages on the far side. Nobody came here anymore, even the local errant youth could think of ten better places to go. Whoever had owned the garages, in a time when the area had promise, now only used them to store junk, had abandoned them or, Sunny guessed, died. The entire plot, about the size of half a football pitch, and with rows of lock-ups on either side stopping it being fully seen from the street, was dirty and overgrown with weeds. Brickwork crumbled and when it rained you could smell rust.

Sunny used a crowbar he'd hidden in the bushes to jimmy open a garage with a dented door, where behind the rusting shells of an old washing machine and a mattress's skeleton of springs he had constructed a secret den. It was comprised of a broken stool, torn world map pinned to the wall and a wind-up radio that only received a Gujarati-language station he'd established was devoted to cookery.

"Welcome to headquarters," he said. Bobby noticed the sole chair facing the map, as if it were the view from the porch of an old folks' home. This scene was made all the sadder for knowing that it was where his best friend spent so much time alone.

"It's excellent."

"It's a little messy but it will do. I was wondering if news of you would ever surface. I was going to plot on the map where you'd gone with colored pins and strings." Bobby sat down on an upturned bucket, split down the side, buckling under his weight. They reminisced about school. Sunny did his impression of Mr. Oats (even funnier now that his face retained a hint of misanthropy). Despite the months apart there was no space between them, no lost tooth, no hole tender to the tongue that had returned to explore it.

"In the story you told me," Sunny said, "did the Boy ever find the Robot?"

"Yes," Bobby said, "he did."

Sunny rubbed his forehead. He had been hoping for a different answer. "I'm not a robot, Bobby. I'm not a cyborg. I'm not anything. I'm just a boy with some metal in his arms and legs whose face doesn't work. I'm not a part of the story. That kind of thing doesn't happen to people like me."

"You're wrong," Bobby said, "I know you're wrong."

For the next three hours they went to work tidying up the garage. Bobby scrubbed the walls clean of cobwebs clagged with dust. They cleared the floor of scrap. A tumble dryer, a fridge, the washing machine, white goods once deemed essential by someone, but now forgotten. Sunny repaired the rip in the map with parcel tape. Bobby tightened the stool's wonky leg. Joe came to help, salvaging wood from old furniture and using it to build a set of shelves. Val filled it with books from the mobile library and soon Sunny had quite the collection of his own. Rosa told him which he might like best.

Bobby went into night mode. He jacked up the doors of the other abandoned garages and sifted through what detritus had been left there. Before long Sunny had a scuffed leather office chair, an oak desk with a scratched marble finish and a Persian rug only one-fifth eaten by moths. It smelled musty, but that would clear if he hung it up to air. In the corner was an empty liquor cabinet in the shape of a globe. Next to it, positioned to appear as though it was inspecting the Indian subcontinent, was a life-size dressmaker's mannequin. He even had a sofa, threadbare in places but comfortable enough, perfect for sleeping.

By the time they had finished, and Sunny had stolen the padlock from his mother's garden shed to secure it, the garage was transformed. Baron's drawing room, eighty feet wider, with opulent pillars holding a ceiling aloft among the gods, could never have housed half its soul.

Joe rolled a perfect cigarette from the tobacco pouch Sunny had stolen from his mother's handbag and they stood back to admire their handiwork. As a final seal of approval, Bert walked four complete circles and lay down on the rug. Captain perched on his back, kneading his flesh with her talons.

Night fell, silencing the birds in the trees. Val made cocoa so hot it scalded their tongues, and the cookies they ate tasted of burnt sugar. The mobile library glinted orange under a solitary flickering streetlight. So dim was its glow that none of them, sitting on the steps blowing steam from their mugs, noticed Mr. Munro peer over the wall that separated the garages from the street. Arthritis riddled his hips, and it took him far longer than he would have liked to get home. Reaching his front door with glacial pace he searched his pockets for the key and realized that he had locked himself out. His only hope of getting to the telephone and calling the police would be to climb over the rickety back fence. With the reward money, he'd be able to afford a new one.

After such a lonely few months, Sunny reveled in the company of his new, and old, friends. Seeing Bobby's affection for Joe, Val and Rosa, and the way they repaid it so wholly, he knew these weren't the people on the news. They were the Caveman, the Queen and the Princess.

They sat outside the mobile library. Joe, still exhausted from the drive, held Val tightly, kissed her and announced that if he didn't sleep soon he'd fall over.

"Good night, love," she said.

"Good night, love," he said.

The thought of Joe being put back in prison stuck in Val's mind as she listened to him snore. Willfully distracting herself from this sadness, she watched the two boys play-fighting on the gravel, and Rosa acting as referee.

"Don't hurt each other," she said.

"We won't," Sunny said, "we're good boys."

"Oh, sure you are." She winked at Rosa. "Like Tom Sawyer and Huckleberry Finn."

Bobby stopped. He scampered into the mobile library, reemerging with a smile on his face and a book in his hand. Its hardback cover was well worn, the spine cracked and feeble. Perhaps a thousand pairs of eyes had read it.

"Here," he said, pressing it into Val's hands. It was an old copy of *Tom Sawyer* by Mark Twain.

"You want me to read it to you again?" she asked.

Bobby was speechless. How could she not see the answer in the pages, right there on her lap? They must have read it together three times or more. He leafed through the pages for her, eventually finding the right one. The warm gold of aged paper bounced off her skin.

"Look," he said. Val did. Tom and Huck had run off to play pirates on an island in the Mississippi. Bobby imagined the vast channel of water rushing by, play-fighting in the foam smashed against the rocks on the shore.

"Huh?" she said, "you want us to become pirates? In a mobile library on the seven seas?"

Rosa laughed.

"No," Bobby said. "Why are they free to go and do whatever they want?"

"Why?" Val said.

"Because the townsfolk think they have drowned in the river."

She pictured the mobile library by the ocean, on a clifftop. Its doors were open, swinging gently in the breeze. On the beach, four pairs of shoes were half buried by sand. The police would wait for the water to give up its secret, but the tide would break its promise. They would wonder how Joseph Sebastian Wiles had met Valerie, Rosa and Bobby. They would wonder what had caused them to walk into the sea with their pockets full of rocks. Somewhere else entirely, they would be together, with a dog and a macaw that knew them all to be alive and well.

Val saw that it was a preposterous plan. They might as well jump in the Mississippi for real. But isn't that life? Its currents drag you this way and that. Sometimes you're washed up, sometimes smashed against the rocks, no matter how hard you kick. What the past few months had taught her was that it wasn't the swimming, but who you clung to on the way that was important. That was what was with you in the end. She had to cling.

Tomorrow, once he had rested, she would tell Joe and they would make a plan. But for now she was content to have Rosa and Bobby by her side, where both of them should always be.

An electric blue flash briefly changed the sky's black complexion. Bobby assumed it was distant lightning and listened out for the clap of thunder. It didn't come. Whatever it had been, it riled Bert, who began running around the clearing between the garages, barking at the clouds. Perturbed by this sudden rodeo, Captain dismounted from the dog and flew into the back of the mobile library, dazzling Sunny with her plumage. They waited, but the night returned to deadened form.

"What was that?" Bobby asked. Sunny shrugged. They walked together to the back wall, from where they had a decent view of the road that, within ten miles, spread out into many smaller lanes, which, like the tributaries of a river, eventually led to the ocean. But for the occasional window lit by the glow of late-night television, there was no sign of life. Bobby scanned the darkest alleyways, just to be sure. Everything was as it should be, in a suburban street when the moon is up.

Sunny led Bobby along a thin pathway at the side of the garages that had been overrun by nettles. Four side steps with his back to the pebble-dashed wall. Eighteen long strides around the brambles. A five-second scurry to the gate. There, crouched behind a fence post, they had a view of the street's far end, where the cars turned off the road into the garage lot. Joe had been hard at work earlier building a crude blockade out of bricks and logs, and the fruits of his labor impressed them. Though it was not especially sturdy, no ordinary vehicle would have been able to pass through it. Again, the view was clear.

"Wait," Bobby said, "up there." He pointed at the house next door to Sunny's, to the first-floor bathroom's window.

"That's Mr. Munro's house," Sunny said. "He's just a lonely old guy, sits up there watching the comings and goings all day."

"But it's gone midnight."

"So?"

"He's still there." To Sunny's surprise he found that Bobby was right. There, in the blackness, he could just make out the familiar shape of Mr. Munro's bald head, occasionally catching the glint of the stars.

"How did you see that?" Sunny said, but Bobby was busy following Mr. Munro's sight line down the road. Though he had to climb through another crowd of nettles to do it, a raised red rash rolling down his arm, he was eventually able to see exactly what Mr. Munro was watching. A police car, parked in wait. A second arrived. Then a third. Soon, there were seven lined up at the end of the street. By then, Bobby and Sunny were running toward Val and Rosa, who had been preparing for bed and were justly alarmed by the speed of their approach.

"They're here," Bobby said. Val leapt up.

"We have to go," she said.

"Should we wake Joe?"

"No," she said, sealing the back of the mobile library from the outside, then hurrying Rosa and Bert into the cab, "there isn't time."

The engine roared into action, seeming to have understood the urgency with which she had twisted the key in the ignition. She turned to find Bobby standing with Sunny beside the truck.

"Come with us," Bobby said.

"No," Sunny said, "I can't."

"Why not?"

"Because I'm the Robot now."

They embraced, wetness sticking their cheeks together. Sunny felt them on his face this time, he was sure of it. Bobby's tears, where nothing had been felt in so long. The mobile library began to move, its great mechanical wings taking shape.

•   •   •

On hearing the mobile library's engine, several officers rushed toward Joe's blockade, hoying the bricks and wood into the trees on either side. With many hands it was done quickly, and the route was clear enough for the squad cars to pass through. They came at speed and in convoy. Entering the court between the garages, they found what they had been searching for. The mobile library, now painted white, its full-beam headlamps filling the space with blinding light.

Val revved the engine and the vibrations traveled up through the windscreens of the police cars, rattling steering wheels and stinging the hands that held them. Its rear tires kicked up great plumes of dust. Gravel rained down onto the metal bonnets of the squad cars with deafening force. They were trapped, or so it seemed, until the mobile library shunted forward, into the wall in front of it. The brickwork began to crack, then topple as the truck pushed onward. The mobile library edged over its ruins, crushing bricks that exploded in clouds of red powder, before continuing down the incline and onto the road unimpeded. Behind it, destruction, and an entire police response unit outdone.

There, where the dust had just started to settle—a thick blanket of dirt and grit the sterile gray of bone—on the ground, was the body of a boy.

CHAPTER TWENTY

THE CHASE

A young officer leapt out of the nearest squad car and rushed to the boy's side. She hadn't seen a dead body before, but had been warned that when she did it could appear almost serene, more as if it were sleeping. Serenity described him perfectly. Though no older than twelve or thirteen (it was difficult to judge beneath all that dust), the boy looked as though he was clasped in the grip of a pleasant dream.

"Is it Bobby Nusku?" said the radio clipped to her breast pocket.

"I think so, sir, it's difficult to tell," said the rookie.

"Well, is he dead?"

"Yes, I think he is."

She slid her arms beneath the boy's body. Cradling his head in one hand, and with her other under his knees, she started to lift.

"No," Sunny said, opening his eyes, moist wells in the desert of his dry, dirty face. "You'll need to drive over me." The rookie screamed and dropped the boy.

She ran back to the car, still screaming, and slammed the door behind her.

Another, more experienced, officer found that he couldn't lift Sunny either. When he tried the boy stiffened his arms and swung them around in the air, catching him flush on his left eye socket, where a bruise immediately blushed.

"I'm a robot! Drive over me," he yelled, "drive over me!" The officer tried again. The metal plate in Sunny's arm caught him sharply on the bridge of his nose. Blood stained the collar of his crisp white shirt. "I am a robot! I am a robot!" Swallowed by the commotion was another order through the radio receivers, this time in crackled unison.

"Just move him!" And they did, after almost five minutes of trying, two torn police jacket lapels and a badly cut constable's chin. It took one officer holding each limb, and another at the head, to carry Sunny to the garage doors, where he was arrested. By the time his protest was over, the mobile library had a lengthy head start on the cars that sped off in pursuit.

Bobby Nusku was right, Sunny thought, barely capable of containing his glee. Stories did happen to people like him.

"We must get to the coast," Val said, "all we have to do is get to the coast."

"To the seaside?" Rosa asked.

"Exactly, to the side of the sea."

The mobile library seemed easier to drive than it had before. It was an extension of her, its wheels her feet, its windows her eyes. The books in the back were things she had done, places she had been to, people she had met. The same could be said for all of them. The library had imbued them with its gift. Words. Microscopic traces of human experience that would be forever carried in their blood. Every decision would be made with the hindsight of a thousand characters whose lives were contained within its walls. Every problem they would face had been solved in countless next chapters already. Love, loss, life, death, these mighty winds that test us, had been weathered on the pages so that they would not be faced alone again.

"We had an adventure, didn't we?" Bobby said. Despite the speed with which they hit the corners of the lanes, and how the truck's enormous body smashed overhanging branches from the trees, Val was able to look over at the boy beside her in the cab. Bobby Nusku, who had changed her life.

"It isn't over yet," she said.

The white paint had now been all but flayed completely from the mobile library's livery to reveal its flecked green underlayer, and so, from a distance, speeding through the patchwork countryside, it did indeed look like a mirage moving on the breeze.

Rosa wound down the window and let the fast air whip her hair into a nest of snakes. Bobby held her by the waist so that she could lean out further still, combing the leaves with her fingertips when the mobile library pulled close enough to touch the trees.

Val floored the accelerator, vying to beat the sunrise to the horizon. Disappearing would be easier by night. Disappearing is what night is for. The mobile library vibrated more violently than ever. Parts of its underside shook themselves free, clanking as they hit the road and spun off into the past, as if it were alive and shedding, preparing for the end.

As the roads narrowed, the mobile library was forced to slow. The sea came into view before them just as the first police siren appeared in the rearview mirror. Above, a helicopter was chopping up the sky. They were too late.

"We didn't make it," Val said. Bobby kissed the soft skin where her neck became her collarbone, then picked the bubble of a tear from her cheek and let it search his hand like a tiny spider.

"We did," he said.

The police convoy gained on the mobile library, but the roads were too slim for them to overtake it. Val slowed the pace and led them through the sleepy clifftop village, a funereal procession toward the sea at dawn.

Detective Jimmy Samas, thanks to some uncharacteristically assertive radio instruction, was able to muscle his car through to the front of the pack behind the mobile library. As the mobile library's front tires came to a stop on the very edge of the clifftop—the slightest tickle of the accelerator could have sent it plunging over—he called a halt to the slow, surreal pursuit. Now just a few hundred feet of grass separated the police, with him at the front, from the people for whom he'd searched for months. Any closer and he worried that the woman might be spooked by their presence. With a three-hundred-foot drop just below them he didn't want to provoke any rash decisions. Clearly she'd be sensitive, sleep-deprived, a real test for the negotiation training he had recently passed with flying colors. He needed to talk to her, to look her in the eye. The helicopter now buzzing overhead reported a woman and two children in the cab, but no sign of a man. The detective instructed it to stand down. The noise from its propeller was disconcerting. Who knew how it might frighten the children. After it had flown on, and the sirens on the police cars muted, the morning, now beginning, sounded just like any other, when it was anything but.

"Keep your weapons trained on the back of the truck," he said into his radio, "do not aim them at the cab. The danger here is Joseph Sebastian Wiles."

CHAPTER TWENTY-ONE

THE END

Lips, sticky, not how his mother kissed. He only considered the difference in their ages whenever he tasted her makeup.

"Are we in trouble?" Bobby asked.

"No," Val said, "not anymore."

Val watched in the wing mirror as Rosa and Bobby walked past the young-looking detective toward the ice cream van. Behind them was Bert, his bottom swinging to and fro. She swallowed, the salty sea air forming a film in the back of her throat. Bobby had told her that his mother had planned to escape by the sea. She felt honored by the prospect of fulfilling this promise for the son they had come to share.

The detective approached, hands stuffed deep inside his pockets. He nervously ran through various ways of introducing himself as he neared the door, which seemed odd. He knew the woman better than he knew anyone, despite their never having met.

"Hello," he said through the open door, "my name is Jimmy Samas."

"Hello, Jimmy," she said, "I'm Val."

"Oh," Detective Samas said, smiling, "I already knew that."

She remained behind the steering wheel, but turned her legs and faced him as he stood on the ground looking up. Early sunrays hit his eyes through the windscreen, and he shielded them with a trembling hand. He noted two things, the first more important than the second. She was calm, and she was far more beautiful in the flesh.

"An awful lot of people have been looking for you, Ms. Reed," he said.

"Please, call me Val."

"You're quite elusive for a lady in a giant truck."

"But that's all over now, isn't it?"

"Yes, I guess it is." He noticed that she was whispering, and presumed this was so that Joseph Sebastian Wiles in the back of the truck would not be able to hear.

"I'd like to do this calmly and at your pace, Val, if I may. Rosa and Bobby are safe with my colleagues now, so I guess that's a very good start."

Val looked up the hill, past the police line to the ice cream van, where the two of them were holding hands and deciding which lolly to eat.

"Okay."

"Good." The detective motioned toward the back of the mobile library. "Val," he said quietly, "is there anybody in there?"

"Uh-huh," Val said.

"Would you care to tell me who that person is?"

"That person is somebody I believe you may know to be Joseph Sebastian Wiles."

The detective muttered something Val couldn't hear into his radio transmitter. Back at the police line, with their target confirmed, the gathered officers trained their arms even more keenly on the back of the mobile library. Below, the waves broke with a crash that briefly distracted them both.

"I'd like to come down from here," Val said.

"Then you may." He held his hands out toward her, shaking and actually shaped as if clutching an olive branch.

"But first I should explain," she said, "I need you to understand that we only intended to go for a day, not more."

"I understand."

"Bobby Nusku came to me. He was covered in bruises. Have you been to his home, Detective?"

Jimmy Samas thought of the size of Bobby's father's hands, the ugly missing digit.

"Yes," he said, "I have."

"Then you will have met his father. I wanted to take Bobby away, to somewhere safe, away from him. The mobile library was the only vehicle I had access to."

"That stands to reason. But may I ask . . . why would you not come directly to the police?" Val flicked a strand of hair from her eyes.

"Because I had made a complaint to the police just a month

or so before. About an attack on my daughter?" The detective guiltily remembered it now, he had seen it written in her records. "And nothing happened. I considered Bobby's life to be in danger. I wanted to do something that would draw your attention to just how serious a matter it was."

While she spoke the detective reevaluated the risks. The clifftop had induced vertigo in him, a spinning sickness he'd not experienced before, which made the grass around his feet seem farther away every time he glanced down at it. He wanted this to be over, but he wasn't willing to let Val know as much. "We drove to some woods. We were going to camp there, just for a night."

"And . . ."

"That's where we found a man hiding. That man was Joseph Sebastian Wiles."

"What was Wiles doing there?"

"Hiding. From you. He said that he had been put in prison for beating up another soldier."

"That's correct. He is a very violent, dangerous man."

"He said that he escaped."

"He did."

"I hope that he didn't harm anybody doing it. You hear terrible stories in the news all the time, of riots and prison guards being taken as hostages."

The detective scratched behind his ear with a pen and considered an uncomfortable truth. "Actually, his escape was quite the opposite of that. Joseph Sebastian Wiles got out of military prison because of a clerical error. A case of mistaken identity. He was served with somebody else's documents by accident and they opened the doors for him to walk straight out of there. So he did. By the time anybody realized their mistake, he'd disappeared, as quickly and simply as that." Val fought to suppress a smile, imagining this giant walking free, tipping a nod to the warden.

"He took us," she said, "he made us act as though we were his family, so that he might hide from you more easily."

"Did he hurt you?"

"He scared us."

"But did he hurt you?"

"He took us to Scotland, to his father's. He made us parade like man and wife, as if to prove a point. The old man abandoned him, you see."

His father? This was news to the detective, a fact he was far too ashamed to admit. He made a mental note to have Baron arrested for lying to a police officer.

"And you did?"

"Yes. But I had no choice. I'm not a kidnapper, Detective. I am frightened. I am frightened that he will harm me. I am frightened that he will harm the children."

"You don't need to be frightened anymore."

"And I am frightened of what you'll do to me, Detective. You think I'm bad, don't you?"

"Ms. Reed, it is not for me to judge you."

"I'm not bad, Detective. I'm not bad at all. I'm a mother. All I want is for you to assure me that Bobby Nusku will not have to go back to his father."

"I understand, and of course, if what you claim is true, then it won't happen. We'll need to speak to Bobby about that."

"Good. I want him, in time, to be able to stay with me."

"This is a conversation for the future."

"It's why I locked Wiles in the back of the mobile library for you."

"I appreciate that. With the help you've given us bringing him to justice, I'm sure what you've done can be looked upon favorably." The detective could feel the negotiation coming to a natural end. He handed Val a tissue from his pocket.

"Thank you," she said, wiping tears from her eyes. The words were pleasant on her tongue, lingering like the taste of fine wine.

"I must ask you . . ."

"Yes?"

"Is the mobile library locked?"

"Oh yes."

"So he can't get out."

"Not without the keys."

"And where are the keys?"

"Right here, in my handbag."

"Then if you'd step down from the cab, we can take it from here."

"Of course, Detective . . ."

"Jimmy," he said.

"Just let me gather my things."

The detective turned away to light up a celebratory smoke. Negotiations by their very nature were complex, each exponentially different from the last. This one, the conclusion to a hunt that had been reported all over Europe and North America, had ended about as well as it could have.

This was his second and biggest mistake in the entire investigation. The negotiation was not finished, the investigation not complete. It wasn't up to him to decide when the story ends, something he'd been taught on his very first day in the job—far longer ago than the smoothness of his skin suggested.

Val stroked the cab's leatherette, closed her eyes and rested her head against the dashboard. This was her unseen goodbye to the mobile library. She picked up her handbag from the footwell. Adjusting the buckles to maximum length, she tied a loop in the strap and hooked it over the handbrake, which she pressed the small red button to unlock.

"I'm coming, Jimmy," she said. "The mobile library is all yours."

The detective turned in time to see Val jump from the cab, and behind her the strap of her bag snapping taut, releasing the handbrake. She shrieked, let go of the bag and scrambled toward the detective, who pulled her to a safe distance and watched in disbelief as gravity conspired with the incline of the clifftop and the slippery gloss left by morning dew on the grass. The mobile library was moving, sliding, rolling, the weight of a whale, toward the drop.

Once the front wheels went over the edge its momentum was set. The cabin tipped over the side and the gunshot snap of the axle echoed along the cliff face. The rear of the mobile library vaulted into the air. Its metal walls crumpled under their own weight. Now completely upright, this doomed structure saluted the waves, and from a distance, a mile away up on the hill from where it could still be seen, it seemed to collapse, to concertina, as it dove over the edge toward the ocean, splitting in half and releasing its cargo. Hundreds, then thousands, of books took flight, flapped and swooped, fluttered and fell, like a flock of birds dive-bombing into the sea.

The cab hit the rocks below, thundering into the ground, and the tiniest spark lit a trickle of fuel. With a deafening bang, the mobile library became a tower of fire, burning its shadow into the chalk.

Somewhere in there, thought the detective as the heat crawled through his skin and clothes, is Joseph Sebastian Wiles, an inferno claiming his remains. Somewhere in there is an ending.

Bobby and Rosa watched the flames burn, letting ice cream melt over their fingers. Charred book pages twirled through the smoke, an endless snowfall of cinders fluttering around them. And there, in the sky, a blue and yellow macaw, in free and glorious flight out to sea. They walked through the police line toward Val on the clifftop. Brother, sister, mother.

CHAPTER TWENTY-TWO

A CHILDREN'S STORY,
PART TWO

The Robot saw the dragon on television. It had breathed fire for the first and last time, said the newsreader, who appeared just as shocked as everyone else. They showed footage of the smoke left behind, filling the sky above the ocean for miles and miles. The Robot was so surprised by the news that his eyes flashed just like they were supposed to.

The first thing he did was tighten the bolts on his arms and legs. The second thing he did was rush all the way to the workshop he had recently built, which was full of maps and chairs and human things.

The third thing he did was tell the Caveman, who had been sleeping in his workshop. The Caveman was delighted to hear the news. Now that the dragon had breathed fire, it meant that no one would care about a humble Caveman anymore. In fact, it meant they would think he no longer existed, and you can't search for something that doesn't exist. He sat back and waited for his family to arrive. The Boy, the Princess, the Queen. He would wait for as long as it took them to come.

ACKNOWLEDGMENTS

No Paul Whitlatch, no book. A massive thank-you for talking me down off the ledge, and a hundred or more other things. Thank you to everyone at Scribner—Nan Graham, Colin Harrison, Roz Lippel, Kara Watson, Mia Crowley-Hald, Tom Spain, Charlotte Gill, Karen Fink, David Lamb, Alexsis Johnson and Lauren Hughes. Thanks to Gray318 for the cover, and David Goodwillie for the party.

Gigantic thanks to Francesca Main for doing a perfect job. I see a happy future. Thank you to everyone at Picador—Paul Baggaley, Nicholas Blake, Sandra Taylor, Lucie Cuthbertson-Twiggs, Jodie Mullish and Katie Tooke.

Thank you to Cathryn Summerhayes, my agent, and her rapidly expanding family of beauties, for everything, as ever.

Thank you to everyone at WME, especially Claudia Ballard, Laura Bonner and Siobhan O'Neill, as well as those from back in the day, Becky Thomas and Eugenie Furniss.

Thanks to Francis Bickmore, Jamie Byng and Canongate for adventures past.

Love to Mum, Dad, Alison, Glenn, Darren, Alex, William, Oliver, Anna, Thomas and Jonathan, to the rest of my family and to the Jakemans.

To TC, a boy's best friend.

Love to my friends, and all three of their jokes.